# Dragons of the Past,
## Visions of the Future

By: Lilia & Jarek Barć

ISBN 979-8-218-47097-5

Book Cover by Lilia & Jarek Barć

Illustrations by Lilia & Jarek Barć

First edition 2024

To my family and friends, especially Charlotte, Lorrie and Melinda, for keeping me motivated throughout this writing journey.

# The Known World

IceLava Fields

Frostfall

Mt. Skytop

Great North River

Sagestone

Ravensthorn

Humans
Dwarfs

Grapevine

Cloud Hill

Etherbald

Littlewing

Talonwing

Sheepy Isle

Farfling

Emerald Isle

N
W    E
S

## PROLOGUE

Thunder slashed angrily at the sky as Honeywing flailed through the air. She was so close to the sea below that waves crashed into her side and seawater stung her eyes and flooded into her nose. She knew that she was going to crash into the water. Then, she caught a glimpse of the reason why she was out here; a narrow, wooden ship with a tall, slender mast. Then, a powerful gust of wind slammed into her side, and she lost control. She plunged into the dark water. She emerged gasping for breath and fighting to stay above the surface. With her other hand, she gingerly touched her chest where an object was strapped. Honeywing felt the smooth shell of her precious, beautiful egg. *I haven't lost you*, she said to herself in relief. Suddenly, a huge wave knocked the air out of Honeywing and her stomach lurched. *No no no,* she thought. *Why does this storm have to come at the worst possible time*? Her frustration turned into fear as the currents started to drag her under the surface again. The darkness of the depths seemed to beckon to her. She'd been fighting this storm for what seemed like days. She was so tired. But she could not give up. Honeywing kicked her back talons powerfully again and again as her lungs burned. She emerged once again above the surface, gasping for breath. The wind seemed to die down. It became quiet. The rain was no longer coming down in sheets. The waves were no longer relentless. Did she dare to hope? Then, out of the corner of her eye, she spotted a welcoming sight. Mountains! Land! But as she turned her head, she realized something was wrong. Those tall cliffs along the horizon…were moving. *Waves!* she screamed to herself. Disbelief gave way to panic. Honeywing began swimming frantically, swinging her tail through the water with all of the remaining power she had. She swam in desperation away from the fast-approaching wave. She heard the rumbling of the rushing water behind her. Then the wall of water hit her like a hammer and pain seared across her body. She tumbled in the oncoming wave, completely losing any sense of which way was up and where she was. She was desperate to find air again, but all she found was more rushing water. Moments later, or was it hours, she lay flat on her belly on what felt like sand. She was so weak that it took her ages just to roll over and get her head to stop spinning. She was…alive? She couldn't believe it. But then she brought her hand to her chest to look for the familiar smooth edges of her egg still resting in its sack. The egg was gone. *Noooooo!*

## CHAPTER ONE: THE ORPHAN DRAGON

Lavender trudged through the dark woods, branches scraping her sides and pine leaves dropping onto her snout, making her nose tickle. The strong tang of pine trees was lingering in the air."H-hello? Is anyone here?" Lavender called. She was a sleek, long, thin dragon with strong talons and an unusually long, slender tail. Her fine scales were a dark purple, and her eyes were a midnight blue. Her back spikes were sharp as razors, and so were her teeth. She was fast and she was quiet. But just now, she should have been quieter. Suddenly, she heard rustling coming from her left, not far away, but close…very close. She froze, crouched down, perked her ears and sniffed at the air. A long moment went by, as if time stood still. Lavender tensed her muscles and prepared to fight….or run. Then, from behind one of the trees emerged a dark figure. There was no doubt that the figure saw her as it started stepping forward in her direction. The steps became faster and started to become trots…and then the lumbering beast charged towards Lavender. She let out an ear-piercing scream. Startled by the sound, birds fluttered past her. She felt sand under her talons. There wasn't time to run. Reality came crashing down on Lavender's head and she felt the air itself tense the moment before impact. Then...a sound brought her back. Not the sound of her impending doom. But rather-

"Wake up, sleepy head!" exclaimed a familiar voice.

Lavender came out of her dream, or nightmare, with a yelp. Instead of a dark, creepy forest, her eyes were greeted with a warm, sunny day.

"What happened to the forest?" Lavender asked, a little too loudly.

"What forest? This is math class" replied her teacher, to the giggles and laughter of the other students. Lavender, now fully aware of the reality she belonged to, suddenly felt embarrassed.

"Never mind," Lavender replied with her face flushed bright red.

"Well then let's get back to learning, and this time, no day dreaming" said Lavender's teacher, Miss Pepperwing.

She was a gray-scaled dragon with purple wings and a long, narrow snout. She has the nurturing, rational air of a teacher who's been teaching for a very long time. Her schoolhouse was perched on an overlook with a spectacular view of the dragon town of Talonwing. Dragons had settled in Talonwing a millenia ago, and the entire town was carved out of a dull white stone. Everything from the narrow streets to the homes and shops- even the interior furniture- all carved out of stone. It was said that the ancient dragons used a sort of magic to shape the stone into such fine shapes; a skill that has since been lost by the dragons. Inside the schoolhouse, dragons used their talons and a soft rock called pumice to scribble the answers to the various questions and assignments the teachers gave them on a small, rough piece of wood. The schoolhouse was dark inside- as were most of the stone structures in the town, as they only had small windows. Even though it was a bright, sunny day, the interior had a gloomy feel. At night, the dragons would use torches to light up the gloom so that the streets would not be entirely dark. And so it was now that Miss Pepperwing noticed Lavender wasn't the only dragon who was on her way to falling asleep again. She picked up a long, wooden torch and placed it in its holder along the wall. Then, with a snap of her talons, she created a spark that lit the torch on fire.

*I wish I could do that*, thought Lavender. It was a trick all of the students always found entertaining.

"Now then, where were we…oh yes, you students were about to recite your times tables for me," said an overly cheerful Miss Pepperwing. A collective groan made its way around the classroom.

A few hours later, as the sun began to descend behind the jagged peaks that surrounded the valley the town was located in, Lavender made her way out of the schoolhouse and towards the place she called home.

"Wow, that must have been quite a dream," she heard coming from behind. It was Cecil, a small, bright green dragon who seemed like he was always talking. "Yeah you really let out a yelp there, haha it was funny," continued Cecil. Lavender just acknowledged him with a quick smile and nod. "So…what was it?" asked Cecil.

"What was what?" replied Lavender.

"Your dream of course! What was it about?" he asked.

Lavender briefly contemplated the intense realism of her dream; the sights, sounds, even smells…all of it seemed so real. And the feeling of fear- that was the most real of all.

"I don't remember now," she lied. Lavender wasn't the talking type. A disappointed Cecil continued on to blabber about how much he hated times tables. Lavender's thoughts drifted as she walked towards the main square in Talonwing. She thought about her life and how she'd gotten here; about how she was found on a beach by a fisher dragon and brought back to the town. She thought about how she'd grown up in the orphanage, cared for by the dragons who worked there and befriended by other dragon hatchlings who had experienced equally sad stories. She pondered on how where her parents were- if they were even alive. Thoughts that she'd let roll through her brain so many times on so many different days. Today would be no different. The smell of freshly-grilled fish brought her back to the moment. She had walked all the way down to the market. Cecil was nowhere to be seen. She thought it was scary how she could just walk on auto-pilot like that, especially that the worn-out stone streets were uneven and slippery. Suddenly, she remembered that it was her turn to cook dinner for her roommates at the orphanage. Conveniently, she was at the market already. At this hour, the market was very busy and dragons everywhere were scurrying around, yelling out orders and wrapping up food. The jingling sound of sapphire tokens could be heard everywhere. She was given enough tokens that morning to buy dinner. Or so she thought.

"That'll be four tokens dear," said the shopkeeper at the grilled fish store. He was a large, squat dragon with spikes all over his tail in seemingly random spots. Lavender looked into her satchel.

"Oh" she said, disappointed. "Then I'm one token short. Perhaps I could pay you back tomorrow?" she asked. The smile fell from the shopkeeper's face and he frowned.

"Aren't you one of the orphanage dragons?" he asked. She hated that term. Orphanage dragon. Like dirty laundry. Like day-old fish soup.

"I can have it for you first thing tomorrow," she stated, ignoring the original question.

"Er…I'm afraid not. Sorry." He said.

*Three fish for four dragons….hardly enough*, she thought. She felt frustrated and a bit angry. She gritted her teeth and at that moment, for reasons that she really cannot explain, Lavender closed her eyes. She focused on the problem, thinking only of that missing sapphire. The room turned hazy…and then disappeared. She was outside on the main street. Vendors and customers were everywhere, screaming over each other. It was raining, and the street was muddy. In the madness, a mother dragon with her baby bumped into another and spilled her groceries all over the road. The baby began wailing. In her frustrated effort to pick everything up, she dropped something. Lavender watched as it fell from her satchel…slowly turning in the air, as if in slow motion. It fell to the muddy ground, not with a jingle, but with a *plock*. In the craziness of the scene, it quickly got pressed into the mud. One sapphire. She came out of her vision with a gasp of air. What had just happened? She looked around…the shopkeeper was staring at her looking totally lost.

"Are you…all there?" he asked, waving his crimson red talon in front of her face wildly. Soon, the world came back into focus. She quickly reviewed what happened, and what she saw. She then glanced out of the shop and onto the busy market street.

"One moment," she told the shopkeeper urgently. She then strolled on the street, acting casual, recalling the exact scene she had just witnessed in her vision. The mother with the baby…where was that…the corner shop…there. She quickly arrived at the location and began scanning the ground. The mud had mostly disappeared now as the rain had passed many hours ago. She got down and looked carefully at the gaps between the stones on the street…and then…she saw it. Covered in mud but for a tiny spec of shiny blue. One sapphire. She couldn't believe it. She quickly brushed it off and went back into the shop. The shopkeeper- curious about the strange young dragon- watched her through his tiny shop window. He was equally amazed by her discovery.

"Here you are. Four sapphires for four fish," she said. The shopkeeper stared for a moment, in a shocked daze, and then got her order wrapped. She felt a triumphant happiness wash over her as she skipped back to the orphanage with four fish grasped in her talon. She had seen something…the past? This wasn't just some daydream. This was real. All her life she had felt that being different meant being an orphan. Now, she felt that being different meant she could do something others couldn't. It meant that she had a gift. Later that evening, after she finished cooking and eating dinner, the caretaker approached her.

"Lavender, how did you manage to get four fish for three sapphires?" she asked.

"What?" asked Lavender.

"You brought back four fish. But you only had three sapphires," continued the caretaker.

*Woah, is everyone just full of supernatural powers now?* thought Lavender to herself. "How did you know I only had three sapphires?" asked Lavender.

"Because" said the caretaker, "when you put them into your satchel, one slipped out and fell onto the cushion" she said. "I found it here later. But you still haven't answered my question," she said, now looking very carefully at Lavender.

"I convinced the shopkeeper to lend me one which I promised I would pay back first thing tomorrow" said Lavender, hoping the caretaker wouldn't press the issue further.

"I see," she said. "Well then ...you'd better fulfill your promise and take this to him tomorrow," she said. Lavender took the sapphire from the caretaker's hand. As she did, the caretaker closed her hand on Lavender's and said in a low voice, "just remember- anyone caught stealing will have to find a new place to live." Lavender swallowed hard as she released her grip.

"Yes, ma'am," is all she managed to say in reply.

That evening, after everyone was in bed, Lavender decided she had to try an experiment. She tried once again to focus her mind hard- she tried to return to the mother dragon with the baby. She tried to glance a little further into the past- where did she go? But she didn't get anywhere and with a disappointed knot in her stomach, went to sleep, exhausted from the effort.

The next day she walked past the fish shop, where the shopkeeper was eagerly poking at every rock and stone by the foot of his stall, trying to find any sapphires like Lavender did last night. When he saw her, he nervously looked away and ran back into his stall. She passed the corner shop again where the mother dragon with the baby lost her sapphire. She stood for a moment and she started to feel light-headed. She closed her eyes. Suddenly, she was peering into the past again. The mother was walking quickly, the rain making her all wet. She' was carrying her baby. The baby is crying- why is the baby crying? She witnesses the weighty groceries in the mother's sack, the squirming baby. The cold rain. The squelching sound from the puddles as she quickly trudged home…her home…at the far end of a narrow alley near the bookstore. Lavender came back to reality with a loud "poof" that she could almost feel in her head. She'd done it again. Now she made her way to the house- down the narrow alley next to the bookstore, to a large stone doorway. She knocked. The door creaked open, and a tired-looking mother dragon peeped out.

"Yes?" she asked wearily.

"I believe you dropped your sapphire at the market yesterday. I'm here to return it," said Lavender. She held up the shiny sapphire.

"What…you found it?" asked the mother dragon, completely flustered.

"I did, and it's yours." Without another word, Lavender handed her the sapphire and left hurriedly before the mother dragon could question her more. On her way to school, she pondered on these visions. They felt so real. She wasn't just watching a scene play out as if she was watching a play. She saw and heard and felt everything at that moment. It was as if she was really there. It was beyond strange. And totally cool.

## CHAPTER TWO: THE ORPHAN BOY

Farflung was a fishing village that fell on hard times. It was located on a beautiful lake with sparkling water, surrounded by lush pine forests. Humans had inhabited this area for thousands of years, and Farflung was a very old human settlement. For a long time, the fish that lived in the lake were considered the tastiest delicacy in the human kingdom, and the fishermen of Farflung grew wealthy from selling these fish to other cities and towns. Horse-drawn carts filled with ice and fresh fish made their way as far north as Ravensthorn- the capital of the human kingdom. Farflung grew rapidly and attracted merchants, craftsmen, shopkeepers and artists. The artists loved to paint scenes of the town, which was unlike others for it was situated right on top of the water, with the houses and buildings supported by long, wooden pillars. But this age of wealth and good times would not last. Eventually, the greedy fishermen fished all of the fish out of the lake, without thinking about what would happen if all the fish were gone. Eventually, they cast their fishing nets into the vast lake, but always brought them out empty. And so the town became poor and run down, and many of the people who moved there grudgingly left. Some of the houses became abandoned, and with nobody taking care of them, some even fell into the lake. The town became a center for criminals. It also became home to an orphanage, where unlucky kids who had lost their parents ended up. One of these kids was a scrappy boy named Malon. He had lived in the orphanage for many years, and he was one of the older kids there. He didn't know much about his father; only that he was a soldier that died fighting in some battle. His mother was poor and they moved around a lot, but he doesn't really remember much about his past. He was very young. It was on one of their journeys that he became an orphan. They were on a ship that got caught in a terrible storm. The ship sank, and everyone aboard drowned. Everyone, except Malon. People called it a "miracle". Malon himself doesn't remember how he'd survived, only that he woke up floating on a piece of wood in the middle of the ocean, and a few hours later, a rescue ship picked him up. Everyone felt sorry for him then, but that only lasted a short while. Then he was sent to this orphanage, and the world has been trying to forget about him ever since. This made Malon bitter and angry. He was cold and rude to the other kids and to the caretakers at the orphanage, and he caused trouble in the town. For this reason, they kept Malon away from the other kids and his bunk was put in a small storage closet inside the orphanage. This insult made Malon even angrier, and he snuck out of the orphanage at night whenever he could to cause trouble. His favorite method of troublemaking was to steal items from shop stalls in the market, and then sell those stolen items to shady characters in dark alleys. In this way, Malon was able to make some money, but he was also robbed and beaten once, and after that day, he decided to stash all of his stolen treasures inside the mattress of his bunk. There was one treasure in particular that he loved more than anything else; it was a book. The book was large, heavy, and very old. He found it sealed in a display case with the words *The Tale of Doomswing* etched into the fine leather casing. "If it's in a display case, it's worth a lot," Malon thought as he breathed in a sharp breath. He picked the lock carefully and undid the latch. He then rushed home to read the book. It was written in a way that made it hard to read, but Malon eventually got used to it. It was a story about an ancient dragon. The dragon was named Doomswing, and he was the most fearsome creature that ever lived. He attacked human cities and towns, and seemed to be unstoppable, until an army of dragons came after him. Through an immense amount of effort and sacrifice, they chased him into a cave and managed to trap him there. But they knew that no normal force would hold Doomswing, so they used magic. Doomswing was very strong and nearly unstoppable, but he wasn't very smart. The dragon wizard who finally trapped him in the cave did so by challenging him. He told Doomswing that if he could solve a riddle, he would be free, but if he couldn't, he would be trapped forever. Doomswing believed he was very clever and could solve any riddle, so he agreed. But he was wrong. He ended up trapping himself in that cave, with the magical lock sealing him in. He could free himself at any time, but he was never smart enough to solve that riddle. Malon sometimes wondered if the story was real, and if Doomswing really existed and was trapped in that cave to this day. Malon felt imprisoned himself. He felt trapped in the orphanage and in a world that didn't care about him. But not for long, because Malon was planning his escape.

He knew that what he needed more than anything else to free himself from the orphanage was money, so he continued his nighttime stealing. This continued for months. He knew that his days at the orphanage were numbered, and so he planned to run away with the stolen goods and make his way to a different town, where he could start a new life. He was very close now...all he needed was one more treasure. He had spotted a beautiful pearl necklace on display at one of the jewelry merchants' stalls. That necklace would be the biggest prize in his collection, and with it, he could easily afford to run away. He waited until the moon was hidden behind the clouds, and a foggy gloom covered the town. One way or another, this night would change his life. He waited until most of the kids were fast asleep, then made his way to the hole he had dug under the wooden fence in the back of the playground. It was covered by bushes with sharp thorns, but Malon knew exactly how to get around them. The hole in the fence led to an alley behind one of the taverns, and within a few minutes, Malon was free of the orphanage and on his way to the market. He covered his head with a hood and wore oversized glasses as a disguise. He silently crept through the dark back alleys of the gloomy town, being spotted only by a black cat. *It's bad luck to let a black cat cross your path*, he thought to himself. But then he remembered that his luck couldn't get any worse. Or so he thought. As he crossed a small side street, he caught a glimpse of the lake. The water was calm, and looked black in the gloom. Then suddenly, a large wave came and bashed against the peer, causing boats to bang against each other. He stumbled back and fell to the ground with a yelp. That wave reminded him of his childhood, and the day he lost his mother to an angry sea of blackness. He was very young, but he remembered that moment well. They were traveling across a sea, on their way to some island where his mother promised they would find a better life.

But all he found was grief and sorrow. They never made it to that island. The boat they were sailing on was caught in a terrible storm. The strange thing is, Malon remembers clearly seeing a shadow in the sky, like a gigantic bird, following the ship. Some other people on board noticed it too, but the wind and rain and lightning means it could have been anything, or nothing. Malon remembered a wall of water that threw everyone around, and he was separated from his mother. He was flung into the sea, and tried desperately to keep his head above the gushing waves, but in the darkness and panic, he wasn't sure which way was up. He somehow managed to swim his way to the surface but just as he caught his breath, the sky lit up with lightning and he saw the creature once more, this time as clear as day. It was a dragon with a long spear-shaped tail and scales that glistened in the rain. And then it was gone, swallowed by the waves. He called out to his mother and waved his arms vigorously. But in a flash, the ship was gone. He eventually grabbed a hold of some wooden planks, and was able to stay soaking wet but afloat until the morning. Half a day later, the storm had passed, and he was eventually rescued by a boat that was passing by. He was the only survivor. Nobody believed his dragon story, believing instead that the poor boy was delirious with grief over losing his mother. But Malon knew that dragons were real, and that's why he liked the Doomswing story so much. Nobody else believed in dragons. Everyone dismissed him. Nobody took him seriously- ever. But that would all change, starting tonight.

Malon put away the bitter memory, and returned to focus on his task. He was close to the market now, and he could hear the sounds of merchants shouting over themselves, trying to attract buyers. The street ahead opened up to a large open square, which was lit up by street lamps and merchant stalls. He was about to walk right into the open square, when out of the corner of his eye, he noticed a man standing in the shadows. A tall hat and shiny belt buckle made it clear that this was one of Farflung's police officers. Malon quickly darted back down a dark alley. Had the police noticed him? Clearly the market was now being closely watched, as thieves like him were more and more common in the town. He thought for a moment that he should quit and go back to the orphanage empty-handed tonight, but then his dream of running away would have to wait, and he couldn't accept that. It was now or never. He decided that he needed a distraction to pull this off. He spent some time looking around, until he found just what he was looking for. Up a side street, one of the carts used to haul away rubbish had been left unattended. It was parked on a slight hill, with two rocks being used to keep it in place. All Malon had to do was move the rocks, give it a good push, and it would roll all the way down to the market, where it would collide with one of the stalls. Then, as the police officers went to investigate, he would quickly sneak over to the jewelry merchant, steal the necklace, and sneak away before anyone knew what had happened. His plan was perfect. He quickly kicked the rocks aside and pushed the overloaded cart as hard as he could. The stench of the rubbish made him gag, but he knew this was good as it would add to the effect. Once the cart was rolling, he ran at full speed down a side alley and back around towards the market, hoping he could arrive just as the cart hit the stall. As he rounded the last corner, he heard a crash and some screams. He quickly got himself into position behind a bunch of barrels, where he could see the market. The cart had crashed, but not into the stall as he had hoped. One of the cart's wheels must have been crooked, and the cart crashed into the side of a building and rolled over, spilling the rubbish onto the street just in front of the market. He watched people running away from the stench and two policemen walking over to investigate, but the commotion wasn't enough. The other vendors were already starting to look away, and he couldn't be sure if any other policemen were on patrol. He decided to go for it anyway. He crept behind the stalls until he had reached the jewelry stall. The merchant at the stall was still looking over at the commotion caused by the rubbish cart, and asking the merchant next to him what had happened. The necklace was displayed right at the front of the stall, within sight of anyone passing by. Malon crept to the side of the stall and was just within reach of the necklace. The police investigating the rubbish cart then called for the rubbish collector to come clean up the mess, who began to argue that he wasn't responsible for it. The argument was just what Malon needed. Everyone likes to watch an argument, and so the shopkeepers and customers were all momentarily fixated on the scene. Malon made his move. He silently grabbed the necklace and crept away into a side alley. He then walked at a fast, but not suspiciously fast pace back towards the orphanage. The sound of a new commotion began to develop behind him as the jewelry shopkeeper noticed his missing necklace. As Malon rounded the corner, he could hear someone yell "thief!", but it wasn't aimed at him. As far as anyone could tell, Malon was never there. He repeated the steps to sneaking back into the orphanage, and finally made it back to his bunk. He took out the necklace and admired his prize. The adrenaline was wearing off now, and he was able to savor his work. He had risked everything and won. Just like he would continue to do, he thought to himself. He went to sleep with dreams of living in a different town and having his own thief hideout, where he would become a legend and recruit his own gang of thieves. He would be someone. He would matter.

The next morning, Malon was awoken to the sound of banging on his door. That was a first...the orphanage caretakers mostly ignored him. "Open up boy, we know you're in there," said a loud, booming voice. This was no caretaker. This could only be one thing- a policeman. Malon felt the rush of panic, and began to tear open his mattress. The banging continued. His treasure spilled out all over the floor. *Why didn't I go last night?* he cursed himself. He grabbed as much as he could and stuffed his pockets, putting the necklace into his hood. There was one other way out of this room, but he would wait until they broke in and then make a run for it. Moments later, the banging turned into booming as the police began to kick at the door. It didn't take long for the door to fall off of its hinges and collapse into the room. Malon was quick, and he dived through a gap and rolled into the hallway and past the policeman. Just as he thought he might have a chance at escape, one of the caretakers grabbed him. Soon the police were on him, and he was caught. With stolen goods literally falling out of his pockets, it was the definition of being caught red-handed. The police tied his hands, and made him sit on the floor as they collected all of the stolen goods. The caretakers looked on, and Malon could tell that they were pleased. They would finally be rid of him. He wondered how they found out about his stealing, but in the end it didn't really matter. He was caught, and all that he had been hoping for was now ruined. The police took him down to their office, where he signed some papers about promising never to return in exchange for not going to jail. And so in some sad way, Malon got what he wanted. He was free of the orphanage and free of Farflung town. The police escorted him to the town gate, where they threw him out into the mud. All he had was the raggy clothes sticking to his back. He had no idea where he was going, or how he would survive. All he could do was to start walking.

## CHAPTER THREE: THE SEER

Over the next few weeks, Lavender grew more and more
comfortable with her newfound ability. She could peer into the
past and see what happened before she arrived. The further back
she tried to see, the harder it was, but looking back a few
moments was not hard at all. And so Lavender decided to use this
to her advantage. She volunteered to help out at the next
fundraising booth for the orphanage. That morning, she helped set
up their stall in the market and put up signs. Two other orphanage
dragons, Cecil and Celeste, were there to help. They expected
another boring day in which a few dragons would give a few
sapphires out of generosity to the poor orphans. But not this time.
This time, Lavender had a better idea. She had fashioned a silly
hat and cloak out of leftover clothes she found at the orphanage,
put on her outfit, and started yelling out to the crowd of

passersby, "come one, come all to see the amazing Lavender, guesser extraordinaire!"

"Guesser extraordinaire?" questioned Cecil, wondering what Lavender was on about. But Lavender paid him no mind and just continued.

"If I can guess what you had for breakfast this morning, you donate one sapphire to the orphanage," she shouted out to the crowd. A few dragons looked at her as if he was crazy, the rest just walked on. Lavender was disappointed, but pressed on.

"You sir," she said to an older-looking dragon walking by. She then focused her mind for a moment and saw him sitting at his table at home, eating a porridge with some berries. "I bet you ate porridge with berries this morning for breakfast," she said to him just as he was walking away. He turned back to her in surprise.

"Why, that's exactly correct," he said, smiling at her. "That was quite a guess, you earned this," he said, as he deposited one shiny sapphire into their donation box. Lavender was thrilled.

"Thanks very much!" she said, and then found her next customer- a lady dragon carrying a baby in a large satchel. "Hello miss, I bet you had…" Lavender focused again. This time she saw the woman trying to cook some eggs over a fire, but then being startled by the baby dragon who ran up behind her, causing her to drop all her eggs on the floor.

"Why…you missed your breakfast this morning didn't you. I'm sorry about those eggs," said Lavender. The lady dragon's jaw dropped.

"How…how could you possibly have known that?" she asked. Lavender just smiled. "Everyone, everyone this orphanage dragon is truly gifted!" Yelled out the lady dragon. "What else can you see?" Can you see the future?" Can you tell me where I put my bracelet…I lost it last week." The questions started to pile up, not just from the lady dragon, but from several others who were now very interested in her. Soon, the booth was surrounded by dragons wanting questions answered. Lavender suddenly felt overwhelmed.

"What have you started here?" Yelled out Celeste, as she was pushed aside by the gathering crowd. Lavender tried her best to manage to answer the questions, but in all the commotion, she was unable to focus her mind.

"Please, everyone, I'll answer all your questions, just not all at once!" She yelled. The crowd gradually settled down and Lavender was able to use her ability to help dragons find missing items and recall things they had forgotten, or just to be entertained by her amazing ability to peer into the past. By the end of the day, she was completely exhausted. She fell onto a bench while the other orphanage dragons took their stall down.

"That was pretty amazing," said Celeste, as she walked over and sat next to Lavender.

"Oh yeah, how much did we get in donations?" asked Lavender. Celeste brought over the donation box. It was heavy with sapphires.

"But that's not all," said Celeste, as she pulled out a satchel which was also full of sapphires. "We got so many donations that they wouldn't fit in the box!" she exclaimed. Lavender was thrilled. She had used her gift to help all her fellow orphans.

"Now maybe we can finally get some better food at the orphanage, instead of the usual fish stew with a side of slop," said Celeste. They both laughed.

The next day, Lavender made her way up the hill and into the schoolhouse. She expected to hear all kinds of questions about what she did at the fundraiser. Miss Pepperwing and the other teachers were indeed suspicious, but nobody could find anything wrong with what she had done, so they let her be.

"Well, are they kicking you out for being amazing?" asked Celeste during their lunch break.

"No, but they didn't so much as thank me for a job well done," replied Lavender. "They always think the worst about us....as if we are always trying to cheat or steal. It's very annoying," she added.

"Well, we all appreciate you," replied Celeste. Lavender smiled. But despite her big contribution to the orphanage, nothing changed- especially the lunch menu. The orphanage dragons asked and asked, but the teachers were firm in saying, "we spent that on improvements to the building."

The dragons were distraught. So Lavender decided to do something nice for all of them. Over the next few weeks, Lavender spent her free time at the market, taking donations in exchange for her visions of the past. She took all the sapphires she made and invited all of the dragons at the orphanage to a delicious dinner. They ate fresh fruits, breads, exotic fish and even had five different kinds of dessert. The orphanage kids were so happy. One of them even cried because she had never tried mango ice cream before and it was so good. Lavender was thrilled that her newfound ability was bringing so much joy to her friends.

Then one day, Miss Pepperwing called Lavender to her office after dinner. When Lavender arrived, she saw a distraught-looking lady dragon sitting there with Miss Pepperwing.

"Lavender, this is Miss Scalesworth, and she has come here asking for your help," explained Miss Pepperwing. Lavender sat down and said hello, though she wasn't feeling very comfortable being there. Clearly, this wasn't going to be another *let me guess what you had for breakfast* kind of situation.

"It's my daughter," started Miss Scalesworth. "She's missing. It's been two days and nobody has seen or heard from her. The police haven't found anything. It's as if she simply vanished!" she cried. Lavender listened and felt very bad for Miss Scalesworth. Miss Pepperwing looked at Lavender.

"Lavender, you've gained something of a reputation for having an uncanny ability to see into the past," she said. "I really hope you haven't been lying to people, because now there is a real situation where this so-called gift of yours could save this dragon's life." Lavender resented Miss Pepperwing's tone, but her eyes grew wide when she realized how serious the situation was.

"Can you help me?" begged Miss Scalesworth.

Many thoughts flashed through Lavender's mind. *What if I try and fail? Worse still- what if I find out that something terrible happened and then I have to share that news?* But looking at the miserable, desperate dragon, Lavender couldn't help but agree to try. That very evening, Lavender went with Miss Scalesworth to the last place that her daughter, Taly, was seen. Lavender brought Celeste with her for emotional support.

"She would always play with her ball on this playground," said Miss Scalesworth. Lavender looked around. It was dark, so she could only make out the silhouettes of tall trees surrounding a small park with a grassy circle in the center.

"Do you have her ball?" asked Lavender.

"No, both the ball and Taly are nowhere to be found," said Miss Scalesworth. It was time. Lavender closed her eyes. In her mind, she watched the clouds above move in reverse and the sun go from setting to rising, to setting again. Then, she saw a small dragon run onto the playground, tossing an orange ball in the air. There she was! Lavender felt a breeze against her scales and heard the sound of the trees rustling. The visions were so real that it always scared her a bit when she realized all of this had already happened. Taly kept throwing her ball higher and higher. She giggled as it sailed through the air, touching tree branches. Then, she missed catching it and it rolled out of the park and onto the street. Taly ran after it. Lavender followed her. The ball rolled all the way down to the market, where some vendors were loading a cart up with hay. The ball settled next to a large pile of hay. Taly came running down the street with such speed that she couldn't stop in time, and ended up plowing head-first into the hay. Before she could emerge, the vendor took a huge shovel and threw the entire pile into the cart. He then closed the back of the cart and yelled to the cart driver to be on his way. And just like that, Taly and her ball left the market. Lavender chased after the cart as long as she could, but the further she got away, the murkier her vision became. The last thing she remembers seeing is the cart making its way out of the town through the main gate. Lavender opened her eyes.

"I know what happened to Taly, but I don't know yet where she is," she said. She then relayed the vision to Miss Scalesworth, who immediately called the police. Lavender had to repeat her story again, and by the time she finally got back to the orphanage, it was well past midnight. She was exhausted, but satisfied that she did what she could to help. The next day, while sitting at lunch trying not to taste the food, Lavender heard a commotion in the hallway. She walked over to see what was happening. It was Miss Pepperwing, running toward her.

"They found her! They found her!" she yelled at the top of her voice. It took Lavender a moment, but then her heart leaped.

"Taly? They found Taly?" she asked, as she wanted to be certain.

"Yes! After hearing your vision, the police sent messenger dragons to fly to every town nearby and check if anyone unloaded a cart full of hay. They found that one farmer had a cart that had arrived recently and was ready to unload. They quickly got to it, and found Taly inside, tired and miserable, but alive and healthy. You did it! You saved her life!"

All of the orphans looked at Lavender as if she was a celebrity. And pretty soon, she was. The whole town celebrated, and Lavender was honored with an award. The police even made her an official deputy, hoping that she could help them solve cases in the future. The story was reported in the Dragon Chronicle- the largest newspaper in the dragon kingdom. Miss Scalesworth insisted on adopting Lavender right then and there. She was thrilled at all of the attention and overjoyed that Taly was found, but this was all happening way too fast for Lavender. She felt that something which started as an odd quirk had now spiraled out of control. She just needed some time to think. Meanwhile, far away, in the dragon capital city of Sagestone, a dragon picked up the newspaper and started reading. She stopped, and read the story again. *Oh my,* she thought to herself. *Could you be her daughter? Could you really be alive?*

A few weeks passed, and the excitement surrounding Lavender's detective work settled down. She was still a big celebrity in town, but dragons no longer constantly bothered her with requests for help. One day, as she sat down at her desk for class, she noticed that Miss Pepperwing was nowhere to be found. All of the students were in their places, chatting and scribbling on their pumice boards, but the teacher wasn't there. Lavender waited for a while, then decided to look around. She glanced out onto the top floor balcony where the teachers like to spend their break time. There she saw Miss Pepperwing speaking to another dragon. She had never seen this dragon before. She was a emerald green color with beautiful, shiny scales. She has elegantly-folded wings, and was carrying a beautiful, embroidered pack. The two dragons were having an intense conversation. At that moment, Miss Pepperwing let out a loud "nonsense", and walked back towards the classroom- and directly towards the snooping Lavender. Miss Pepperwing's eyes widened when she saw her.

"Lavender! What…What did you hear?" was the question Miss Pepperwing settled on.

"Um…nothing, I was just looking for you. I was worried that…"

"You know that spying on people is impolite!" said Miss Pepperwing, but her words were full of tension and she was clearly shaken from whatever she had been talking about with the strange dragon. Then, Miss Pepperwing's eyes softened. "Oh child," she said. "There are some things we need to discuss," she continued. Lavender suddenly felt very scared. She'd never seen Miss Pepperwing this serious before. Her mind raced.

"Miss if it's about that slop that got onto the ceiling yesterday, I promise I didn't throw it up there!" she blurted out the first thing she could think of. Miss Pepperwing looked confused.

"This has nothing to do with slop. It is something else entirely. Lavender, this is Peacefinder," Miss Pepperwing introduced the strange dragon, who was now standing behind Miss Pepperwing. "She's come all the way from Sagestone to meet you." Lavender looked at the strange dragon, now known to her as Peacefinder. There was something unsettling about her. She had a piercing gaze, as if she knew something about Lavender that Lavender herself didn't know. It was then that Peacefinder spoke for the first time,

"Hello, Lavender," she said with a smooth, mellow voice. Lavender took a step back, her back talons quivering slightly. Apparently Peacefinder noticed this and said, "please don't be alarmed; I just wanted to talk to you and get to know you.'' she reassured Lavender. Peacefinder put her warm talon onto her shoulder. Lavender pinned her wings close to her back and flattened her ears. She spotted that Miss Pepperwing also looked uncomfortable with this visitor. Lavender let out a deep sigh and murmured,

"What would you like to know?"

"Well you see, I read about your amazing ability, and it reminded me of another dragon who had the same ability. That dragon was a close friend of mine. I believe that dragon was your mother, Honeywing." Lavender's heart skipped a beat and her body became shaky.

"Are you ok Lavender dear? You look like you've seen a ghost." Miss Pepperwing questioned, placing her talon on top of hers.

"I-Im perfectly f-f-fine." she stammered. Miss Pepperwing gave Lavender an unsure look and then turned to face Peacefinder.

"And you're sure that she's this ability-dragon you're looking for?" Miss Pepperwing asked. Peacefinder nodded. Miss Pepperwing looked displeased.

Lavender gulped and started to protest- how dare this stranger talk about her mother- but then, she said she knew her? How?

"Your mother was special, just like you," continued Peacefinder. "She had visions. Visions of the past. She was what we call a Seer. This gift is very rare and often passed down from generation to generation. But this ability- it comes with danger. There are dragons in this world that would fear you...or try to use you for their own gain." Lavender's head was swimming. She wasn't even sure if this conversation was really happening. But Peacefinder wasn't done yet.

"Your mother was part of a group of dragons who worked together to advise King Everwise and help him rule the kingdom. I am still part of that group. I have the gift of seeing the present. I can see far away lands and the dragons who live there. And a third and final member of our group could see the future. But sadly, he too has disappeared." Lavender latched on to this final statement.

"What do you mean disappeared? My mom died and left me alone!" she cried.

Peacefinder sighed. "Your mother disappeared at sea during a storm. Losing her was a terrible blow to all of us," she continued. "But now- with you- we have renewed hope. But I don't want to tell you any more for now," Peacefinder said. "In order to continue, I'll have to show you." At this moment, she held out her talon. "You have the power to find out if all I've told you is true. You know how to do it. And now is the time for you to use your power to understand your past- and why continuing the work your mother started is so important," Peacefinder said. Lavender felt overwhelmed. All of this information- all of this secrecy and newly-discovered facts about her mother- it was all too much to handle. And now, she was expected to join some group of magical dragons that were supposed to- what- save the world? It was all too much. Lavender suddenly felt light-headed. The room began to swirl as she tried to regain her balance. "I think…I don't feel too well" is all she could manage before collapsing snout-first onto the floor.

Cold talons shook Lavender out of her sleep. She spread her wings and coughed loudly.

"I-Is she awake?" asked a hesitant voice. Lavender opened one eye to see her friend Celeste. She had a frown plastered onto her face, but when she saw the whites of Lavender's eyes glowing in the night, she beamed.

"Hi Celeste," Lavender said painfully, as she sat up and pressed the wet leaves that lay on her bed to her forehead.

"What happened?" asked Celeste, as she took a bucket full of cool water over to Lavender's bed. Lavender took the leaves, dunked them into the icy water, and pressed them to her forehead before having a proper look around. Lavender just realized that she was in her bed, back at her orphanage, but none of the others were in their beds. Lavender scanned the room again but still… no young dragons. She blew out a breath and thought about what was best unsaid.

"I…I guess I fell down," Lavender said simply. She squinted her eyes and leaned forward, trying to make out the silhouettes of the dragons standing on the opposite end of the long, dark hall. She strained to see them…but she could not. She focused on her ears now and told Celeste to be absolutely quiet…and the sound of the voices came to her ears.

"This can happen," said the first voice- a deep, slow tone that she recognized as Peacefinder. "She has been over-stretching her mind while she explores the limits of her abilities." Lavender raised an eyebrow.

*When I used my powers to find that sapphire, I didn't feel overworked or tired,* she thought to herself, as she swirled her finger in the iced water bucket.

"Will she be okay?" asked the second voice, which Lavender instantly recognized as Miss Pepperwing.

"She will. She just needs coaching. And now you see why I must take her with me," said Peacefinder.

"Yes...I have to reluctantly agree. She needs someone who can help guide her. Nobody here can do that for her," Miss Pepperwing admitted. At this moment, Lavender knew her life would change forever. She gazed out of the stained window with glassy eyes and saw the other dragons from the orphanage running around and pouncing on each other without a care in the world. She wished she could play outside along with them. But her destiny was about to take her out of this simple life. Celeste was chatting now, but her words fell on deaf ears. Another moment, and she would be asleep.

The sky was still dark when Lavender awoke. Sitting not far from her bed was Peacefinder. She was glancing out the window and absent-mindedly dabbing a wet towel on Lavender's forehead.

"You're awake." she said, when she turned to Lavender, "and you are probably aware of what Miss Pepperwing and I spoke about last night" said Peacefinder, somewhat surprising Lavender.

"Yes, I heard your conversation," she replied. "Your fainting spell was a result of you over-straining your still undeveloped abilities. You'll have to be more careful in the future. But I will guide you." said Peacefinder.

"Guide me? I still haven't agreed to any of this!" exclaimed Lavender. Peacefinder fixed her with an appreciating glance.

"No. No you haven't. And it was selfish of me to assume you would. I'm sorry. Sometimes I forget that...well...that you are very new to this. All of this. And that it all seems overwhelming." Reluctantly, Peacefinder then said, "if you need some time to think about it, I can return in a few weeks." Lavender paused. Something inside her stirred. All of her life she has felt out of place; as if she was destined for something different. Something extraordinary. This was it.

"No," she said finally. "I don't need any time. I want to become better at controlling my abilities. I want to learn more about my mother and her mission, and follow in her footsteps. I want to help." said Lavender, with more confidence than she thought she had.

"Wonderful" said Peacefinder. "Then our journey begins tomorrow."

The morning sky was painted in a tinted orange and a salmon pink. The first of the sun rays danced over Lavender's scales and made little flecks of orange shine all over her. She smiled at the glimmering sun. Lavender saw Peacefinder approaching with a large pack strapped to her back.

"We have what we need." she said. Just then, Lavender saw Miss Pepperwing and Celeste emerge from the orphanage.

"I'm very proud of you child," said Miss Pepperwing. "You've come a long way and I know you have what it takes to face anything this journey- and your future- throws at you." Miss Pepperwing looked sad, but she managed a smile.

"We'll never forget you!" said Celeste with a smile. Lavender hugged them both, and in that morning sun, she captured a bittersweet moment she would always look back on as the end of her first life, and the beginning of her second. Lavender then came over to Peacefinder.

"We have a long way to fly," she told Lavender.

"Wait, what? We're flying? I'm not very good at flying," Lavender replied.

"That's ok," said Peacefinder. "None of us are. But I have something that will help. Our first destination is the very center of dragon culture and society, and a place where your mother and I spent a good deal of time."

"You mean, we're going to Sagestone?" asked Lavender with a look of wonder. She'd read about the capital of the dragon kingdom, and all the amazing things there. She never dreamt that she could go.

"Yes, Sagestone," replied Peacefinder, "I see you have been studying," she said, clearly pleased. "I need to review our notes about the Future Seer, and I'm also waiting on a message from one of my messengers from the far western lands. Hopefully it'll be there when we arrive" explained Peacefinder. And with that, they set off, wings flapping up dust. Lavender looked back at her teacher and classmate, at the village she called home her entire life. She wondered when she would return- if ever.

## CHAPTER FOUR: MALON'S EXILE

Malon walked all day down the rocky dirt road that led away from Farflung and into the unknown. He knew enough about the world to know the names and locations of nearby towns and villages, but he also knew that Farflung, as was clear by the town's name, was far away from just about everything. Nobody walked to or from Farflung. Horse-drawn carts were the only way to travel there, and he had heard travelers complain about the multi-day journey to the nearest town. A multi-day journey on horse cart would take three times as long on foot, not to mention the dangers of wolves, cougars, and bandits that he might find along the way. Malon felt like he was walking to his own grave. On the first night, he slept up in a tree because he thought it would keep him safer from the wolves which he heard howling not too far away. He wrapped himself in a pile of moss to stay warm. It helped, but only a little. The problem with sleeping up in a tree is that it's impossible to get any sleep. That's why he didn't bother on the second night, and just slept in a patch of bushes. The ground was wet and cold, ants crawled on him and earthworms weaved through his fingers through the night. He was so exhausted though, that he was able to ignore his discomforts and managed to sleep. He woke up with the moon still shining, and his stomach rumbling. His fingers were dug into the coarse dirt. He only ate nuts and berries he found by the side of the road, and he now longed for that orphanage porridge which he despised before. When he finally gathered the strength to get up, he noticed a strange rash had covered his arms and legs. It seems that he had slept in a patch of poison ivy. The road he was walking on had once been paved by cobblestones, but these had now worn down or washed away. The road made its way through a forest of tall oak trees, who's leaves were orange and red with the changing of the season. The sun shone through and a gentle breeze rustled the leaves, causing some to fall onto the road and covering it in a tapestry of color. The fallen leaves crunched under Malon's boots and fluttered upward everytime a slight breeze hit them. *If I wasn't cold and hungry, I might actually enjoy this hike,* he thought to himself. And so he continued through the seemingly unending forest.

On the third day, it started to rain, and the air became bitter cold. The forest now became gloomy, and his mood darkened. His soaked-through, mud-covered clothes were now really rags. At one point, he walked past a puddle and was able to see his own reflection. He looked like a beast. Then, he heard the distant sound of horse hooves coming from behind him. Malon froze, straining his ears. He then darted into the nearest bush and craned his neck over the cluster of leaves. He turned to look, but he couldn't see anything from over a slight hill. He knew he had to attack whatever came over that hill. He would risk everything again…as he felt he had nothing more to lose. He picked up a heavy rock and climbed up into a tree, which had a thick branch hanging over the road. Moments later, he saw a single horse cart with a covered top making its way down the road. This meant that the cart carried passengers, not goods. That wasn't ideal, but he would attack it anyway. There was one man sitting at the front, just behind the horse on a bench. He was wearing a dark gray jacket and a helmet with a pointy top. This was the driver. The carriage was a dark blue color, but the paint was faded and chipped, and the copper bolts and door handles appeared old and rusty. As the horse cart passed under the branch, Malon jumped onto the top, partially collapsing the roof as he did. He lost his footing but quickly grabbed the front of the carriage and took out his rock. As the driver looked back to see what was happening, Malon bashed him on the side of his helmet. The driver fell from his seat, dazed. The horse then slowed down and Malon took the driver's place. He would hijack the entire horse and carriage. He heard screams from inside the carriage, and a voice demanding that he stop. Malon kept looking back, and then saw a man who looked like a guard peer out from one of the side windows, a crossbow in his hand. When the guard saw Malon, his eyes grew wide and he hesitated for a moment, not sure what to make of the raggedy creature that he saw. Malon glanced at the crossbow that was ready to fire at him any moment. He moved quickly, jumping onto the carriage roof and kicking at the crossbow before the guard had a chance to aim. He heard a "thump" as the crossbow fired, but the arrow went high into the air, and Malon now kicked at the guard again, this time causing him to lose his balance and fall out of the window. The guard recovered and tried chasing after the carriage, but it was moving too fast. Malon quickly returned to the driver's seat and urged the horse on. A few moments later, he felt a crossbow bolt soar by. Malon was thankful that he missed and he kicked the horse hard, causing them to gallop around a bend. The guard disappeared from view. There was still shouting and screaming coming from the carriage, but nobody came out. Eventually, the shouting stopped, and Malon found a place to stop the carriage. He couldn't go all the way to another town with a hijacked carriage, and he would need to move fast before another traveler came along to help. He jumped down from the driver's seat and went to the back of the carriage. There was a luggage chest in the back, but it was locked. The door to the carriage was locked as well, but the window the guard had smashed allowed Malon to see inside. He saw an older woman, and a child, who now started to scream again.

"Open the door and come out, I won't hurt you, I just want the carriage," said Malon, in a raspy voice. He didn't sound like himself. When he didn't get any reply, he began to pound against the door with the rock. "Don't make me climb through that window," he said, though he knew that in his current weakened condition, he wouldn't be able to put up much of a fight. Eventually, the door opened and the woman came out, holding a spear in one hand and the child in the other. A look of wild fear crossed her face as she saw Malon. The child actually stopped crying at the sight, and began to cower behind the woman.

"I'll have you know that, I'm the countess of Larson, and I have many friends at the capital. You bandits will be severely punished for this," she said, trying to keep a steady voice, but failing. She was clearly no warrior, but even so, the shiny tip of the spear could easily kill Malon, so he was very careful not to make the wrong move. He scoffed.

"If you're as important as you say you are, you wouldn't be traveling in a single-carriage with a single guard," commented

Malon. "But in the end, I don't care if you're the queen of Ravensthorn," he continued. "I'm going to take this carriage, and I'll have that spear as well," he said. He felt surprisingly calm, as if he really didn't care what happened next. If the woman decided to lunge at him, he might be able to dodge, but at this moment he felt so tired and weak, that she could just as easily kill him with a single swipe. But he did look like a wild beast, and his raspy voice made him sound a lot older than he was. This intimidated the woman, and in the end she put down the spear in exchange for a promise that he wouldn't hurt them. He kept his promise, and took the carriage, horse, and key to the luggage chest. But when the woman asked him if she could take some food and water while they waited for rescue, he said no. "Farflung threw me out with nothing," he said. "Now you get to experience what that feels like," he continued. "Good luck, you're going to need it." And with that, he urged the horse forward and left the two people by the roadside. *Someone will come along for them eventually*, he thought to himself. Once he was a good distance away, he stopped and looked through the carriage. There he found food, and ate so fast that he nearly choked. He found elegant clothing in the luggage chest, which he quickly changed into. The carriage even had a small heater, which he turned on by lighting the fire inside. For the first time since his exile from Farflung, he wasn't hungry or cold. He savored the moment, knowing that it wouldn't last for long. He could now turn his thoughts to something other than survival. Based on this success, he wondered if he could become a roadside robber, waiting for carriages to go by and hijacking them. But he remembered that most of the carriages that came to Farflung were full of cheap goods, and even those were usually well-defended because they traveled in groups. He just got lucky. So he decided to stick to his original plan of making it to the next town and taking it from there. But he couldn't take the carriage with him. The moment that woman got rescued, every traveler on the road would be looking for the carriage, so he decided to unhook it from the horse and leave it there. In addition to the clothes and food, the carriage had a few trinkets that he could sell. It wasn't much, but it would be a start. He then mounted the horse…and was quickly thrown off. Malon never learned how to ride horses, and this one didn't even have a proper saddle. In addition, the horse held no value to him because selling a stolen horse was nearly impossible as nobody would buy it, and it would eventually be recognized. So since he couldn't ride it and he couldn't sell it, he decided to set the horse free. And with that, he once again started walking down the dirt road.

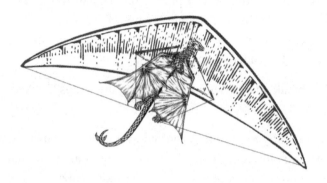

## CHAPTER FIVE: LAVENDER'S JOURNEY

Birds are graceful and efficient flyers. They use the wind and glide majestically....dragons, not so much. Dragons are heavy, and their wings, while fully extended could be quite large, aren't large enough to be able to keep them in the air for very long. Dragons use flight for traveling short distances and for hunting or fighting. They are not masters of the sky, and are much more comfortable on the ground. But dragons are more clever than birds and can build things. That's how dragon science created some tools to help dragons elevate their flying ability.

"It's called a Gliderwing," explained Peacefinder, holding out a long, narrow tube with some material folding around it. "We use these when we want to fly far," she said. She carefully unfolded the material and pressed a button on the side of the tube. two additional tubes popped out, creating a "T" like shape, with the material hanging out on both sides, secured by tight strings.

"Oh, it's like a kite!" exclaimed Lavender.

"Exactly, but there's no long string to control it because we ARE the kite, and we control it by pulling on these strings here" explained Peacefinder, demonstrating the use of the strings. "Now, let's get these on," she said, as she moved to attach the awkward kite to Lavender's back.

"Won't it break apart when I start flapping my wings?" asked Lavender.

"You don't really need to flap your wings much when using a Gliderwing. You only open it up when you are high in the air and then use it to glide…not flapping all the time like a crazy chicken" Peacefinder teased. "Don't worry, watch me and follow what I do, you'll be fine." After fiddling with the harness and making sure all the straps were tight, Peacefinder took to the air with several powerful flaps of her wings. Lavender followed, feeling annoyed by the added weight of the contraption on her back. By the time they got high enough for Lavender to be able to see the distant mountains and rivers ahead, she was already tired. "Now, you'll need to dive quickly and open the Gliderwing as you fall" said Peacefinder to a rather worn out Lavender. "Just watch me do it first," she said as she tucked her wings in and dove head-first towards the ground. Moments later, Lavender saw the kite's wings open to their full size. It was impressive- the kite's wings were at least twice as large as Peacefinder's own, which were already big for a dragon her size. Right after the glider opened, it caught the wind and Peacefinder jolted upward, then made a graceful arc back towards Lavender. "There now, you see?" shouted Peacefinder, who was now gliding above Lavender. At this point Lavender's wings were burning with the strain of just keeping afloat, so the idea of diving head-first didn't scare her as much. She dove. The initial feeling of relief from flying quickly changed to the terror of falling. She started flapping her wings again out of fear, but then remembered that she's supposed to open the glider instead. She pulled on the strings the way Peacefinder taught her. Nothing happened. She pulled again, harder this time. Nothing happened! Panic entered her brain again as the ground below her rapidly approached. She still had time to get out of this, if she flapped her wings as hard as she could right now….but her wings were out of power from all the flapping she just did! Suddenly, she felt a jolt as she hit something; it wasn't the ground, and it wasn't a tree or anything else like that. She realized then that it was Peacefinder, who had swooped down next to her and caught her! Lavender was now riding on Peacefinder's back, just above the glider. Peacefinder regained some distance from the ground and then spoke to Lavender, "It's ok, don't be upset. Most dragons struggle with the Gliderwing. It's just that…most dragons struggle once they get it open. You're not on that level of struggle yet." Lavender felt like she should defend herself, but instead decided to enjoy the ride. "We'll work on it and you'll become a Gliderwing master before you know it," said Peacefinder, trying to brighten up the mood.

Over the next few days, Lavender worked on learning how to use the glider. She managed to get it open, but then managed to flip herself over in the air every time she tried to turn.

"You're pulling too hard," yelled Peacefinder, trying to make herself heard over the sound of rushing wind as she flew next to Lavender. It was a tricky thing, the Gliderwing. Pull too hard, and it flips you over. Pull too gently, and it doesn't do anything. After a few hours of training, they landed next to a small pond to have lunch. Lavender was exhausted. After folding her glider elegantly back into its tube, Peacefinder pulled some dried meat and fruits out of her sack. "We'll need to get to the next village soon," she said. "Either that, or go fishing." Lavender looked dismayed. They had already eaten up most of their rations and barely got out of Talonwing. "Once you master the Gliderwing, we'll make quick progress," said Peacefinder, sensing Lavender's frustration. The air was warm and the pond was a cozy little spot, with small trees and stones surrounding it. Lavender was so excited at the start of a new adventure and a new life, but she had no idea it would be so much work! She just wanted to lay about this pond for the rest of the day. But as soon as her lunch was finished, Peacefinder said, "let's go." Lavender forced herself up with a groan. "Wait. Sit for a moment, let me show you something," said Peacefinder, as she prepared her glider for takeoff. "I want to show you what this thing can do," she said, as she flapped hard and took to the sky. Lavender watched her closely. So far she only knew the glider was good for flying comfortably over long distances. What she saw next amazed her. Peacefinder unfurled the glider high above the pond, but this time only unfurled it halfway. She lunged down, directly at the water! Lavender shrieked with fright, but at the last moment, Peacefinder unfurled the glider fully and pulled hard on the control strings. The glider made a loud "whooshing" noise, and Peacefinder made a swift arc right above the water, grazing the surface with her talons. She then did a triple spiral straight up into the air before somehow ending upside-down and doing a loop! Lavender's jaw had dropped by now and she was gawking at her in awe. Peacefinder continued doing amazing acrobatics in the air. Quick turns, loops, spirals, dives…the glider was like her own wings that she could control with such ease. Moments later, Peacefinder landed, a look of exhilaration on her face.

"That was amazing!" yelled Lavender. "How did you learn to do all that?" was Lavender's first question.

"I had a good teacher, and I worked really hard. I've been flying Gliderwings longer than you've been alive dear." Lavender was still in awe. Seeing this, Peacefinder said, "My teacher taught me everything she knew about flying, and I will teach you. You'll be as good as I am, if not better, but it'll take time and lots of work." After seeing that amazing display, Lavender was motivated again. Over the next few days, Lavender made great progress, and flying was feeling less like a hassle and more like enjoyment. Not only were her glider skills improving, her wings were getting stronger as well. She loved feeling that she was improving with each day. She felt like a bird, gliding over the world and seeing far across the horizon. They were flying above a cobblestone road that linked many of the major dragon towns.

"Does this road go all the way to Sagestone?" Lavender questioned, while they glided together.

"It does," replied Peacefinder. "This is the Everroad. It was built by King Evergreat, one of the first kings of the dragon world," explained Peacefinder. "He named himself Evergreat, which is quite a statement, but in fact, he wasn't wrong. The things he built to unite the dragon kingdom are still around today. Like this road, which allows us to transport goods between towns and helps make the kingdom what it is today," said Peacefinder. "He wasn't a Seer, but Evergreat had a vision of the future beyond himself and his time as king." Lavender pondered on this.

A few days after their lunch at the pond, Lavender and Peacefinder flew into a small dragon village along the Everroad. The sun was starting to set and Lavender felt tired. "We'll sleep here tonight," said Peacefinder. "There is a small guest house here." After sleeping outdoors for the past week, Lavender was thankful for a warm straw bed and hot meal. The village was called Littlewing, and the name fit it quite well. The Everroad passed through the middle of the town, which was built mostly out of wooden structures which were short, small cottages and shops. The dragons who lived here were mostly farmers. Lavender noticed many wagons full of corn and wheat and barrels and cartons. These carts would be pulled by large beasts called Tuks, which looked mean with their wide horns and large bodies, but were actually very calm creatures. Dragons have been using Tuks for hundreds of years to help pull heavy things and build houses. The town itself was small but everything looked nice. There was fresh paint on the signposts outside of the shops, and the dragons here were friendly and cheerful. Up ahead, Lavender saw the largest structure in the town- a guest house with a restaurant full of dragons eating and singing songs. She smiled. This place looked fun. They went inside and were welcomed by a cheerful waitress who seemed to recognize Peacefinder. Some of the dragons looked up from their meals and their eyes grew wide at the sight. Peacefinder seemed to have an effect on dragons, but Lavender wasn't sure why. They were given a small table near the back of the restaurant. In fact, Lavender had never been outside of Talonwing before. She read about the fancy dining halls and banquets in Sagestone, and how the menus at those places could take an hour to read through. But there was no menu here.

"Welcome to Littlewing Inn your honorship!" said a voice from out of the kitchen. A short, lively dragon with vibrant red scales walked out to greet them.

"Thank you Sigmund, it's been awhile," replied Peacefinder.

"Indeed it has, too long!" he replied in a grand sweep of his arms. "We are always honored to have a member of the King's Council at our humble village," said Sigmund. *King's Council? Wow she really is famous*, thought Lavender, more curious than ever about who exactly Peacefinder was.

"I am grateful for your support," was Peacefinder's only reply to Sigmund.

"And how is the king?" he continued. Peacefinder was clearly in no mood to discuss, especially now that the entire restaurant was clearly listening in on the conversation.

"The king is…well," she said with some hesitation. Realizing she was now speaking to the crowd, she raised her voice and said, "the king sends his praise to the good people of Littlewing. May your crops be plentiful and your spirits high," said Peacefinder, in a dignified voice that Lavender had not heard her use before. At this, the entire room erupted in cheering. Now the music was louder than ever and several dragons began to dance. Soon, Lavender had a big bowl of porridge in front of her. It was filled with vegetables and a red sauce she never tried before. It was delicious. She ate two bowls full. Peacefinder smiled. "I'm glad you like it. Now let's hurry off to bed before they start asking us to dance." They thanked Sigmund again and Peacefinder attempted to give him sapphire tokens to pay for the meal and the room, but he flatly refused. They made their way up a creaky staircase to the room. It was small, but cozy, with two straw beds and a torch-lit dresser in between. Lavender's belly was full and her eyes were heavy.

"What was all that about the King's Council?" she asked, half yawning.

"You'll find out all about that when we get to Sagestone," replied Peacefinder. "Now get to sleep, we have a long day ahead." Lavender didn't need to be told twice. She welcomed the straw bed gratefully and immediately fell asleep.

Peacefinder woke her up while it was still dark out. Lavender was in no mood to get up this early, but she was an adventurer after all, and adventurers woke up early. This was the image Lavender now took to heart. She was no longer an orphan in a sleepy town. She was now an adventurer on important and dangerous quests. She flew with a Gliderwing and hung out at guest houses. She was somebody.

Peacefinder dropped an envelope on the dresser on their way out.

"What's that?" asked Lavender.

"Payment for the dinner and the room" said Peacefinder. "He even stocked my sack full of provisions," she noticed. "Such kind dragons in these parts. I know he insists on us staying and eating for free, but I included a letter saying it was a wonderful stay and that the king insisted on repaying him. He cannot refuse that." Lavender thought of this.

"But the king doesn't even know we're here," she said finally.

"No he doesn't," replied Peacefinder. "But the king believes in fairness, and it's only fair that we pay our own way," she told Lavender.

"But does that mean- Peacefinder do you actually know the king himself?" asked Lavender, a look of awe on her face. Peacefinder noticed her look.

"Like I said, there is a group of dragons that advise the king in all things. This group meets regularly in the Everhall- the king's grand throne room at Sagestone," she explained. Lavender knew all about Everhall. It was described in detail in one of the books she read in school. The Everhall was said to be the most grand and beautiful room in the entire kingdom. "I am a member of that council," said Peacefinder, jolting Lavender out of her daydreaming about Everhall. "But it's not like the stories might say," continued Peacefinder. "Being a member of that council is very stressful and very hard work. We are responsible for advising the king in the best way we can, and if we make a mistake, it could lead to disaster for the kingdom," she said with a serious tone. "That is why we are standing here," she continued, while strapping on her Gliderwing. "I am on a mission to avoid a terrible disaster...a calamity. You are part of that mission." Lavender's eyes grew wide. Suddenly her idea of being an adventurer took on a much more serious meaning.

Two days later, Lavender spotted a gleaming silver spire over the horizon. There, on a large hill next to a river, was the capital, Sagestone. They were still far from their destination, but it already looked like nothing she had ever seen before. The tallest spire was part of the Kingsden- the ancient home of dragon kings for hundreds of years. Surrounding it were many shorter spires, all gleaming in different shades of turquoise, amber, copper and gold. Gentle smoke could be seen wafting out from hundreds of chimneys, and the Everroad branched out across three bridges that led to three grand gates. The bridge in the center had two large statues on each side, which must have been statues of the two kings who came together to form one kingdom over a thousand years ago. All around, she could see activity. Tuks pulling carts, dragons walking the road and many on Gliderwings, landing or taking off from several circular towers located along the outer wall. The entire scene was like something out of a storybook. Lavender was in awe.

"Follow me," said Peacefinder, clearly amused by Lavender's reaction to seeing the capital for the first time. "I remember my first time seeing the capital," said Peacefinder. "I was younger than you are now, but it's one of my most vivid memories. I was riding in a cart pulled by a Tuk. We had been on the road for days and I was tired and uncomfortable, but the sight of this place- the first time I saw the spires over Kingsden...I'm sure I was just as overwhelmed as you are now," she said, while gazing in the direction of the capital. As they approached, Peacefinder removed a silver and red colored flag from her sack. She draped it down and it hung from her talons.

"What's that for?" asked Lavender. "This is for the city watch. They must recognize every dragon flying into the city. This tells them where I am intending to land and who I am," explained Peacefinder.

"So what happens if I don't have a flag?" asked Lavender. "That's why I told you to fly close to me," said Peacefinder. "If the city watch spots a dragon without a flag...well, let's just say they will politely ask them to land outside of the city walls...and if they don't, they will ask impolitely," said Peacefinder. Lavender never considered how important this place was and how dragon warriors were keeping it safe. The king lived here after all. They landed on top of a flat tower which had the same silver and red flag flying above it. There, they were greeted by a small, green and yellow dragon and two larger warrior dragons who were carrying spears. They wore shiny, ruby-colored armor which was painted to look like scales. It was the first time Lavender had ever seen a warrior dragon, and they were intimidating.

"Welcome back to Sagestone your honorship!" exclaimed the small dragon. "Thank you Goldflake," said Peacefinder, dropping her sack and unstrapping her Gliderwing. Lavender did the same. The warrior dragons eyed her with caution. Then, Peacefinder spoke, once again using that formal tone she heard her use once before. "I would like to announce the arrival of the long-awaited Seer," she said to both Goldflake and the two warriors. Immediately their faces changed from suspicion to awe. "Lavender, this is Goldflake. She will help you to your room and get you a meal."

"Pleased to meet you," said Lavender. Goldflake was clearly surprised by what Peacefinder just said, but kept her composure and welcomed Lavender. She then spoke in a low voice to Peacefinder,

"Your honorship, your messenger arrived not half a day ago. But…he's in rough shape. He is currently at the medic house, recovering from both wounds and exhaustion." Lavender caught a brief look of fear across Peacefinder's face, but she quickly returned to her professional look of total calm.

"Then there is no time to waste. I must seek out my messenger immediately," said Peacefinder, clearly in a hurry now. "Lavender, I will meet with you tomorrow," she said, as she made her way down the spiral staircase of the tower. Peacefinder's rapid departure left Lavender with Goldflake.

"You must be exhausted after your journey," Goldflake said gently. "I'll show you to your room immediately." Lavender's face brightened up, after all of the flying, confusion, and pure exhaustion, she would love to sit on a nice, cozy bed. They descended the spiral staircase of the tower and emerged into a long hallway with tall ceilings. Torches lit up the hallway and Lavender could see several doorways on one side. All of them were closed. They then proceeded down the hall and into a much larger room which held a long wooden table in the center and benches on either side. The room was decorated with tapestries of various colors and statues of great warriors on either side. Lavender was impressed, but it didn't look like she thought it would.

"Is this Everhall?" she asked. Goldflake let out a small laugh, then quickly controlled herself.

"I'm sorry, I didn't mean to laugh, I just didn't realize this was your first time to Kingsden. This room is called the Hall of Spears, and it's used to honor the warrior dragons who protect the capital and the kingdom. The Kingsguard normally eat dinner here, if they are not on duty," explained Goldflake. They made their way through the room and through a large double doorway on the other side. Now they were inside a long, narrow courtyard with a small fountain in the center. The surrounding building had fancy columns carved out of stone and white marble staircases leading to the various floors. "These are the guest quarters," said Goldflake. "Your room is just at the top there," she said, pointing to the far end of the courtyard where a tower rose over the rest of the building. As they walked up the stairs, Lavender noticed more warrior dragons keeping watch.

"Are there always so many warrior dragons around?" asked Lavender.

"No, it hasn't always been this way," replied Goldflake. "The Council has ordered additional security all over the capital over the past few months."

"Do you know why?" asked Lavender.

"I'm just a squire," replied Goldflake.

"What's that mean?" asked Lavender.

"Oh, squires are young dragons who are chosen to live and work inside Kingsden, doing various chores like cooking, cleaning, and helping the noble dragons with their daily tasks," she replied with a hint of pride. "I was very lucky to get this chance." They soon arrived at the guest room. Goldflake opened it with a large, copper key which she then gave to Lavender. "Let me know if you like the room," said Goldflake, as she lit a series of candles inside. The room was large, with a feathery bed on one side and a wooden dresser on the other. Above the dresser hung a glass mirror- something that was considered an incredible luxury back in Talonwing. The room had dark red curtains which, when Goldflake pulled open, showed a small balcony overlooking the city. The view was marvelous, and Lavender moved quickly to the balcony to take it all in. "There you can see the Six Feather School, and there is the Jade Dragon statue, and there's the Royal Bathhouse, and over there is the Great Sage Museum," explained Goldflake, pointing out the various landmarks so quickly that Lavender barely had time to spin her head around.

"I wish I could see them all," murmured Lavender, half to herself and half to Goldflake. "But I fear my time in Sagestone will be short," she said. Goldflake gave her a small smile.

"You can always come back here though! You're more than welcome." Goldflake showed her how to use the water pump inside the room to brighten up the  mood and then left Lavender to relax. She would fetch her again when it was time for dinner. Lavender wasted no time hopping onto the feather bed and melting into it. It was just as she imagined- the softest, most comfy thing she had ever experienced. She dreamed of one day sleeping on a feather bed. Today, that dream was coming true. She was jolted away by the sound of bells clinking. Had she fallen asleep? She looked out the window- sure enough, the sun had already set.

"Lavender? Are you ok? It's Goldflake. I'm here to take you down to dinner," said Goldflake through the door.

"Coming," replied Lavender, her eyes still heavy. She got herself off of the feather bed and opened the door slowly. Goldflake stood on the other end, her scales dancing in the moonlight. She led Lavender through more long hallways and through another courtyard. They finally arrived at a large building with vines curling around the stone tiles. Flowers blossomed from the vines and there were small bits of quartz embedded into the walls. Birds perched on the two trees that stood in the courtyard. It was a magnificent building that had a peaceful aura. Lavender stood there, mesmerized. Goldflake cleared her throat loudly and beckoned for Lavender to come to the door. She trotted over to her and murmured a small, quiet "sorry." Goldflake took out another key- this one made from silver. There was a small click and the door opened to reveal a massive hallway with gold stripes studded into the walls for decoration. Moonlight filtered through the windows and cast shadows on the wall. Torches were placed along the columns to light the way. Lavender's heart pounded so loud that she was pretty sure the birds outside could hear it. She pinned her wings against her side and her claws curled tightly onto the smooth, cold stone. There were huge stone carvings along the walls, some showing great battles, others showing meetings between what must have been important dragons in history.

"The Hall of Great Deeds," said Goldflake, anticipating Lavender's question. Eventually, they arrived at a huge golden door with flowers and glittery silver pearls scattered around it. Placed next to the door on the wall was a wooden sign with swirly, neat handwriting engraved onto it. The sign read:

KEEP OUT! COUNCILLORS ONLY

"This is as far as I go," said Goldflake, who was already moving away, as if the door itself was repelling her like a magnet.

"Wait...what?" questioned Lavender, but Goldflake was already gone.

## CHAPTER SIX: THE BLOOD-RED GANG

Malon's exile had lasted nearly two weeks, and he was tired of walking. The elegant clothing he had stolen from the carriage was already looking ripped and muddy, and the food he had stolen had run out. He was back to looking like a beast of the wild again, but this time he at least had a spear. The landscape had become more rocky, and the road now followed the bottom of a steep stone cliff. Ahead of him, he saw a large rock formation; two large stone pillars with the road passing directly in between them. He noticed a rope hanging between the two pillars, connecting them at the very top and crossing high over the road. He also noticed some poorly-constructed wooden stairs hanging off the side of the stone pillars. As he got closer, he noticed a broken-down wagon sitting on the road, right in between these two pillars. Malon knew immediately what this was- a trap. But it wasn't a trap for him, he thought. Someone walking was moving slowly enough to notice all of these details. A horse-drawn carriage would come across this scene very quickly, and would have to stop as the broken-down wagon was blocking the road. This trap was set by bandits. He took cover behind some bushes and waited. It took nearly all day, but just as the sun began to sink below the horizon, a caravan of three carts was spotted, rumbling towards the trap. The lead cart stopped and six guards jumped off, looking in all directions. That's when the bandits attacked. They started by throwing rocks down onto the caravan from above, while several bandits jumped out from somewhere behind the rocks and attacked with wooden clubs. The guards carried spears and crossbows, and although they were out-numbered, they were also better trained and better armed. The bandits had to battle the guards, while the rocks continued to fall. One of the bandits throwing rocks got hit with a crossbow bolt, and fell to the ground below. Several other bandits got hit with the rocks that their friends were throwing down, and a few others got swiped with spears. The entire attack was a disaster that ended with the caravan breaking past the broken-down wagon and losing nothing, while many of the bandits were either dead or injured. Malon saw an opportunity. Later that night, he crept around the bandit camp. Without being seen, he was able to steal most of their weapons stash. He then hid the weapons and approached the bandits, who were now sitting around a fire, tending to their wounds. When they saw Malon, they quickly ran to their weapons stash, only to find nothing there.

"You guys are clowns," said Malon, still using that raspy voice which he had now grown comfortable with. "But I can help you," he continued. The bandits were still running around trying to find their weapons, but Malon reassured them that the weapons were safe. "I watched your attack today, and I'm sure I could do better just by myself," he said.

"Oh yeah, why should we believe you, you look like just a kid," replied one bandit, who managed to find a bow and had an arrow pointed at Malon. But Malon showed no fear. He was once again risking everything, because he had nothing to lose.

"Fine, I'll prove it to you," he said. The bandits were unconvinced, but since he did manage to steal all of their weapons from right under their noses, they decided to give him a chance. The following day, Malon instructed the bandits to remove the broken-down wagon and any obvious signs that their trap existed. He then told them to dig several long trenches along the road leading up the rocky pillars. They then had to fill the trenches with sticky mud, and cover them with leaves. He then used wood and scraps of leather and cloth to fashion new "uniforms" for the attacking bandits. He remembered how his wild beast look affected the woman in the carriage. This taught him that intimidation was a powerful tool. He then told the other bandits sitting on top of the pillars to make thumping sounds all at the same time, and for a few of them to point- but not shoot- arrows at the target. The point of this was to make the caravan guards believe there were way more bandits then there really were. Finally, he said that he would be the one to negotiate with the caravan guards, and that nobody was allowed to attack them unless he ordered them to. The bandits were still skeptical of this plan, but Malon's craftiness would be proven on the very next day. When the next caravan approached, it was very similar to the one that the bandits failed to rob before. Three horse-pulled wagons with no fewer than half a dozen guards. As they approached, the first wagon got one of its wheels caught in the trench, and quickly stopped. The second wagon's wheels fell in right behind it. The third stopped in time, but that didn't matter. The wagons couldn't move forward or backward now, and it was at this moment that Malon came out from behind a bush and walked casually to the front of the caravan.

"It seems you have a problem," he said, casually poking the end of his spear on the ground. The guards immediately formed a line, spears pointing at him.

"Or maybe you're the one with the problem, bandit," said one of the guards, smirking.

"Here's my proposal," said Malon, completely unphased by the spears pointing at his head. "I'll have my crew help get your wagons out of this mess, and charge you a fair price for the service. And from now on, every time you drive by here, we'll charge a road tax to keep this road in good working order so that you never have to waste your time like this again," said Malon. The guards all laughed.

"You're just a puny little kid, we'll just run you over and forget you were ever here," said the smirking guard. At this, Malon gave the command. Bandits who were hiding behind the rock pillars now emerged, running wildly at the caravan guards. They had what looked like wings sticking out of their backs, and were painted black and red. They carried clubs that were painted completely red, so much so that the wet paint was falling off the clubs and looked like blood. At the same time, terrible booming noises came from above, and the guards could see a line of archers pointing arrows at them. The guards were stunned, not knowing which threat to deal with. Then Malon walked right up to the smirking guard- who was no longer smirking, and with his spear right in his face, ordered him to tell all of the guards to drop their weapons. They did as he asked.

"Now, let me ask you again, will you take my deal or not?" Malon asked smugly. The guards agreed reluctantly. "Great, but the price just went up," said Malon. The bandits then used planks they had ready to get the wagons unstuck. Malon collected a hefty fee in silver, and reminded the guards that they would be expected to pay a road toll from now on. They grudgingly agreed, but Malon knew his road toll idea would not be so easy to accept. That evening, the bandits celebrated their victory, and couldn't believe they achieved it all without even fighting. "Every trick works the first time someone sees it," said Malon, sitting just outside of the fire's light. "But once they know the trick, it won't work again. That's why you need me. I can keep coming up with new tricks." The bandits' leader had been killed in the last failed robbery attempt, so Malon's arrival as their new leader was unchallenged. And so, Malon became the leader of what would later become known as the Blood-red Gang, named after their use of red paint on everything.

Malon ran the Blood-red Gang with great success for years. His road tax became a commonly accepted cost of traveling, and his methods of luring caravans into traps became legendary. So much so that one day, the king of the human realm decided to rid the roads of all bandits, and sent the army to deal with them. When he heard this, Malon knew their days were numbered, so he decided to try one final robbery- the most ambitious of any thief who ever lived. While the king sent his army out to find Malon, Malon would come to the king's castle and rob him.

## CHAPTER SEVEN: THE JEWEL OF DRAGONSMIGHT

King Steadfast the Twenty-Fifth ruled over an ever-expanding human kingdom. His great, great, great (and so on) grandfather fought a war against the other human kingdoms, and had come out victorious. Legend has it, King Steadfast the First had the power to ride and control dragons. These creatures only existed as myths in the human world for hundreds of years, and nobody had seen a dragon in generations. But the world is large, and a good part of it is unknown, so the king believed that it was possible that dragons still existed. The legends went on to say that King Steadfast the First became greedy in his lust for power, and eventually sent his dragon armies against the realm of the dragons themselves. This resulted in another, much more terrible war, in which the free dragons fought against the dragons whom the humans had enslaved, eventually destroying King Steadfast's entire dragon army, and killing the king in the process. Then, in revenge for enslaving dragons, the victorious free dragons attacked the human kingdom, burning entire cities to the ground with their white-hot flames. What was left of the human armies eventually banded together to stop the dragons, and a peace was reached. In this peace, humans promised to never again enslave or enter the realm of the dragons, and the dragons promised to never bother the humans. Maps were drawn with solid red lines, showing where the human realm ended. All humans, whether they be soldiers, merchants, or explorers, were forbidden to venture past those lines. But over the next generations, the human realm expanded, and soon the solid red borders became troublesome. And so humans began to ignore them and build settlements beyond the red lines. Nothing happened to those settlements, so humans continued to push further, setting up mines, farms, and villages well beyond the original borders. Eventually, the maps were updated and the red lines disappeared, and with the passage of time, everyone forgot about the peace agreement. Dragons became legends, and legends became fairy tales. In the modern human world, nobody believed that giant, flying, fire-breathing beasts existed somewhere in the unknown wilderness. But King Steadfast the Twenty-Fifth liked to believe that dragons did exist, and he had one piece of evidence to support this: the Jewel of Dragonsmight. This broken fragment of crystal was very special to the king, and it was believed to be the only surviving piece in the world. Legend has it that the Jewel of Dragonsmight was the only recovered fragment of the orb used by King Steadfast the First to control dragons. Where the king found this orb, who made it, and how…are all mysteries lost to time. But the fate of the orb was known. In the final battle between free dragons and enslaved dragons, King Steadfast the First rode on a huge and terrible dragon he called Doomsflame. Together with his army of dragonriders, he fought against the forces of the free dragons in a battle that would shape world history. The king's army was

63

outnumbered, but his dragons were terrifying and strong, and for a moment it seemed like they would win. But then, a small, quick dragon dived through the air at the king, broke through his guards, and swiped a talon directly at the king's heart. However, the talon was stopped by what the king was holding in his hand-the orb of Dragonsmight. The impact of the talon against the orb shattered it into a dozen pieces, all of which fell to the ground far below. With the orb broken, the enslaved dragons suddenly regained control of their own thoughts, and stopped fighting for the humans. Doomsflame quickly spun through the air, knocking off the king and sending him falling to his death. The other dragons got rid of their human riders in the same way, and just like that, the humans lost their advantage, as well as the war. The Orb of Dragonsmight was no more, and humans were forbidden to ever try to use such a power again. But years later, one of the pieces of the orb was found, and given as a gift to the new king. The king ordered that the shard be shaped into a jewel and made into a fancy necklace. And so, the Jewel of Dragonsmight came to be. King Steadfast the Twenty-Fifth now gazed upon the necklace, and the shiny red jewel at its center. The jewel always made him shudder to think about those terrible, legendary beasts...but it also made him wonder. Would the jewel, now only a small fraction of the original orb, still work? The king returned the jewel to its chest. He used two golden keys to lock the chest, and returned each key to its hidden space inside the king's dresser. The Jewel of Dragonsmight was his most prized possession, and whenever he wore it in public, everyone would gaze upon it in awe. Whether or not it worked to control dragons was unimportant. The king went to bed, and that night, he dreamt about flying atop a dragon.

64

When the king issued the order to wipe out all roadside bandits, he did so out of anger. The bandits had become so bold as to pretend they were tiny kings themselves, forcing citizens to pay a so-called "road tax". This could not stand. And so, in order to guarantee swift success, the king ordered his entire army to the task, leaving only his personal guard to defend the capital. His critics called him reckless, but the king wasn't worried. There weren't any serious threats against the kingdom in centuries. The human realm had been united, and he had no challengers that would be eager to try to overthrow him. In fact, he was so certain of himself, that he declared a feast be held once the army reached Farflung and cleared out all the bandits. When word reached Malon that the king was holding a feast, he saw his chance. He took a few of his most trusted bandits and rode hard for the capital.

Ravensthorn was the capital of the human kingdom. Unlike most large cities, which were located along rivers or on top of hills, Ravensthorn was built into the side of a mountain. The town itself was located in a valley surrounding the mountainside, but the king's castle was actually carved into the mountain itself. Ravens liked to gather on the tall trees that grew in the area, and so the town got its name. The king's castle was called Ravenstone. The castle was built after the Dragon War, when the old capital was burned. The king at that time was so afraid of dragons that he ordered his castle to be built into the side of a mountain, where the thick rock could give protection against dragonfire. Over the generations, the castle was expanded and made more grand, with towers, ballrooms, grand halls, and even waterfalls built into the mountainside. Even so, the original chambers, hidden deep inside the mountain, were still kept and used as storage spaces. But the king had no interest in living in such dark, damp places, and instead lived in the king's Royal Chamber, which featured a beautiful balcony and floor-to-ceiling windows that overlooked the entire valley. It was said that the Royal Chamber was so high up that the king saw sunshine even when it was raining in the town below. Malon had arrived in Ravensthorn a week before, and had spent his time gathering information about the Royal Chamber and the treasure inside. He chatted with locals, listened to legends and rumors, and even bribed guards to get as complete a picture as he could. He also bought climbing equipment and learned how to use it, practicing on the mountain outside of the city at night. On the next day, the king would be busy at the feast, and all of his guards would have their hands full guarding the king and all of his guests. That's when Malon would have his chance.

The night of the feast arrived. Malon thought back on his journey to this point. At each turning point in his life, he was willing to risk everything because he had nothing to lose. Now, once again, as his bandit life was coming to an end, he had to risk it all. How many times would he need to do this before he finally felt like he was someone that the world respected; someone that mattered. He didn't know, but he did know that if he pulled this off, it might just be enough.

The king's outfit for the feast featured a white fur coat studded with jewels, a crystal crown which was said to come from the fabled Icelava fields, and a necklace featuring twenty six sparkling diamonds- one for each of the provinces he ruled over. The necklace was especially grand, as it was a recent gift from one of his dukes, and had never been seen in public before. As much as the king loved the Jewel of Dragonsmight, he had worn it many times, and it was only fitting that he wear his latest necklace on this occasion. And so, King Steadfast the 25th left the Jewel of Dragonsmight in its chest that evening. The feast was already in full swing when the king entered his grand ballroom riding in on a white horse with glimmering, silver wings attached to his back. The wings weren't real of course, they were made from silk and embroidery. The effect was stunning, and together with his crystal crown and dazzling diamond necklace, the king really out-did himself in his grand entrance. He felt on top of the world- as any king should. Unknown to the king however, at that very moment, two men were silently climbing up the side of his mountainside castle. Malon and his deputy were nearly an hour into their climb and about to reach the king's balcony. They had timed their break-in to the king's castle perfectly, and with so few guards around, they had their chance. However, something was bound to go wrong. That's when his deputy slipped and fell. The rope caught him, but he still fell nearly three stories and landed on a rooftop with a bone-crunching thud. It made a terrible noise. Malon saw torchlights coming in his direction from one of the ledges far below. He had no choice but to cut his rope and jump for the balcony, with nothing but air between himself and the ground far below. He leapt into the air and grabbed the stone ledge above. The stone was hard to hold onto, and he felt his grip slipping. The muscles in his arms were already worn out from the climb, and now they were burning. He managed to hold on just long enough to pull himself up and over the ledge. Exhausted and drenched in sweat, he had arrived on the grand balcony of the Royal Chamber. Malon didn't stop to admire the view; he was on a mission. The king was careless in leaving his balcony door wide open, so Malon was spared the long task of breaking in. This was good. Torchlight lit up the inside of the chamber, which was even grander than Malon had imagined. His eyes went straight to the center of the room, where a huge chest decorated in jewels and gold stood. It seemed too obvious, and Malon looked all around for traps, but found none. Once he reached the chest though, Malon realized that getting to the treasure wouldn't be so easy. The chest required two keys, which could be anywhere. If the king kept one or both of the keys with him at all times, his plan would be finished. But Malon knew that the keys must be big and heavy, and the king would not be interested in carrying them around. They must be here, somewhere. After searching and searching, Malon thought about what the king loved best- himself. He opened the dresser drawer below the huge mirror where the king would admire himself. He threw out all of the brushes and jewelry, and at the bottom he found two compartments. Each compartment contained a large, golden key. Malon couldn't believe it- he was one step away from success. Quickly, he moved to the chest. Was there some special way of putting the keys in? He decided to put them both in at once and turn at the same time. With a creak, the chest opened. Malon expected gold and jewelry to be overflowing from the chest. He anticipated that the treasure would completely fill the sack he brought with him, and be too heavy to even carry. When he peered inside though, he was amazed to find it was empty. Empty- except for one object, a fancy, golden necklace with a ruby red jewel shining in the center. Whatever this was, it was priceless. Malon quickly took it out and stuffed it into his sack. He thought back on Farflung and how he got caught stealing there because he stayed too long. He wouldn't make that mistake now.

He made his way out to the balcony, but he heard a commotion below. His deputy had been discovered. Malon thought fast, and went back inside. He went to the king's closet and pulled out a bunch of elegant robes. He picked one and put it on. He fixed his hair in the mirror and strolled out of the king's chamber. His heart raced as he walked into the grand ballroom and past the guests. There must have been a hundred people there, and nobody paid attention to him. As he made his way to the exit, he swore he saw the king himself glance over at him. But by the time the king could wonder if that was his royal robe, Malon was gone. He walked out of the castle through the front gate, with nobody questioning that he belonged there. He then mounted the horse that he had prepared, and rode right out of Ravensthorn. And so the theft of the Jewel of Dragonsmight would become the greatest legend ever told among bandits and thieves alike.

And that should have been the end of his story. Malon became a legend among the criminal world, having tricked the king so completely that the human realm would secretly laugh at the king for years to come. The king so missed his prized necklace that he even offered a huge reward and a full pardon to Malon for returning it. But Malon didn't take the offer. For one, he didn't trust the king, but more importantly, the necklace became a symbol of his ability and fame. He wore the necklace day and night. It made him important. But Malon still didn't understand why the king treasured this necklace so much. The one he wore to the feast that night was much more grand and certainly more valuable. Then one night, while sitting around a campfire, one of the bandits that made up Malon's group started talking about a legend he had heard while sitting in jail back in Ravensthorn.

"That jewel Malon stole isn't just some trinket, it's got real power. Magical power! It's called the Jewel of Dragonsmight, and it can control dragons!"

The bandits gathered around the fire laughed.

"Come on, dragons? Next you'll tell us it can also help you talk to trolls!" yelled out one of the bandits standing in the back. Malon listened for a moment, then came out of his tent.

"Who told you this legend?" he asked the bandit. The bandit suddenly got quiet, wondering if he was in trouble.

"I...I just heard it from another thief, and he said he had read about it in a book." Malon was curious.

"Anyone who brings me that book will get one hundred silver coins," he announced to the entire camp. One hundred silver coins was a small fortune, and the bandits instantly started to scramble for information about the book. Less than three weeks later, Malon had the book in his hands. The book was big, heavy, and burned on one side. It looked like it had been rescued from a fire. It reminded him of his favorite book back in Farflung. *The History of the First Empire*, he read to himself. The book was written in the same difficult to read text that Malon already knew, and he skimmed through it. This was how Malon learned about the necklace's history, and especially what the Jewel of Dragonsmight was fabled to really be.

Malon became obsessed with the legend, and felt an overwhelming need to find out if the jewel still had any power over dragons. He remembered the story about Doomswing, and imagined what it would be like to have such a powerful dragon under his control. And so, Malon set out to the outer reaches of the human realm and beyond, in order to find a living dragon, and maybe even the legendary Doomswing. Most people laughed at him and said that he had gone mad. Dragons didn't exist after all. But Malon had already proven that he could do what seemed to be impossible, so his closest bandit gang believed in him and followed him. After a long and difficult journey, the bandit gang arrived at the farthest edge of the human realm, past the Great North River, where only small hunting and fishing villages existed. The locals told them many tales of dragons, but one stood out. There were rumors that there was a group of bandit dragons who would sometimes swoop in and attack trade caravans that ventured too far into the deep forest. Malon decided that they would set a trap. They put together what looked like a trading caravan, and started down the deepest, darkest paths into the unknown regions of forest that they could find. They made all kinds of noise while they moved, but day after day, nothing happened.

They were camped on a large field surrounded by forest one night, when they finally got what they were hoping for. Wings flashed in the dark, and an unnerving screech could be heard. Then, with incredible speed, four dragons swooped down on them, talons swiping at them. The complete shock caused two of the bandits to freeze in place. They were slashed to pieces, as were three others who started to run. The rest of the bandits picked up spears and bows and began to defend themselves, but the dragons swooped down again and again, taking them out one by one. Arrows seemed to do nothing, as they just bounced off of the dragons' scales. Malon hid behind one of the wagons, watching the carnage but doing nothing to stop it. The speed and ferocity of the dragons made his blood run cold. But then, the dragons finally landed and started walking around the camp, and Malon's initial fear turned to curiosity. These dragons weren't nearly as scary as the dragons he'd read about in the ancient books. The dragons of legends were huge. These dragons weren't much bigger than horses. The dragons of legends had wingspans as big as entire fields. These dragons had wings so small that it looked like they could barely fly. Most importantly, the dragons of legends could breathe fire, but there was no sign that these dragons could do any such thing. These dragons were nothing like Doomswing. But their speed and strength was still overwhelming, and he was the only human left alive to see it. The dragons then began to raid the caravans. They made noises as if speaking to one another, but it sounded nothing like human language. But based on their gestures, Malon believed he knew which one the leader was. A large, dark red dragon with wings that were battered and torn in many places. He had a long scar crossing his snout. Malon was about to take the ultimate risk once again, but he wasn't sure why. He just knew he had to. He stood up, walked towards the dragons, held the jewel up to the leader, and shouted "Bow to me, dragon!"

The dragon turned quickly, startled by the sound. When he saw the small, frail human standing in front of him, holding some sort of glowing rock, he began to laugh. The other dragons came over and started laughing as well.

"Looks like we missed one," he said to the others.

"No weapons, no armor….does he expect to bore us to death?" asked another.

"That jewel….that looks valuable." The dragon reached out a talon to snatch the jewel from Malon, but as he did, his arm began to tremble. His eyes glazed over and he stepped back. The others looked at him with worried expressions.

"Hey boss, you ok?"

"I'm....I'm feeling like we need to help this human. I think we should....yes. Yes, we should listen to him. He's got some good ideas."

The other dragons stood there, speechless. Had their boss gone mad? Then, the dragon dipped down and Malon jumped onto his back. The others couldn't believe it.

"I'm going to follow this human for a while. I think he'll make us rich. You guys should come along," said the dragon, in a calm, dreamy voice. The other three dragons weren't sure what to do, but decided to follow along just to see what would happen next. Malon took another big risk with his life, and once again, it paid off. He was now the only human alive who had power over dragons.

Over the next few weeks, Malon would go on a rampage, tearing through human villages and settlements on the fringes of the human kingdom. The dragons helped him steal what little valuables the villagers had. Word had soon spread that dragons were terrorizing the countryside. Malon's rise to power had just begun.

## CHAPTER EIGHT: THE COUNCIL OF KING EVERWISE

Lavender stood at the doorway, all alone and unsure of what to do next. Just then, a loud "clunk" came from the door, and it slowly swung open. Standing inside was Peacefinder.

"Welcome to the council chambers," she said with a smile. "Very few dragons have ever been inside Kingsden, and fewer still inside the council chambers…you managed both in the space of one afternoon," said Peacefinder with a joking tone. This put Lavender more at ease.

"What am I doing here?" she asked.

"All will become clear to you this evening," replied Peacefinder. Inside, the room was dark except for the light of candles and torches. The room itself was not very large, and contained mostly just tables and a large, wooden globe towards the back of the room. Six dragons sat on worn red cushions studded with gold. There was a long, wooden table that stretched all the way from one side of the room, to another. The dragons were in deep conversation, but suddenly one dragon that was perched on a taller, grander spot on the far end slammed his fist down onto the table, making the candles rattle.

"Silence!" he yelled. All the dragons snapped their heads towards his glare, but as he spotted Lavender, a warm smile creased his wrinkly, freckled face. "Hello there Lavender! Welcome back Peacefinder!" he said cheerfully.

"Greetings, Your Majesty." Peacefinder said, bending her haunches and spreading her wings into a bow. She nudged Lavender with one of her outstretched wings and Lavender bent down into a slightly crooked bow.

"Hello, King Everwise," she murmured shyly.

"Please, sit down," he rasped, gesturing to two seats at the very end of the table. Peacefinder nudged Lavender gently as she gracefully slithered over to the seats, Lavender right on her heels. As they took a seat at the table, King Everwise began to speak again. "We have urgent business, but none more urgent than dinner," he said, and at that moment he dinged a small bell on the table. Immediately, the door behind the king's chair opened and servants came out, carrying dishes out to the table. Lavender was really hungry, so seeing the fresh fruit, fish cakes, fish stew, dumplings...they all made her mouth water. After all the dishes were served, the king spoke again,"Please, eat." Lavender didn't need to be asked twice. She began to chomp down on the fish cakes, quickly moving onto the stew which she downed with a spoon that she wished was bigger. The food was delicious. She was eating so fast that she didn't realize that everyone was staring at her. The king let out a jolly laugh. "If I didn't know any better, I'd think you haven't fed her since flying out from Talonwing," said King Everwise to Peacefinder.

"We had a long journey, Your Majesty," replied Peacefinder, somewhat flustered.

"So tell us, is she truly a Seer?" asked the dragon sitting to the left of the king. She was old, but her eyes blazed a bright green. Her scales were silvery-gray, and she wore a fancy crimson-colored scarf around her neck.

"She is a Seer, and the daughter of Honeywing," replied Peacefinder. Several of the council members gasped at this.

"How can you be sure?" asked another one of the councillors, this one with dark blue scales and long, white whiskers.

"She has her mother's gift, of that there is no question," replied Peacefinder.

"Then, she is exactly what we need. She can use her vision to help us uncover what happened to Daybringer!" exclaimed another councillor, this one distinguished by her long, narrow snout and dark orange scales.

"Her ability is still in its early stages," replied Peacefinder. "She can only see a very short time into the past," remarked Peacefinder. The councillors all seemed to deflate at this remark.

76

"How long before she is ready?" asked another councillor, this one with a short, fat snout and a constant look of worry in his eyes.

"I will help train her along the way," was Peacefinder's reply.

"Along the way? Why- you don't even know where to go!" exclaimed the fat-snouted councillor, whom Lavender decided she didn't like.

"This brings me to my next point," said Peacefinder, turning towards the king again. "I've visited with my messenger. You were all aware that he was seriously injured on his way back to Sagestone. "The situation is, unfortunately, even worse than we thought," said Peacefinder. The room was silent. "For years, we've known about bandit dragons living in the forests and mountains on the fringes of our territory. These bandits have only ever been a nuisance, requiring travelers and merchants to take extra care when traveling on dark, forest-covered roads. Those dragons sometimes also attacked the human settlements on the far side of the world. But now, my messenger tells me that they have become bold, organized, and acting as if someone was in control of them. They have attacked human villages and towns, causing havoc to that part of the far away world," explained Peacefinder." The room seemed to chill at the sound of those words. But not every dragon was concerned.

"So what," uttered the fat-snouted councillor. "Who cares if they are attacking humans so far from here that it might as well be on another world," he continued. Peacefinder looked at him with anger, but it was the councillor on the far end of the table that spoke.

"It matters because what do you think is going to happen next? The humans will retaliate, sending their armies to our doorstep; or, those bandit dragons will start looting our towns!"

"Indeed" said the king. "This is chilling news and we must act."

"My messenger got too close and was nearly killed," said Peacefinder. "I'm not sure if they realized that another dragon was spying on them, but one thing is for sure; time is working against us. We have to hurry." The council now erupted with questions and shouts.

"But what should we do?", "How can you be certain?", and "Are we all going to die?" were shouted just as loudly as "send the army", "defend our borders" and "run and hide". The king shouted out and waved his talon, so much that he accidentally hit the dinner bell again. The room went quiet, and confused servants came in.

"Nevermind the dinner bell!" shouted the king. He then turned to Peacefinder. "Send your messenger my personal thanks. His bravery will be recognized by the kingdom," he said. "And as for this Council…" he trailed off, turning to Lavender and losing some of his anger. "My apologies, these councillors can be a little…over-excited sometimes. I don't know what has gotten into them. Actually, I do know," he said whilst eyeing the council members. "Fear." Lavender's eyes grew wide. "Have you read about humans in storybooks?" asked the king. Lavender, realizing she needs to answer, did so with a squeaky "yes".

"Well," continued the king, "the characters in those stories are real." Lavender couldn't believe it. Only baby dragons believed in humans. Small creatures who walked on two legs and with funny, stick-shaped bodies. It was absurd. But here he was- King Everwise himself, telling her these creatures actually exist! "It's been a thousand years since the last time dragons and humans came into conflict," the king continued. "That war nearly destroyed both humans and dragons alike. Since then, dragons have settled far away from humans, and for all of this time, dragons have been forbidden to make any contact with them. Over the centuries, the deep forests and tall mountains that separated our two species made sure this law remained unbroken. Humans eventually became a myth to dragons…like a story you tell to the little ones. But we know the truth, and we know how dangerous humans can be if provoked. That is why we must take action immediately to stop these bandit dragons from bringing the human armies to us," said the king. "I will meet with my commanders and decide on a course of action," he continued. "And you, Peacefinder, what is your plan?" Peacefinder was prepared for this question, and she now looked to Lavender.

"The decisions we make today in the face of this crisis could shape the future of all of the dragon world," she said. "This is why I want to take Lavender with me to Frostfall and try to find Daybringer again." At this remark, the fat-snouted dragon let out a laugh.

"Daybringer?" he said through continued laughter. "It's been ten years! We sent so many out to look for him then, not to mention Honeywing. All efforts failed. We've heard nothing from him since. What makes you think that old kook is even alive?" Peacefinder looked at him with some disdain, but she was certain his question was something many of the other councillors were also thinking.

"You're right, and maybe he's long gone. But Daybringer didn't go up there for no reason. With Lavender's help, I believe I can retrace his steps. If we cannot find him, perhaps we can find what his purpose was," said Peacefinder.

"His purpose? He had no purpose! He was mad!" said the fat-snouted dragon. Once again, Peacefinder kept her cool.

"Maybe he was, but Honeywing wasn't. And she risked her life to carry out his plan. We don't know why, but now Lavender, the daughter of Honeywing and a Past Seer, has come to us. I believe it's all connected." The council was quiet once again. Then, they heard a new voice.

"What am I even doing here?" said Lavender, in a low voice. She looked up and realized she said that out loud. Her snout grew red with embarrassment. Peacefinder noticed and quickly stepped in.

"I'm sure you are confused, Lavender, so let me explain. There are three types of Seers; Present Seers can see the world as it is now. Past Seers can see how the world was before, and Future Seers see how the world might be. I am a Present Seer. So I can tell you where every dragon in Sagestone is right now, and what they are doing. You are a Past Seer, which is why you are able to see events that already occurred. Then there is the rarest form of Seer- the Future Seer. These dragons have the ability to peer into the future," explained Peacefinder. Lavender knew of these mythical Seers, but she didn't believe they were real- until now.

"The king's last Future Seer was a dragon called Daybringer. He was an ancient dragon who served on the council for longer than most of us have been alive. But he disappeared over ten

80

years ago," continued Peacefinder. "Before he left, he kept seeing visions of a great calamity. He spoke of it frequently, and became obsessed with trying to alter events in the present to stop this from happening. He became frustrated and very erratic. We were all worried about him. And then, he just disappeared without a trace." Lavender was fixated on Peacefinder's words. "Honeywing, your mother, was the last dragon to speak to Daybringer. For reasons unknown to anyone but the two of them, she decided to immediately set out on a journey of her own...and she had you with her." Lavender was now breaking into a cold sweat, realizing where this story was going. "In her last message, she wrote that she had to help in any way she could, even if it meant her life, and that we should follow Daybringer north, towards Frostfall. It was the last we heard from her," said Peacefinder, in a solemn tone. Her words seemed to melt into the stone. There was absolute silence in the chamber now. "We'd lost Daybringer, and then Honeywing with her unhatched egg. We sent an entire squad of dragons on a search & rescue mission. They spent the better half of an entire year searching for her. We believed that she had traveled all the way to the human kingdom, but we lost her trail there. In the end, they found nothing. Years had passed, and we lost all hope. And then you came along," said Peacefinder.

"We don't know how you survived, but you are a miracle," said a dragon who had not yet spoken before. A member of the council sitting on the far end of the table, with dark, matte gray scales and gentle, purple eyes. "I knew your mother dear," she continued. "You resemble her very much. We are very happy to have you here," she finished. Lavender felt overwhelmed. This was all so much to take in. Finally, she gathered her wits and spoke, this time on purpose.

"So…if you're a Present Seer, why can't you just see where Daybringer is and go get him?" Peacefinder gave a small smile.

"I wish it were that easy. But just like you cannot see too far into the past, I also cannot see that far away. If he is close to us, I'd be able to find him. But I've tried that and failed. I've never been close enough to see him."

Lavender looked dejected. "That's exactly the problem. My visions are short. I see what people had for breakfast. I cannot possibly see what happened over ten years ago. If I could, I would know what happened to my mom." She didn't mean to say that last part; it just came out.

"You're right," replied Peacefinder. "Visions are like dreams; murky, vague, sometimes disjointed and confusing. They are also limited by time and space. But I will help you improve your ability along our journey, and hopefully we'll be able to find some clues that will bring us closer to Daybringer."

*Our journey?* thought Lavender.

"Your Majesty," said Peacefinder, turning to the king. "With your permission, I would like to take Lavender to Frostfall. It is the last known location of Daybringer. If there is even a small chance that she can gaze into the past to retrace his steps, it's worth trying." The king showed his agreement with a small nod, but he held up a talon.

"We value you very much Peacefinder," said the king, then hastily adding "and…Lavender too. We will need your ability if it comes to war. I cannot allow you and Lavender to follow in the footsteps of Daybringer and end up lost to us. Therefore, I am sending one of my own Kingsguard to protect you on this journey." There was a hint of disapproval from a few council members, but nobody could deny the value of having a chance to bring back Daybringer. And with that, the council dinner was concluded.

The councillors slipped out of their seats and made towards the exits. Peacefinder grabbed Lavender by the talon and led her to another golden door.

"Wait here," she whispered, and hurried towards a shelf loaded with ancient-looking books. She rummaged through them whilst skimming the pages of some of the books. Eventually, after all of the councillors were gone, Peacefinder, who was carrying a stack of books, stumbled towards Lavender. "What you learned in school isn't everything there is to learn," said Peacefinder.

"Oh I knew that already," replied Lavender, "but what are these books?"

"These are the ancient texts that will help you understand…well, everything. They were outside of the council chamber now, walking down the barely-lit, deserted hallways. Lavender took one of the books from Peacefinder's pile. The book was large and heavy, bound in a dark leather with metallic hinges along the spine. Despite looking very old, Lavender had never seen a finer book.

"The History of Dragons in the Human Kingdoms," she read the title out loud. "Is this….is all of this real?" She asked Peacefinder in bewilderment. They had made their way back onto the courtyard now. Peacefinder replied to her question with a smile.

"I bet you feel a long way from Talonwing right now."
Lavender thought about this for a moment.

"Seers, kings, humans, bandits, wars ... .it's all so much, it's
unbelievable," she said in reply.

"Unbelievable indeed, and also true," replied Peacefinder.
They headed back to their room in the tallest tower. After such a
long and crazy day, all Lavender wanted to do was relax. She was
eager to try the water pump. Back at the orphanage, they had to
drink water from the river that flowed down into the village. She
rushed into the room, grabbed a cup from the kitchen and dashed
over to the small corner of the room where Goldflake had shown
her how to use it. Lavender placed the glass cup underneath the
pump and held down the stone button. Crystal-clear water came
spilling out of the pump and filled the glass rapidly. Lavender felt
a hint of pride as she drank from the cup.

"I see Goldflake showed you how to use the water pump,"
Peacefinder observed from the other side of the room. Lavender
nodded. "But did you notice the bathtub?" asked Peacefinder.

"The what?" asked Lavender. Peacefinder then showed her
what appeared to be a large, shallow stone bowl.

"You see that water pump over there?" asked Peacefinder,
pointing to another pump similar to the one Lavender just used,
but bigger and pointing into the tub. "Press the silver button," said
Peacefinder. Lavender did so, and water immediately began to
pour out of the pipe and into the tub. Lavender was amazed, but
her amazement level hit the roof when she realized with a yelp,
"the water is warm!" Back in her village, dragons only ever
bathed in the stream or in lakes. Having a bath inside your house

was unheard of, and warm water was simply unreal. Lavender hopped in and instantly melted in the warm, steamy water.

"If I told you a month ago that warm flowing water baths existed inside rooms, would you have believed me?" asked Peacefinder.

"Of course not!" said Lavender.

"And if I told you in the same sentence that humans were real, you would probably say the same about that," said Peacefinder. Lavender realized what she was trying to say.

"So we're going to Frostfall?" Lavender asked, her snout barely sticking out above the water.

"Yes. It's very far, and a perilous journey," replied Peacefinder.

"Oh good, then I will have time to read all of these books!" said Lavender with excitement. Back in her ordinary life, books were her whole world. They would keep her company every single day. All the other orphans hated reading; they didn't even like reading about their favourite topics like food or arts. It was all play play play; eat eat eat; sleep sleep sleep for them. But Lavender's day was more like: read read read; eat eat eat; sleep; wake up in the middle of the night; read read read.

"Yes," said Peacefinder, breaking Lavender out of her thoughts. "But please just bring one, as we will be flying and the books are too heavy to carry." Lavender was unhappy about this because she wanted to read them all. A single, ancient, ten-thousand page book simply wasn't enough for a long journey. But she understood Peacefinder's point.

"So when do we leave?" asked Lavender.

"I suggest you get to bed soon," replied Peacefinder. "We depart tomorrow."

## CHAPTER NINE: DOOMSWING RETURNS

It had been several months since Malon stood before a group of bandit dragons, holding a jewel which, for all he knew, held no power at all, and putting his life on the line. What he found out that night was that the jewel did work, and he was able to bend the will of the leader of the bandit dragons, but he also learned that the jewel didn't have nearly the power that the orb which it shattered from did. The orb was said to be able to control all the dragons it surrounded, and that those dragons could only be released from its control if the human carrying the orb allowed it. The jewel on the other hand could only control one dragon at a time, and even then the control was not complete. So while Malon was able to influence the bandit leader, he still had to convince the other bandit dragons to follow him. Without being able to speak to them in their language, this convincing was difficult. But

Malon was great at tricking people, and it turns out he was also great at tricking dragons. He showed them how, with his "help", they would be able to attack larger human settlements and have their share of food and riches. Because Malon knew where the human settlements were, how they were defended, and where they kept their loot, he could use the dragons very effectively against any human force. And then there was the shock value. Humans hadn't seen dragons in a thousand years, so when Malon came riding in on one and raining terror down from the sky, the humans could do nothing but run in fear. One time, he even strolled right into the governing council chamber of a town and declared that he was now the ruler, and that if they disagreed, he would bring his dragons to terrorize the town. Of course, the council laughed at him and threatened to throw him in jail, but moments later, a terrified guard came running in to inform them that dragons were attacking the town. They quickly gave Malon all of their gold and treasure. But Malon knew that this band of misfit dragons wouldn't be enough to conquer a kingdom. In fact, they wouldn't be enough to even win one battle against the king's army. He needed a truly unstoppable weapon. He needed Doomswing. But convincing the dragons to stop their easy plundering of human settlements wouldn't be easy. They believed that they were unstoppable. But that all changed one day when they attacked a settlement which was defended by soldiers with crossbows.

This time, the dragons couldn't simply fly through the arrows and ignore them. To their surprise, the fast-flying bolts got through their thick scales and caused injuries. The dragons were shocked and ran. They now realized that the humans were not such easy targets after all, and that Malon was right. If they wanted to rule this kingdom, they needed Doomswing. But was he even real? The dragons had never heard of this legend. Malon was the only one who believed it. Fortunately, Malon memorized the entire story, including the location of the cave where Doomswing was trapped.

Finding the cave proved to be harder than Malon thought it would be. He soon learned that dragons were not very good long-distance flyers, and they had to make frequent stops to rest. Bad weather and strong winds added difficulty to their journey. More than once, they wanted to turn back, but Malon urged them on. Even after they reached the mountain range where the cave was supposed to be located, they had to travel around for days to locate it. But then, just as the sun was setting after a long day of searching, they found a cave entrance. It was overgrown with vines that made it look ancient. The dragons were too big to get inside, so Malon had to continue on his own. Without the protection of the powerful creatures, he felt vulnerable and small. Also, he took the Jewel of Dragonsmight with him, so he wasn't even sure if the dragons would still be there when he came out. But he was determined to see this through. So he continued to make his way deeper into the cave. Soon he had to light a torch to be able to see where he was going. After what felt like hours of walking down the dark shaft of the cave, Malon reached a large chamber with a gigantic, round stone placed against the wall. The stone looked un-natural, like it was placed there. It had strange inscriptions on it, which Malon couldn't read in the torchlight. There were three huge metal gears attached to the stone. His excitement grew and he knew this was it. But what was he supposed to do now? With the Jewel of Dragonsmight in hand, he closed his eyes and tried to reach out with his mind. He didn't sense any presence at first. But then, from far behind the rock, he heard a voice in his head.

"Who dares disturb my slumber?" rumbled a deep, ancient voice. Malon was startled and opened his eyes. He was back in the cave, alone. The Jewel of Dragonsmight was glowing a dark red color. That voice was only in his head, but it felt so real. Could this really be the voice of Doomswing? This was his chance. Malon once again closed his eyes and reached through the wall with his mind and formed words in his head.

"Are you the dragon, Doomswing?" he asked. A long moment passed, and then a rumbling sound again filled his head.

"Who dares disturb my slumber?" replied the voice.

Malon replied, "I am a human, and I have the power to free you." Then Malon felt a deep laughter rumbling in his head.

"You are not the first to come here and fail," replied the voice.

"So you are Doomswing," answered Malon.

"I am, and I am equally certain that you will fail," Doomswing replied. Malon stood his ground.

"But if I succeed, will you help me conquer the human kingdom and make me king?" he asked. After another long pause, the rumbling voice answered,

"If you succeed in freeing me, you can be the ruler of the entire world." A wicked smile crossed Malon's face.

"Very well, but in order to free you, I will need your help," he said. Doomswing agreed, and Malon asked him to describe the riddle that had to be solved to free him.

"I've pondered on this riddle for a hundred years," said Doomswing. "I cannot solve it, I've given up, and so will you."

90

But Malon insisted, and so Doomswing read the riddle to him. "There are three parts that must be answered in order to unlock the stone," said Doomswing. This is what he read to Malon:

THE RIDDLE

Part 1:

What is darker than the dark?

A shadow cast that leaves no mark,

On a moonless night you cannot see,

But when the moon shines, there I'll be.

Malon pondered this, and asked Doomswing to read it several times. Something to do with the moon....what is darker than the dark? He thought to himself. A shadow cast by the moon...an eclipse?

"No," said Doomswing. "I tried that already." What is darker than the dark he thought to himself. After several minutes, he had an idea.

"It's not the moon that casts the shadow, it's anything standing under the moon," he said. "There can be shade, even at night. It's nightshade!" As Doomswing said the word, a rumbling and shaking started, as if an earthquake had begun. One of the gears on the huge stone slab turned.

"I can't believe it," said Doomswing in awe. Malon was giddy with excitement. "But there are two more parts, and they are harder," said Doomswing. He then read the second part to Malon:

Part 2:

A terrible wind that blows down trees,

Sends the waves and moves the seas,

But this wind only comes at night,

Unlike the bird that sings when bright.

Once again, Malon focused all of his concentration. He listened to each line and each word carefully, looking for hidden meaning. He tried a few things- a hurricane, a tornado, a storm…none of them worked and none of them made sense because of that last line- what does a bird have to do with anything, he thought to himself. He was stumped. After over an hour, he had nothing. He decided that he was tired and needed a break. He ate some dried fruit and fell asleep in the cold, wet cave.

"Are you giving up?" rumbled a voice in his head. Malon was startled awake. It took him a moment to realize where he was.

"No, no I was just resting," he replied. Now, with a fresh mind, he approached the riddle again. This time he considered if all three riddles could be related. That's when it hit him- it's a type of bird, and the wind is a type of wind, and what links them is….

"It's a Nightingale!" he yelled. He sent the answer to Doomswing, and soon the rumbling came again as the second gear turned. Malon's heart beat faster- he was so close now. Even Doomswing seemed to get excited now.

Part 3:

When you fall asleep tonight,

You may receive a terrible fright,

A beast with hooves will come at you,

Until you wake, you'll think it's true.

Malon knew that this one had to be related to the other two.
The other two started with "night", he thought to himself, so this
one should as well. But what is an animal with hooves that starts
with "night"? Once again, he thought of all the hooved animals he
could think of and came up with nothing that fit. But then he
focused on the first part of the riddle. What scares you at night he
thought ...realization came to him- a nightmare! It's also a type of
horse- a mare! As he passed the answer to Doomswing, a
rumbling even stronger than before knocked Malon off his feet.
The third gear turned, and the stone slab began to move. It made a
terrible grinding sound as it slowly opened, and after several
minutes, everything stopped. Malon got up and looked to the
opening. Then the most feared creature of the ancient world
emerged. Unlike the dragons Malon had seen before, Doomswing
was huge. Even in the low light of the torches, he could tell that
he was at least ten times larger, with huge talons and scales so
thick, they looked like they were made from stone. But the
ancient dragon didn't move with strength and confidence. In fact,
he could barely move at all. Doomswing was pulling himself
along, his huge body looking impossibly heavy to move. Malon
remembered that Doomswing was over one hundred years old,
which may not be super old for dragons, but he's also been stuck
in a cave all that time. Some type of magic must have kept him
alive, but that magic must be fading now. Doomswing finally

came right up to Malon, his eyes glowing a dark red, much like the Jewel of Dragonsmight. Then, Malon saw a beam of light travel from the jewel to Doomswing. It became hot, and a red glow covered the entire dragon. It was as if the orb gave the dragon new life! After a few moments, Doomswing stood up and looked much different; stronger, and meaner. He sent a thought to Malon,

"You hold an orb of power, that's how you were able to communicate with me." Malon was afraid, but he tried not to show it. He held up the glowing jewel and sent a thought back,

"That's right, and now I command you, dragon!"

Doomswing flinched at this, but then replied,"I know of this magic, but yours is incomplete. You only hold a part of the orb. Maybe you can control smaller, weaker dragons, but I am much too strong for that." Then Doomswing raised one of his massive talons and prepared to strike Malon. Malon closed his eyes, knowing that he was powerless to stop it. But Doomswing couldn't do it. The jewel had power over him after all. Then he put his talon down and laughed. "Very well human, it seems you are the one thing I cannot kill. You want to be king, I'll make you king." Malon had been close to death many times before, but this felt the closest he had ever come. And each time, he came out of it stronger than ever before. This time would be no different. Doomswing used his tail to smash through the overgrowth covering the cave entrance, and Malon walked out of that cave with the most fearsome dragon in existence following behind him. Malon thought of all that had happened that led him to this moment. He did it; nothing could stop him now.

Malon quickly realized the four bandit dragons that had come with him to the cave were gone. He expected this, and wasn't worried. He didn't need them anymore. *When the world sees Doomswing, anyone with a brain will want to join my army*, he thought to himself. He then jumped onto Doomswing and told him to fly towards the borderlands where he could recruit more bandits and outlaws, both human and dragon. The huge dragon had no need for Gliderwings; he could fly just as well without them, as when he unfurled his wings, they were unimaginably large. Malon flew through the air like he already owned everything he could see. *I need a symbol, or a flag*, he thought to himself. *I need to let everyone know that the Blood-Red Army is back.*

Whenever he saw a bandit camp or trading post, he would land. The horror and amazement of seeing Doomswing made everyone listen to him; and just like he predicted, everyone wanted to join him. He got hold of some red fabric, which he painted a black dragon onto. The Blood-Red Army was indeed back, and this time, they were a force that would shake the entire world. The bandits and thugs even began to call him "king". It didn't take long for his army to grow. Tales of Malon's army, and especially his dragon, soon reached every part of the kingdom, and bandits, thieves, thugs, and every kind of criminal made their way to him, hoping that he would add them to his army. He welcomed them all. Even disgruntled soldiers joined his army, and they were particularly useful as he got them to train the criminals. Even dragons heard of the tales, and came to him, including the original four bandit dragons he had first met. With thousands of humans and dozens of dragons, Malon was already a force to be reckoned with, but with Doomswing as his personal dragon, Malon was the most dangerous human alive.

## CHAPTER TEN: THE COUNCIL OF KING STEADFAST THE 25TH

King Steadfast the 25th was in disbelief when he heard about what was happening in the far eastern end of his kingdom.

"This simply cannot be true!" he screamed to the special council he called together to decide on how to deal with the threat. "We crushed the so-called Blood-Red Army, how can they be back? It must be an exaggeration. A dragon the size of a castle? Come on!" But none of his advisors took it lightly.

"The reports are coming in every day", said one of his advisors. "They all say the same thing." They all looked terribly worried.

"We must act now," said a general in the king's royal army.

"My messengers tell me that the big dragon has only been seen twice. Most people have seen about a dozen dragons, and nobody has ever seen them breathe fire," said a tall, slender woman sitting on the far side of the table. "They are also quite small," she continued, "so it is possible that people are just exaggerating about the big one."

"The fact that we are sitting here arguing about the details of how many dragons he has is ridiculous!" said a voice from somewhere down the table. The King's Council had so many members these days that the king himself couldn't remember who they all were, or when he had even appointed them.

"Who cares how many and how big they are, he has dragons! Dragons! Beasts straight out of fairy tales are now terrorizing our towns," continued the voice. King Steadfast now recognized who that voice belonged to; it was Veralus, one of his most capable generals. "Which is the reason why we need to act now," said Veralus, pounding his fist on the table to add emphasis.

"Our last report states that this Blood-Red Army has made it to the edge of the Great North River," said the king's cartographer, pointing at a large map in the center of the table. "That means they are still 400 leagues from Ravensthorn, but only 50 leagues from Grapefine," continued the cartographer. The king felt overwhelmed. He still couldn't believe that this little thief; this kid who first terrorized his roads and then came right into his private chamber to steal his most prized possession, is now laying waste to his very kingdom.

"We've already seen mass evacuations from Grapefine and the towns and villages in that area," said one of his councillors. She had a look of kind concern on her face, as if they were discussing

97

an unfortunate rain delay in their outdoor plans. "Those refugees are coming here," she continued. "We'll need to prepare…or close the city gates," she said, looking at the king for a decision. The king just continued to stare down at the table.

"This is all too much," he said. "Fetch me my wine!" he shouted. The general grimaced.

"My king," he began, "if we don't move to defend Grapefine, there will *be* no more wine." The king took a moment to realize that all of the wines produced for the entire kingdom were produced in the town of Grapefine.

"Very well Veralus, what do you propose?" he said finally, pulling himself out of his stunned state. The general straightened up.

"I propose we move our entire northern army to Grapefine immediately. They are within two days of marching. That should be enough to stop a direct attack on the city. We then use the southern army to meet them, trapping the Blood-Red Army. They will be forced to retreat. Then we use our cavalry to chase them all the way back to the Great North River. With any luck, Malon's poorly-trained rabble will leave him, and the dragons will be dealt with using artillery and crossbows. I believe we can have the entire operation wrapped up within one month," said the general, clearly very certain of the army's capability.

"When was the last time our soldiers went to war?" asked one of the councillor's sitting to the left of the general. Veralus balked at the question, replying that the army may not have seen any war recently, but that they were well-trained and ready for one.

"And, if you could general," continued the same voice, "let us know when was the last time our soldiers faced up against dragons?" The room grew silent, but the general had a wicked grin on his face.

"It's true that nobody really knows how to fight dragons. But our ancestors did. And they left us with a gift- one that I will bring to the battle," said Veralus. The council looked puzzled. The king's wine arrived. The servant made his way to the center of the table, the sound of his footsteps was the only sound in the entire huge room.

The king took a sip, and spoke, "So we're going to fight dragons now."

"We are," said Veralus. "Furthermore, if we wish to save more of the kingdom from falling into Malon's hands, then we should move our forces out to meet him. But if we want the maximum ability to defend the capital, then we should move every soldier we have to Ravensthorn and prepare to defend here. The decision is yours," finished the general. The king took another sip of wine. It was cool and sweet, just as he liked it. It would be a shame to live without his favorite wine.

"Ride out to defend Grapefine and the eastern territory," said the king. The decision had been made, and the king now got up to leave.

"My king," called a voice, "what about the refugees?" she asked. "Should we let them in and care for them, or close the city gates to outsiders?" The king sped up and out of the room. He had hoped they would believe that he didn't hear her. He hoped that this question could go unanswered.

## CHAPTER ELEVEN: THE EVERROAD

Lavender was awoken by a loud knock that echoed along the stone walls.

"Who's there?" Peacefinder called as she got up from her seat.

"Kingsguard, please open the door," said the voice that carried so strongly that it seemed to go straight through the thick wooden door. Lavender stood up quickly, a surge of adrenaline pushing her to attention. *What if the castle is under attack?* She thought. But if it was, wouldn't Sagestone be on lockdown or at least there might be some warning from the city watch? What if they found the future seer? Lavender pondered on whether she should be glad or alarmed if that was the case. Peacefinder opened the door cautiously. A dragon with glimmering, crimson armor towered before them. He was so tall that his head nearly bumped against the tall ceiling. His helmet gleamed with shiny pearls embroidered into it and golden lines studded on the metal. A majestic chestplate fit perfectly around his neck and stomach. The dragon's maroon scales were barely visible through the gaps of the armor. Lavender was once again treated to what looked exactly like a character from one of her books. She read that at Sagestone, the guards with crimson armor were the royal guards, while the ones with bronze armor were normal guards and the ones with green armor were patrol guards. Although the dragon standing in front of Peacefinder looked like he could snap her in half without a second thought, she didn't look the slightest bit terrified.

"We'll be right out," she said. Peacefinder turned to Lavender and pushed the old book into her arms. "Is this all you're packing?" Peacefinder asked Lavender. Considering that Lavender didn't bring anything other than the talon full of walnuts and fruits in her satchel to Sagestone, and those had been replaced by the servants with much nicer sugar-coated fruits from the castle candy shop, this book was everything she owned. "In that case, let's go." They stepped out into the hallway and followed the Kingsguard down the stairs and into the courtyard. There, they were surprised to see an entire regiment of Kingsguard standing at attention. Lavender was impressed and intimidated at the same time.

"Attention!" shouted the huge dragon that had met them at their room. "I, Crimsonshield, leader of the Kingsguard, hereby appoint one of our own- the fearless, selfless, and utterly reliable Jadeclaw to guide and protect our two Seers on their journey." A smaller dragon then stepped forward from the center of the row of assembled Kingsguard. Her armor was just as impressive, but

Lavender couldn't help but think that she'd prefer the gigantic Crimsonshield to protect them.

"I, Jadeclaw, accept the honor of protecting our Seers and will do so with my life," said the warrior dragon, with such conviction and power that Lavender instantly banished any doubts she had.

"It is with great honor that we accept you as our protector, and give thanks to the Kingsguard for sending one of your own," said Peacefinder, as diplomatically as ever. Lavender was starting to understand the rituals and fancy language of the capital. Nothing here happened without a ceremony. And what happened next was no different. The entire regiment of Kingsguard escorted the three of them to the tower where they would take off from to begin their journey. As they walked through the streets, dragons of all ages, sizes, and colors waved and cheered. It was like being in a parade. Lavender felt embarrassed but also entertained by the spectacle. She then leaned over to Peacefinder and asked, "why is everyone so excited about us going on this journey?"

"Because the king ordered a parade so that you could feel important my dear," said Peacefinder quietly. She then realized that sounded bad, gave an apologetic smile and went back to smiling and nodding at the cheering crowd. Once they reached the tower, they strapped on their Gliderwings and secured their packs. It was at this moment that Goldflake appeared and ran right up to Lavender.

"I'm sad to see you leave so soon Lavender, I think we would make good friends," she said, with tears in her eyes.

"Me too," said Lavender, glad that she was able to say goodbye to Goldflake.

"Goodbye now, and make it back safely!" said Goldflake, as the three dragons lifted off with big, powerful flaps of their wings. As soon as they were properly in the air, Peacefinder pushed the button in the middle of the two harnesses looping around her arms and two extra wings snapped out of the tubes. She instructed Lavender to do so too. Without having to be told twice, Lavender gained two new wings herself and they soared up into the clouds. Lavender sneaked some glances towards Jadeclaw, who showed no interest in making conversation and was probably never going to, so she turned her attention to Peacefinder.

"Is Frostfall cold?" She asked, trying to break the silence.

"Very, they often see blizzards that last for hours, as well as heavy snow. The sun only comes up for a few hours during the summer, and not at all in the winter. Not to mention there has never been a single blade of grass seen there," Peacefinder said, shivering at the thought. "That's why it's so dangerous. Sometimes when it hails, the ice is about this big," she cupped the sun in her hands to outline the edge and showed Lavender, who opened and closed her mouth in horror. "They can knock you off course and your Gliderwing could get punctured by sharp icicles that somehow fly through the air during those storms," Peacefinder explained, gesturing dramatically with her talons. Now Lavender shivered.

"Um...wow that's...terrible," was all she could muster. They reached the north side of Sagestone and continued on. By the time the sun was halfway down the vast, cloudless sky, Lavender could barely fly straight and her shoulders ached. The Gliderwing was indeed amazing and it helped dragons travel long distances, but Lavender still had to flap her wings at times to gain speed and

103

they had been flying all morning without stopping even once for water. Lavender wanted to fly further- so much further, but her body wouldn't let her do so.

"Can…we…rest?" Lavender said through panting, finally giving in.

"Sure! Jadeclaw we shall land now," Peacefinder called in her formal tone. They dived down so that they were below the clouds, and snow-capped trees stretched out as far as the eye could see. Lavender was delighted. They would be soaring over a forest of white. The mountains were silhouettes plastered against the back of the forest and Lavender had to squint her eyes to make out the shadows of dragons bustling around along the Everroad.

"Dip your wings down, fold them a little and tilt them to the right!" Peacefinder instructed as she did so herself. Lavender watched as she pinned her wings to her back and straightened her tail. Peacefinder dipped down so low to the ground that if she reached down with her wings outstretched, they would brush the tips of the pine trees. At the last moment, her wings snapped open and she swooped up so that she was gliding over the trees. Peacefinder opened her mouth as if she was speaking, but the wind carried her words away.

*She probably wants me to do that*, Lavender thought brusquely. She panicked. *What if I crash? Will I crash? WILL I DIE?* She thought. Lavender tried to push away her thoughts. She suddenly wished that she didn't suggest landing. *Tail straight, wings folded, tilt right*, she repeated to herself. Lavender flapped her wings once more before diving straight down. Wind roared in her ears and buffeted her body; the land grew larger and larger. Her vision got blurrier and blurrier. *Snap out of it, Lavender!* She thought. *Focus!* She straightened out her tail and clenched her talons. A second before her gruesome death, Lavender jerked her whole body upward and lost balance. She squirmed around, trying to figure out where up was and down was. She was still in the air, but now instead of a graceful arch, she was spinning out of control. She was dizzy and disoriented. There was nothing she could do. Just then, she felt a jolt and a tug at her side. Her Gliderwing straightened and she could see the form of Jadeclaw directly below her. She used her own glider to stop Lavender's spin, and somehow did so without smashing Lavender or herself to bits. Moments later, they landed together in a clearing, where Peacefinder was already waiting. Lavender collapsed to the ground. Jadeclaw looked furious.

"This journey is dangerous enough without adding unnecessary risks!" she shouted, in the general direction of both Lavender and Peacefinder. "My job is to protect you, and I will. But I will not allow you to be reckless," she continued. Peacefinder looked embarrassed.

"You're right, Jadeclaw and I'm sorry. I've been training Lavender in Gliderwing skills and I rushed into it," she said.

"Peacefinder, you are perhaps the greatest Gliderwing pilot we've ever seen. A simple maneuver for you is considered super-advanced level flying for the average dragon, let alone an inexperienced youth," said Jadeclaw, now in a calm but firm tone.

"Yes," managed Peacefinder. "We will be more careful." Hearing Jadeclaw speak for the first time brought Lavender out of her dizzy, nearly-fainting state.

"Wow," she said, still tangled up in her Gliderwing, "I wasn't sure if you could talk," she blurted out. Jadeclaw shot her a piercing glance.

"When there is something important to say, I say it young Seer, and I don't sugar-coat either," she replied. After a moment of awkward silence, she continued. "Now, we've made excellent time today and seeing as it's already late afternoon, I suggest we make camp for the night." Jadeclaw began unpacking her gear. Peacefinder got to work gathering wood for a fire. Lavender continued to untangle herself from her Gliderwing. They were on a small hill in the middle of a dense forest of evergreens. They could see the mountains looming far beyond, and the sun quickly disappearing behind the horizon.

"I didn't realize the landscape would change so quickly," said Lavender, after managing to untangle herself and get her pack sorted.

"We've been following a northern wind," said Jadeclaw as she shoved the Gliderwing into its tube. "They are rare for this time of year. With any luck, we will arrive at the shores of Frost Lake in three days," said Jadeclaw in a matter-of-fact tone. Peacefinder looked unconvinced.

"We traveled on fresh wings today," she said. "Starting from tomorrow, they will begin to feel heavier and heavier as we get more and more tired." Lavender was already completely worn out. She dreaded the thought of flying again. The fire was cracking now, and the smell of cooked fish made her tummy rumble. "Not to mention that we will not have fresh fish after today," added Peacefinder. Lavender thought about eating the sweet strawberries the servants packed inside her satchel but she ended up filling her growling stomach with a Rainbow Trout.

"We'll have to rely on dried rations, or any food we can get from traders we see along the road," added Jadeclaw. *This journey is sounding less fun by the minute*, thought Lavender. Early the next morning, Lavender was awakened to the sound of "We must get going now, wake up," said by an overly-awake Jadeclaw.

"Aww," complained Lavender. "The sun isn't even up yet; how are we sleeping less than the SUN?" But, after some more complaining, she got up, ate her breakfast, which consisted of porridge, and got her pack together. She lugged her Gliderwing on, and flapped herself into the sky. Her wings were sore, but once she got moving, she felt better. And once the Gliderwing was unfolded, with the fresh wind in her face and the sun rising over a misty forest; she actually felt pretty good. They glided along with the winds, which meant that sometimes they would fly higher, sometimes lower, sometimes left and other times right…it was quite fun at first, but eventually became routine. Still, Lavender was very thankful for the northern wind as she hardly needed to do any flapping of her own. They were following the general direction of the Everroad- one of the smaller, less-traveled sections of the famous road. Lavender was just about to fall asleep with boredom when she remembered- her book! If she was very clever about it, she could just keep it open while they were gliding. She fumbled about for a moment, and in her fumbling her glider started to rock up and down.

"Are you ok over there?" asked Peacefinder, noticing the odd maneuvers.

"Perfectly fine," Lavender yelled back. In fact, she was more than fine. She managed to get her book out and even hold it in such a way as to keep it steady. Now, this trip was perfect. She opened the heavy cover and skimmed to the contents. She had looked through it before they left Sagestone so she had an idea of what the many chapters contained, but now she was looking for a specific one- there. Chapter 87- The Fall of Frosthall. The language used in the book was strange, and there were words that she didn't understand, plus it was written in a scribbly style that made it hard to read, but Lavender eventually got used to it.

*The great dragon city of Frostfall was as splendid as any in the entire kingdom. Built by King Evermore the sixteenth, using stone and a type of ice crystal that only exists in those parts. The entire city gleamed in the sunlight with emeralds, greens and blues, and it was home to some of the most beautiful dragons ever seen- the Glasswings. They were white or light blue in color, with shiny blue eyes and glass-like wings. Legend has it that the Glasswings loved experimenting with magic, sometimes with dangerous results. This is why the largest, most famous school of potions and sorcery was located in Frosthall. However, it was one of these experiments that led to their downfall. According to legend, one day they attempted to use magic to lift the entire city into the air and create a city in the clouds. It worked for a moment, and the dragons celebrated their genius. But something went terribly wrong. The magic created effects they didn't predict, and the floating city began to tilt and crumble. The city crashed back down to earth and broke apart with such force that it left a huge crater in the ground. This was the worst disaster to ever occur except for wars, and after he learned of how this had happened, the king banned magic and sorcery throughout the kingdom. This law remains in force to this day. As for Frosthall-*

*the only thing left was a lake where the city had been, and a tiny portion of the original city which was on the tallest hill in the very center, was now an island in the middle of that lake. That town is a mere shadow of its former self. It is now called Frostfall, as a tribute to the fallen city.*

Lavender was completely into the story. She imagined what the Glasswings looked like, how they lived, and what amazing powers they must have had...before they messed up. *Frostfall...how appropriate,* thought Lavender to herself. Suddenly, a strong gust of wind came at her from the side. Peacefinder and Jadeclaw adjusted their Gliderwings easily but because Lavender was only holding her's with her elbows and not paying attention, she got flipped over completely and started to dive.

"WHHHAAAAAA," she screamed, completely surprised by this sudden terror.

"Here we go again," moaned Jadeclaw. Surprisingly, her lips curled into a simile and she rolled her eyes, as she dived sharply to save the falling dragon...again. But this time, Lavender managed to grasp her Gliderwing controls firmly, shift her weight back and pull as hard as she could. The Gliderwing came out of its dive and straightened out again. Moments later, Peacefinder and Jadeclaw were at her side.

"Are you ok?" asked Peacefinder.

"Yes, sorry," replied Lavender.

"I'm not sure if reading while flying is the best idea," commented Jadeclaw.

"Yeah…you're right…wait, my book!" yelped Lavender. In all of the excitement, she dropped it. She looked below; they were flying above nothing by an endless forest. "Oh no, I need to find it!" she exclaimed. Peacefinder and Jadeclaw looked at each other.

"Ok," said Peacefinder, "it's time for us to take a break anyway. Let's find a place to set down and look around for your book." They circled the area for a while until they found a narrow strip of land that had slightly fewer trees. The landing was rough and Lavender ended up with a snoutful of pine cones. But she unclipped her Gliderwing in record time and dashed in the direction where she believed she dropped her book.

"I've never seen her move like that," said Jadeclaw.

"Well, at least we know how to motivate her now," replied Peacefinder. They watched as Lavender bolted through the trees and leaped over fallen logs. The forest from above looked bright and cheery, with the sunlight beaming down on the trees. The forest from below was another story. It was dark, cold, and scary. Lavender was dashing around at first but as she got further and further from the clearing, she became less excited about finding her book. This forest was huge, every tree looked exactly the same, and she has no idea where she actually dropped her book. But then, she remembered. She sat down on the cold, mossy forest floor. She closed her eyes and focused all of her attention on that moment when she lost control. Her breathing slowed. Her heartbeat did as well. And then…she was there. She was watching it happen, as if she was a bird. She saw how she lost control of the glider- which looked super embarrassing- and then, the moment when the book fell from her grasp. She watched it tumble through the air, almost in slow motion. She had to really focus. It hit the

110

top of the evergreen, and then rolled down until it stopped...on top of a large, flat-topped stone. The stone was nearly as tall as the bottom branches of the evergreen. *Bingo*, thought Lavender, as she popped back into reality. She now knew what to look for. It took her another ten minutes to locate the rock, but when she did, she knew she had it. She leaped onto it and picked up her book-slightly torn on one page and a bit muddy, but still totally fine. *Yes!* she whooped for joy.

"A fine job," said a voice from the ground below. Lavender was startled.

"Peacefinder?" she asked. "What...how did you know where I was?"

"You're not the only Seer in this forest," replied Peacefinder with a smile. "I was watching you with a vision of my own, to make sure you didn't get lost." Lavender was still full of excitement and joy.

"This Seer thing is so useful Peacefinder, I'm never going to lose anything again and I lose stuff all the time!" she babbled, while walking back to the clearing. Peacefinder smiled.

"It's much more useful than that. With enough practice and enough focus, you'll be able to see further into the past. And that is what we will be depending on soon." They returned to the clearing, where Jadeclaw was waiting.

"Wow, impressive. You found a book in a sea of trees," she said, genuinely impressed.

"Thanks," said Lavender. "I used my seeing-thing."

"Your...seeing-thing," retorted Jadeclaw. "Well, I'm happy it worked out and now let's have you put on your flying-thing and get out of here." Lavender didn't mind leaving that spot at all. She had her book. They flew for another two hours or so before it began to get dark. They camped near a small pond along the Everroad. Once again, Lavender was beat, but she was getting used to this rugged adventurer lifestyle. Whenever she felt uncomfortable or afraid or unhappy, she would just think back on what her life was before all of this happened, and she would quickly snap out of it and be thankful. She was finally living the stories that she could only read about before. She wasn't just reading about Frostfall; she was going there! She fell asleep, dreaming of Glasswings.

Lavender awoke to the smell of cooking porridge. She'd eaten porridge every morning for a week now, but something about being incredibly hungry makes any food delicious. The forest wasn't as thick anymore, and the terrain was now a mix of forest, rocky clearings and small lakes and streams. It was becoming more mountainous as well. They set off once again, as they always did, and once again, Lavender got her Gliderwing under control and she used it to catch the wind. Then, she took out her book. *Jadeclaw said it was a bad idea but what's a road trip without entertainment?* she thought to herself. She once again immersed herself in the world of legends. The chapter she started reading dove into the strange world of dragon mages, and one in particular- the ice dragon known as the orb crafter. She continued reading

*When the Frosthall School of Potions and Sorcery was at its height, shortly before the terrible downfall, an ancient mage known as the orb crafter held his workshop on the school*

*grounds. His amazing ability was to capture magical abilities into crystal orbs, which would then allow these powers to be used by any dragon- not just mages. This upset many of his fellow mages, as orbs threatened to make them less important, but at the same time they all realized the usefulness of having orbs. The selling of powerful orbs to other cities and to the king himself made Frosthall incredibly rich and powerful. According to legend, the orb crafter could create wondrous objects- from orbs that could make lightning, to orbs that could slow down time, or even orbs which could make huge, heavy objects float in the air as if they weighed nothing at all. In fact, it was this last type of orb which is blamed for the disaster. The Glasswings of Frosthall believed they were the rulers of the world and that nothing- not even the king, was better than they were. And to prove their greatness, they had the orb crafter create dozens of these orbs and place them in a circle around the city. Their idea was to activate all of the orbs at the same time and simply lift the city off the ground and into the clouds. A city in the clouds would be a wonder that every dragon would come to see, and no dragon could ever doubt that the Glasswings were the greatest. But something went wrong, and they failed. And because they were so proud of their own knowledge and refused to share, all of the books, scrolls, and information that existed about how to craft orbs was located inside the school library. When the city crashed into the earth, all of that was destroyed.*

Lavender closed the book. Imagine all of those books, all that information, gone. It made her sad. The sun was starting to set again, and they were now steering towards the north, where they spotted some large stones on a hilltop. That would be their campsite for the night. Lavender glided to a landing with ease, gently patting the ground. She was very good at handling a glider now, but as she looked up and saw Peacefinder doing a corkscrew in the air and the setting down so gently that she didn't even kick up any dust; she realized she still had a long way to go to becoming an expert.

"This site is good," said Jadeclaw, while folding up her Gliderwing. "We can see in all directions, and look there- a cave. We won't even need the canopies to stay dry." *Jadeclaw was the perfect soldier,* thought Lavender. She was always thinking about things like defense, rations, shelter, and last night Lavender woke up in the middle of the night only to find Jadeclaw sitting there, on watch.

"Jadeclaw, I have to ask a question," said Lavender.

"If you must, then go ahead," replied Jadeclaw, not in an unfriendly, but rather her usual matter-of-fact tone.

"Do you stay up every night to keep watch over us and our camp?" she asked.

"I do," was the quick reply.

"Ok then if you stay up every night…when do you sleep?" was Lavender's next question.

"We have a saying in the guard," said Jadeclaw. "A soldier sleeps when she can." Lavender was puzzled.

"Ok but if you can't sleep at night and you can't sleep during the day…" she trailed off, hoping Jadeclaw would finish.

"Ok Seer, let's see if you can solve this little puzzle," replied Jadeclaw with a smile. Peacefinder was stirring the stew over their campfire, also entertained but this. Lavender once again realized she had her Seer-thingy. She closed her eyes and

114

concentrated. She peered into the past. It was dark now, and there was Jadeclaw, sitting with eyes closed but clearly not sleeping. A sound in the woods- a branch cracking. Jadeclaw instantly on her feet with spear in hand. Woah. It was nothing…a deer. Lavender peered and peered and did not catch a moment when Jadeclaw was truly asleep. She returned to reality.

"I give up," she said. I saw you nearly pummel a deer and scare a bunny half to death, but never did I see you lie down and sleep. Jadeclaw had a look of sly cleverness on her face now.

"Oh great Seer, surely you cannot be defeated by the mystery of the sleeping soldier," said Jadeclaw, in a grand display as if she was addressing the king. Peacefinder laughed, and Lavender did too.

"Peacefinder!" Lavender exclaimed. "Do you know?" asked Lavender.

"The riddle is simple if you think about it," was Peacefinder's reply.

"If she doesn't sleep at night, then…."

"She must sleep during the day!" said Lavender, finishing the sentence.

"There's hope for you yet young dragon," said Jadeclaw, in a playful teasing tone.

"You read your book during our flights, but me, I sleep." Lavender was dumbstruck.

"You sleep while flying??" she exclaimed.

"Sure," replied Jadeclaw casually. "It's not like I will walk into a wall or fall off a cliff. And besides, you experienced the worst thing that could happen, plus I know Peacefinder is always there to save my neck in case anything does go wrong," finished Jadeclaw, now sitting down to enjoy the stew.

"Huh?" remarked Peacefinder. "What makes you think I'm not also sleeping while flying?" Jadeclaw spit out her stew in laughter. All three of them laughed hysterically. Lavender felt warm and happy and cheerful. But as soon as their laughter died down, they heard another sound.

"Wait," said Jadeclaw, all of the joy and fun immediately gone from her face.

"It sounded like...yelling," said Peacefinder, also moving to her pack. She took out what looked like a curved stick. She unfolded it to reveal what it really was- a bow. Jadeclaw had her spear and shield in hand.

"Scout ahead," instructed Jadeclaw to Peacefinder.

"Already on it," she replied. Peacefinder now entered her Seer mode. Lavender had never seen her do this before. Her eyes were closed and her body became rigid, almost like she turned into a statue. Lavender wondered if this is what she looked like when she gazed into the past.

"It's a small dragon, at the entrance to that cave down there," reported Peacefinder. Being able to speak while in Seer mode was something Lavender couldn't do.

"Is there more?" asked Jadeclaw.

"Inside the cave…darkness, wet eyes. Reflecting the light. Too big to be bats, too small to be dragons. They are not friendly eyes," finished Peacefinder, coming out of her Seer mode.

"Ok, Lavender, stay behind us, whoever they are, they already know we are here so let's approach with confidence," instructed Jadeclaw. She took the lead with her speer positioned behind her shield. Lavender had never seen a warrior with their weapon out like this. It was intimidating to say the least. The cave was about two-hundred paces from their camp, and they made their way down with ease, knowing that there wasn't anything out to get them on the way.

"Help!" they heard a raspy, rattled voice yell. At the entrance of the cave stood a small, squat dragon. He was light blue in color with purple spikes on his back. His tail was…strange. As if it had a ball attached to the end. "Oh, oh thank goodness!" he yelled when he saw the three of them approach. "Wait…are you bandits here to roast me on a campfire?" he asked, realizing he should have opened with that question.

"I am Jadeclaw of the Kingsguard, and you are?" asked Jadeclaw, in a rumbling, powerful voice that would scare animals and make baby dragons cry.

"I..I..I…I'm B-b-b-b-bubbletail," replied the small dragon, in a voice that was about as opposite to Jadeclaw's as you could get.

"Bubble..what?" asked Jadeclaw.

"Bubbletail," he replied, now pulling himself together after realizing he wasn't going to be some bandit's dinner.

"Ok Bubbletail, my name is Peacefinder and you seem to be far from home. I also happen to know that there is something in

117

that cave and it's not entirely friendly. So you'd better tell us what's going on here," said Peacefinder, still holding her bow with an arrow ready. Bubbletail, now eyeing both the spear and the bow, realized he wasn't out of danger yet.

"Yes, yes right away," he rambled. "You see, my friend, my friend Firesneezer and I, we…we're treasure hunters! Yes, you know, like the hunt for the magic orbs and such, treasures of the mythic city," he rambled.

"Your friend…Firesneezer? Where is he now?" asked Jadeclaw.

"I was just getting to that," he continued, trying his best not to trip over his words. "He's still inside that cave. We went in and then realized we walked into the living room of a pack of wolves who were not too happy about it…or maybe they were super happy I don't know, anyway we panicked and I ran one way and he ran another and I dropped my torch and fell down but then I got up and a wolf bit my tail so I ran faster and…"

"Calm down, take it easy" said Jadeclaw, noting to herself that they were not about to be ambushed. Bubbletail relaxed when he saw her relax, and then steadily continued.

"So I ran out and they didn't chase me, but I heard Firesneezer saying he managed to climb up onto a rock ridge and was stuck. I wanted to go get help but then I heard laughing, and I started yelling, and now here you are," he finished, exhausted from saying all of that in one breath. Jadeclaw looked at Peacefinder. Lavender noticed that they had some unspoken language between them.

"It's dark in that cave. Good for you. Bad for wolves," said Jadeclaw to Peacefinder.

"Yes, I think I can handle them but I'll need you for backup," she replied.

"Of course," said Jadeclaw. "Lead the way."

Lavender was once again told to stay back and wait. Peacefinder and Jadeclaw quietly disappeared into the cave. Moments later, Lavender heard a commotion coming from the cave; yelps, howls, snarls, and more yelps. Then silence. Several unnerving minutes passed before Jadeclaw and Peacefinder emerged with a small, red and black dragon.

"Firesneezer!" yelled Bubbletail. "You're alive!"

Firesneezer was clearly shaken by his experience, but managed a smile when he saw his friend.

"Where did you find these heroes?" asked Firesneezer after settling down from the excitement. "They are straight out of a comic book," he continued. "This one shot three, four, no… five wolves while in pitch black darkness and then the one wolf that manages to survive lunges at her and boom…gets a spear to the face from captain power-dragon over here," he continued, pointing at Jadeclaw.

"I'm not a captain," said Jadeclaw, "I'm a lieutenant, and you're welcome," she said stiffly. "Oh, yes," he said shyly, "I forgot…thank you." Lavender couldn't help but giggle.

"You two are really silly," she said.

"And who might you be my dear," asked Firesneezer. "Let me guess- you're the brains of this group ... .because they go in to risk their lives while you sit back in safety and…plan," said Firesneezer, in an evil-villain imitating voice that made Lavender laugh some more.

"Actually I'm Lavender and I am…."

"She's with us and we'll be on our way," interrupted Peacefinder.

She nudged Lavender on the shoulder. Jadeclaw was already walking back to camp.

"Wait, wait you have to let us repay you…I mean, we don't have any sapphires or anything, but, we can repay you in kindness!" exclaimed Bubbletail.

"No need, have a nice night," said Jadeclaw, already twenty paces away.

She clearly wasn't interested in hanging out with these two reckless dragons.

"Er, wait," persisted Bubbletail. "You three are, travelers, adventurers, treasure hunters! Yes, and we, we are just like you, and we know these parts well, except maybe that cave ... .where we almost died…but beside that cave we know this countryside like the back of our claws."

Lavender couldn't help but like these two little dragons. "They're funny. Can we keep them?" she asked Peacefinder.

"No," was the immediate, parental response.

"Ok, you're busy, doing ... missions for the king and such, but for sure you aren't going anywhere tonight so at least let us cook you a nice dinner over the campfire," said Bubbletail.

Peacefinder looked at Lavender who was making her biggest, most pathetic sad, wide eyes expression.

"Oh fine, bring the kids for dinner," she finally said.

Lavender smirked in satisfaction. Bubbletail and Firesneezer turned out to be pretty amazing campfire cooks. After bringing their supplies up to the camp, they made a delicious meal which consisted of a thick vegetable stew, salted beans, and a flaky pastry that they must have brought from home. They all ate and ate- even Jadeclaw who never seemed to care about food agreed that it was yummy.

"So tell me, how long have you two goofballs been out here treasure hunting?" asked Peacefinder.

Firesneezer pretended to look offended. "I'll have you know madam that you are in the presence of the foremost experts on ancient artifacts from the Frosthall era," he replied, in his most dignified tone. Lavender chuckled.

"Yeah right," Jadeclaw retorted with a chunk of carrot halfway in her mouth.

"In fact, we have charted no less than twenty-thousand leagues of territory around Frost Lake.

"Frost Lake?" asked Lavender.

"That's what we call the lake that formed around Frostfall," said Bubbletail.

"Twenty-thousand leagues?" questioned Jadeclaw, rolling her eyes.

"Truly!" Firesneezer shot back. "We've trekked across the whole of this land, charting and mapping our progress as we went."

Peacefinder eyed the cart that they had brought up to the campsite. She was curious. "Prove it," she said.

"Gladly!" said Bubbletail, his face lighting up. He went to the cart and removed several scrolls from wooden boxes. "I drew these all myself," he said, handing them over to Peacefinder. Peacefinder gazed at the sheet, and Lavender couldn't help but look over her shoulder. The drawings were excellent, with detailed illustrations of lakes, rivers, mountains and caves. Peacefinder was equally impressed.

"I have to admit, I thought you two were just clowns," said Peacefinder. "But this…this map could only have been made with such detail by someone who actually traveled to these places."

Bubbletail beamed with pride and puffed out his chest. "As I said, we know this territory, and we'd be happy to act as your guides, whatever your mission may be."

Lavender laughed. "Yes yes please let's keep them on, they are great cooks and they can guide us and they are sooo funny!"

Peacefinder looked to Jadeclaw, who only rolled her eyes. She considered it.

"Tell me, have you ever encountered an old, bronze-colored dragon with dark amber eyes who goes by the name of Daybringer?" Bubbletail looked at Firesneezer.

"Not Daybringer," replied Bubbletail. "But I did see the dragon you described once."

Peacefinder perked up. "Go on," she urged.

"Yeah, he was at the general goods store in Frostfall," Bubbletail continued. "I remember he was asking for strange supplies- glass, copper, all kinds of rare and expensive items. That's why I remember him. He took ages to check out. And his name was...Nightfall. Yes. odd name too."

Peacefinder was stunned. Could these two dragons whom they met totally by chance actually hold a clue to the location of Daybringer? She sifted through her pack and took out a drawing.

"Look here- is this him? Is this the dragon you saw?" The drawing showed an old dragon with deeply worn grooves in his snout and oddly-shaped horns.

"Yeah, that's him. I remember the horns," said Bubbletail.

Peacefinder grabbed Lavender, clearly excited about this unexpected breakthrough.

"Lavender, this is our chance to find him!" she said, voice full of excitement.

"Bubbletail, think now," she said. "Can you tell me exactly when this happened? When did you see him last?" Bubbletail took a moment to think.

"I'd say that was, maybe four months ago. It was right before Firesneezer fell off that table and broke his talon," he said.

Peacefinder looked at Lavender. "That's further back than you have ever looked before, but it's not much harder, you just need to focus." Lavender looked concerned, and Bubbletail looked confused. Jadeclaw and Firesneezer just looked on in silence.

"Bubbletail, Firesneezer, as a repayment for saving your lives, I will accept your offer to help us locate what we are looking for," said Peacefinder, back in her diplomacy mode.

"Ok your highness," said Firesneezer in his best impression of the queen. "We're not at Kingsden," he said, "but we're very happy to help."

Lavender chuckled. They concluded their evening with Firesneezer making jokes and Bubbletail singing songs. Lavender was so happy. Meeting unexpected new friends was the best.

## CHAPTER TWELVE: THE SIEGE OF GRAPEFINE

Malon rode Doomswing high above the valley below. At this height, he could see the smoke from chimneys and city walls of Grapefine. This would be the largest town they have ever attempted to conquer. It was also the first which had a stone city wall. Beyond the town, Malon could see a large number of caravans and wagons making their way out, but also a long column of wagons coming into the town. *Why would anyone want to come into the town now?* he thought to himself. He made his way back to his camp. The Blood-Red Army camp was now just as big as that of any royal army, and he could see the tents of his troops extending across the entire field ahead. He landed, and dismounted from his dragon. Doomswing was the most feared dragon in the world, but he was also very old. Sometimes after a longer flight, he appeared dazed and sluggish. But when it was time to fight, the dragon knew exactly what to do, and that's what Malon needed him for. The other dragons were more or less free to do as they pleased, and they sometimes flew off to hunt or do whatever, which annoyed Malon, but there wasn't anything he could do about that. The dragons stayed with him either because they feared Doomswing, or because of the riches they were being given with each victory. Malon discovered that dragons weren't so different from humans in one way- both species were greedy. However, he didn't have to rely as much on those dragons. As long as he had Doomswing, he felt invincible.

Malon walked into his tent, where he had arranged a meeting with his generals. The tent was spacious and decorated with fine furniture they had stolen from the towns they conquered. In the center of the tent was a large, round table with a map on it. Malon's generals were mostly soldiers and mercenaries who generally disliked each other. Malon knew that they would only follow him as long as he was winning them riches, which is why he was careful never to reveal the source of his power. If any of them knew that they could control the dragon by simply taking the jewel that he wore around his neck, Malon would be dead within the hour. But for now, they didn't know, and they all got along well enough.

"I saw a large column of wagons pointing towards the city," said Malon.

"Then it's as we predicted," said one of his soldiers- a man named Swordface.

Malon knew that wasn't his real name, but all of them took on made up names since joining his army. It was as if they had two different lives, and believed that they could just shift back to their old life if this new one didn't work out. Malon knew there was no going back, and that the king would rid the kingdom of every single person who joined Malon if he could. They were all in the same boat together now- either they succeeded, or they were all dead.

"The royal army has come to defend Grapefine," Swordface continued.

The large mercenary named Bolo scoffed at this, saying that the Blood-Red Army would cut through them like a hot knife through butter, but Malon ignored the boasting.

"It changes nothing," said another soldier, this one called himself Connery.

"We surround the city, prevent any food from coming in, and wait for them to surrender. We can wait in comfort, they can't," he concluded.

"But the king will send additional reinforcements and we may find ourselves out-numbered!" yelled Swordface, clearly unhappy with this plan.

Malon thought for a moment.

"How long would it take for their reinforcements to arrive?" he asked no one in particular.

"I believe the closest is the southern army, which could be here in no less than one week," said Connery.

"I flew south a few days ago, and reinforcements are nowhere to be seen," said Malon.

"They could be moving in separate groups, harder to spot with all of the refugees on the roads," said Connery.

Bolo and Swordface disagreed, and Bolo urged an attack on the city right away. But Malon wanted to see if the king would send his entire army to Grapefine, so he made his decision:

"We wait," he said decisively, and walked out of the tent.

## CHAPTER THIRTEEN: NIGHTFALL

Lavender awoke the next morning to the sound of rain and thunder. Their canopies were all wet, and their Gliderwings would be difficult to unravel in the rain.

"Well, even if we wanted to fly, that idea is gone," Jadeclaw pointed out.

"Not to worry!" said Bubbletail, who was already up and making a sweet-smelling corn chowder. "I've got just the thing for explorers in bad weather," he said, as he pulled out what looked like a portable canopy on a foldable stick. "I call it, the rain-stopper." He held it over his head and paraded around. His lower body was still getting wet, but sure enough, his head and tummy stayed dry.

"Clever," said Jadeclaw.

They proceeded to pack up camp and loaded as much as they could onto Bubbletail and Firesneezer's cart.

"I understand why you're called Bubbletail now," said Jadeclaw, when they started walking down the hill and towards the Everroad. "But I've got to ask," she continued. "Why Firesneezer?" Lavender found herself grinning again.

"Oh, you mean our names?" said Bubbletail. "Well yes, mine is obvious. These large, bubble-like tail ends run in my family. Apparently our ancestors would use them to bash predators in the face," said Bubbletail.

"Useful," commented Jadeclaw as she glanced at her own weapon. "But I know you're not about to tell me that Firesneezer…"

"Sneezes fire?" finished Bubbletail.

"I actually have a rare medical condition," said Firesneezer.

"No. Way." interrupted Jadeclaw. "Dragons breathing fire, burning down villages and terrorizing humans? Come on! That's children's book nonsense!" she stated.

Firesneezer agreed, "yes *that* is children's book nonsense, but my condition is real. Sometimes I get some dust in my nose and I sneeze out so violently that it lights on fire."

The entire group was silent for a moment….then burst out laughing.

"You can't be serious," said Peacefinder. "I mean, that's something I would need to see with my own eyes."

"Anybody got some dust?" Jadeclaw asked teasingly.

Lavender continued laughing. Bubbletail and Firesneezer also laughed and soon, the forest echoed with laughter. They spent the day walking down the Everroad, with the landscape shifting from evergreen forest to open, rocky fields, with trees becoming more and more sparse. Most noticeably, it became colder.

"How much further to Frostfall?" asked Lavender.

"Another half a day or so," replied Bubbletail.

The sun was now setting again, as the daylight became shorter and shorter the closer they came to their destination. They kept walking though, helped by a clearing sky and a gentle breeze. Eventually they stopped to make a camp. Bubbletail and Firesneezer, once again, proved experts at camping and quickly built a large, warm fire. Next they made dinner and Lavender wolfed down a tasty pumpkin soup.

"We'll be in Frostfall tomorrow, and our first stop is the general goods store," said Peacefinder to the group.

"Lavender, we need you to try your ability to give us a clue about where to look for Daybringer."

Lavender was concerned about this part of the plan. She had never tested her ability to this level before, and it seemed that everything was relying on her.

"I'll do my best," is all she could say.

Once dinner was done, she curled herself into a ball around the fire and fell asleep.

She awoke to screaming and the heat of a fire. But not the gentle, comforting heat of a campfire. This was something else entirely, and she was somewhere else. Another place, another time. She was in a hut, and she had to escape before it burned to the ground around her. She opened the small wooden door and ran out into the street. The earth shook violently and threw her off her feet. The entire street was tilting downward. Frosthall was in flames. The celebrations of achieving the impossible; of building a city that floated in the sky, had now turned into a disaster. Dragons ran in every direction, shrieking in terror as the ground shook once again, tilting the entire city further sideways. She felt the uncomfortable dread of falling. Smoke filled the air. It was chaos. She looked to the school of magic, where she noticed Glasswing dragons flying away. She tried lifting off herself to escape, but she couldn't. She didn't know why, maybe her wings were damaged, but she tried desperately to escape. Then she noticed one of the elder dragons running down the street towards a nearby water tower. He was old, with greying scales and jagged horns. He carried something in his arms- a bunch of glass spheres. She looked at him and caught his eyes. He was crying, a look of total despair on his face. He looked at her and said

"I'm sorry, child. I'm so very sorry."

He then continued on towards the water tower. The ground beneath her opened up, and she began to fall.

"Wake up, time to fly!" Peacefinder shook Lavender awake.

She jolted up and suppressed a scream. Peacefinder looked at her curiously,

"What's wrong?" she asked.

"Just a bad dream," Lavender mumbled, trying to slow her heartbeat down.

Bubbletail was already bouncing around the stove while Jadeclaw stirred the porridge. Lavender got up, pushed away all her thoughts about the nightmare and headed towards the two dragons.

"Hey Bubbletail," she said.

Bubbletail swung around, his round tail barely missed smacking her in the snout.

"Yikes, watch it!" Lavender yelped as she took a step back.

"Whoops, sorry," he said with not a hint of apology.

"What do you want in your porridge?" Bubbletail asked as Jadeclaw poured a lumpy spoon of it into a stone bowl.

He handed Lavender the bowl and then went off to wake Firesneezer, who was very cheerful in the morning, just like Bubbletail.

"Some honey," she replied.

He spooned the amber liquid into the porridge and passed it to her.

"Thanks!" Lavender swallowed the sweet porridge and went to her satchel. She rummaged through it to find her book. Lavender's claws touched the leather-bound cover and she tugged it out. The book cover was peeling slightly but it was still readable. The familiar scent of old paper wafted through the air as Lavender flipped the book open. Something caught her eye.

*The fall of Frosthall. Chapter 18: The Glasswings who could flee, fled for safety as the city came crashing down. But for many, the sudden and violent collapse meant there was no escape. As to the whereabouts of the orb crafter- he was never seen or heard from again. His magical orbs and the secrets for crafting them, lost with the rest of the city when it collapsed into the earth.*

"Whatcha reading?" Firesneezer interrupted.

"Oh," said Lavender, startled out of her thoughts. "It's just a book about Frosthall." Firesneezer looked over her shoulder.

"It looks old," he commented.

"It is really old."

"Well, there's nothing left of that old ruin now," said Firesneezer.

"Not on land anyway."

"What do you mean by that?" asked Lavender.

"Well, there are rumors that some of the ancient ruins of Frosthall are still intact, but they are at the bottom of the Frost Lake. Which is frozen over for most of the year, very dark, and very treacherous. Did I mention it's cold?" he concluded.

Lavender pondered on the dream she had, and how vividly she recalls being in Frosthall.

"How will we cross the lake?" she asked.

"There are ferry boats which take travelers across," replied Bubbletail.

"Oh, I wonder what those look like," she mused.

"See for yourself," replied Bubbletail. He flicked his tail and pointed further down the road. They had come to a clearing above a flat, empty field. Beyond it, she saw water, and in the center, near the road, a dock with a boat anchored to it. As they made their way closer, she realized that the lake was huge. It stretched across the entire valley, with tall, jagged mountains as its northernmost border. In the center she could just make out a small island. The ferry was a large, wooden barge with a tarp across the center and a tall mast. A tall, skinny dragon greeted them.

"Good day travelers," he said. "Welcome to the best, and only, ferry service to Frostfall. Our next departure is in two hours. Please, come aboard and make yourselves comfortable." Peacefinder spoke to the ferry operator.

"We'd very much like to get going immediately."

"Oh well, there could be more passengers arriving and I wouldn't want to change their schedule," he replied.

"There's nobody else coming," she said, holding out a handful of shiny sapphires.

The ferry operator smiled. "You're the boss!" he said.

He then headed over to a large horn attached to the side of the ferry. When he blew it, it made a low rumble that eventually became a loud bellow that could probably be heard all the way to Frostfall.

"All aboard!" he said, and untied the lines.

Lavender then noticed three small dragons who popped out from below deck. They expertly jumped through the mast's rigging lines and within a few moments, a large, purple, faded sail unfurled. The dragons then took two oars to get the ferry moving. It was a slow process, but eventually the sail caught wind and they were slicing through the waves. The lake was eerily pretty, considering what disaster had formed it. The water was midnight blue, with patches of ice forming around its edges. The waves were gentle, and the ride was smooth. With the cool wind in her face and the sun emerging from behind clouds, Lavender once again felt like the brave adventurer, off to explore new lands.

"What brings you to Frostfall?" asked the ferry operator, once they were on their way.

"We're on business," replied Peacefinder, clearly in no mood for conversation.

"Actually, we are on a mission from the king to locate a lost dragon who goes by the name Nightfall but his real name is Daybringer and Lavender over here will find him by seeing into the past," blurted Bubbletail.

Jadeclaw growled with annoyance while Peacefinder just sighed.

"Wow!" said the ferry operator. "That's quite a tale. Well, I know just about everyone who lives on Frostfall and I can tell you, there's no fellow by that name, or names, living there. And I don't recall bringing any travelers in recently. Though to be fair- we don't get very many tourists."

At this point, Peacefinder realized that a bunch of strangers arriving at a small town like Frostfall would definitely attract a lot of attention, and the locals knowing something about their mission might actually be helpful. She turned to the ferry operator.

"Do you know of any dragons that live outside of Frostfall? In the fields, or mountains nearby? Maybe dragons that only come in once in a while to buy supplies?" The ferry operator laughed.

"Madam, we're in the middle of the wilderness out here. There's wolves, bears, jackals, even very determined racoons. Not to mention the weather- storms that will dump a dragon's height in snow in just a few hours. There's no farms, no hunting outposts, no mines, no lumber mills. The town here lives off of fishing the lake- that's about all we have here. That and looking after the occasional treasure hunters. So you ask if any dragons live beyond the town- no way."

Peacefinder looked disappointed, but she persisted.

"What about these treasure hunters?" she asked. "Are there any who have been out here a really long time?" The ferry operator thought on this for a moment.

"We get some odd ones out here," he said. "Some who travel by night, flying over the lake even. If you ask me, they look more like bandits than treasure hunters. There was one fellow," he continued, thinking hard now. "He was looking for a bunch of odd supplies, hard to find stuff. And he was trying to buy himself a fishing boat down by the dock, though it was plain as day that he wasn't into fishing."

Peacefinder listened intently now. "How long ago was this?" she asked.

"Oh, this was over a year ago," he replied. "I haven't seen him since." Peacefinder sunk back down. Clearly, she hoped that sighting was more recent.

"Did he buy the boat?" asked Jadeclaw, who was passively listening in.

"What- oh, I don't know," replied the ferry operator. "This was just a story I heard from one of my buddies who works at the dockyard. You'd have to ask him."

They were now getting closer to the island at the center of the lake. Lavender could see the first signs of life- dark, wooden structures and the smoke from chimneys. The island was in a circular shape, like a hill popping up from the water, with houses and shops arranged in layers going up to the top of the hill. At the top stood what looked like a tall, narrow stone tower. The ferry operator ordered the sail to be raised, and they floated slowly closer to the dock. They arrived at the shore with a thud. Soon the ferry was tied to the wooden platform. The ferry operator thanked them for their business and helped them off of the rocking boat. Lavender came off first. The captain gripped her arm tightly and she carefully stepped onto the old wood. Bubbletail and Firesneezer came next and Peacefinder and Jadeclaw brought up the rear.

"Someone needs to get these floors checked," Firesneezer commented. "We might fall into the water and then freeze to death!"

"Oh don't be so dramatic, it's fine. See?" Peacefinder said as she pushed the wood with all her might. It creaked slightly but the dock didn't collapse. "Still, we should stay clear," Peacefinder quickly added as it let out another loud creak.

They headed for the narrow streets of Frostfall and stopped to take in the view. The town was made up of wooden houses and shacks, built nearly one on top of the other. The streets were all curved, as the entire town formed a circle around the small island. The houses and huts all had sharply-slanting roofs, built this way to allow the snow to fall off of them easily during snowstorms. The streets were muddy, the houses were dingy and dark, and there were nearly no torches to light the streets at night. Lavender couldn't help but wonder at how far Frostfall had truly fallen from its splendid past. There weren't many dragons out and about, but they heard some noises up ahead.

"That must be the town market," said Peacefinder. "It's also where we'll find the general goods store."

When they approached the market, it was clear that all of the town's activity was centered there. All around them, stalls lined the walls and merchants showed off their goods. As they walked down the street, the merchants came to life, spotting new faces and potential spenders.

"Genuine old Frosthall crystals here," yelled out one merchant.

"Even more genuine Frosthall statues here, get your statues!" yelled another, competing for their attention.

"Lovely fashion from Frosthall's past, I bet this would suit you!" said another merchant, holding out a strange-looking hat to Lavender. The merchants all seemed interested in them.

"This way," Jadecaw yelled over the noise.

The dragons formed a line and she led them over to the entrance of one of the larger structures. The sign across the door read General Goods. Inside, there was a warm, soft light coming from a fireplace. There were jugs and crates and boxes standing everywhere, and various trinkets and curiosities filled the shelves.

"This place is amazing," whispered Lavender.

The only sound was that from the fire cracking, and a humming coming from the back of the store. The group made their way to the back, where they saw an older, grey-colored dragon, busy reading an ancient book and humming an unknown tune.

"Excuse me, sir," said Peacefinder. There was no reply. "Excuse me," she tried again. Still no reply.

Firesneezer was playing with a device he found on the shelf. It was a small, flat piece of wood with some metal and springs attached. It looked like an odd mousetrap. At that moment, the trap sprang shut on Firesneezer's claw.

"Yaaaaa!" he yelped in pain.

The shopkeeper jumped in surprise, torn from whatever he was thinking about. He then noticed the group of dragons around him. Firesneezer was out of the trap by now and trying not to look guilty.

"Hi," continued Peacefinder. "I was wondering if you have seen a dragon called Nightfall come into the store?"

The shopkeeper looked at her as if she had just fallen from the moon.

"Oh, it's not nighttime yet young madam, you see the sun is still up," he replied.

Peacefinder was confused, but Jadeclaw caught on. She then said in a loud, slow voice.

"Not nightfall, we mean the dragon that goes by the name of Nightfall. Have you see him?" she asked, while Peacefinder pulled out the drawing they had of him.

The shopkeeper now began to understand.

"Hmmm…let me think. There was one called Nightclaw…or was it Nightpaw…" he pondered, tapping his chin. He then looked at them again and said, "I have a terrible memory, I don't think I've seen him around here…ever. I'm sorry but you might want to try your luck somewhere else," he said.

Peacefinder look deflated, but Bubbletail stepped in.

"You know, these mousetraps are quite effective. We'll buy some." The shopkeeper now showed renewed interest.

"Oh yes, those are my own design. They'll trap any mouse or rat or rodent that you care to trap," he said proudly.

"We'll take five ," said Bubbletail, "and my friend will see to the payment," he said, looking at Peacefinder, who now understood what was going on.

"Very well," said the happy shopkeeper, "that'll be three sapphires.".

He packed up the mousetraps and handed them to her as she brought out the shiny sapphires as payment.

"You know," said the shopkeeper, "there was a dragon that used to come in here. He's a strange fellow, didn't talk much, wore a hood over his head even when it wasn't raining. He bought a few odd items, then left. He hasn't been back in months though."

This was what Peacefinder was hoping to hear. "Sir, can you tell us a bit more about the last time you saw him?" she asked.

The shopkeeper tried his best to remember the last time he saw the dragon. "It was nearly evening, and there was a smaller dragon in the shop that day as well. In fact, they were both here at the same time. I remember because I rarely get two customers in at once. I think that was right before the spring fish festival," the shopkeeper recalled.

"This should be enough to go on, thank you," said Peacefinder, now turning to Lavender.

They now had a good idea of the time and place he was last seen, so she might be able to find him in the past.

"Can you use your ability to try?" she asked, in a hopeful voice.

Lavender knew all the pressure was on her now.

"Ok, I'll try," she replied.

She then closed her eyes and started concentrating. She began to see the room, exactly as it was, except that now, other dragons were moving through it. Big ones, small ones, some who just wandered around, others who bought things, and some who just came in to chat with the shopkeeper. She saw them and watched them and then moved on to the next. Mostly, she was just watching an empty shop. After hours and hours of looking at nothing particular, she opened her eyes, exhausted.

"How long was I gone for?" she asked.

Bubbletail and Firesneezer were both staring at her.

"You knocked yourself out for about 5 minutes," said Firesneezer.

"What, no I was away for hours...days!" said Lavender.

"It might seem that way when you're in your vision," said Peacefinder, "but in the real world, you're only actually gone a short while," she continued.

Lavender was in disbelief. It truly felt like she had just spent a week sitting in that shop.

"Did you see him?" asked Jadeclaw.

Lavender thought for a moment, but she already knew the answer. "No." she said.

"It doesn't mean anything," continued Jadeclaw, looking to comfort Peacefinder.

"We'll just have to search for more clues around town," she continued. "But first, we need to find the inn and get some food and rest. We've been traveling for a long time. We all need a fresh start in the morning."

Peacefinder looked for a moment like she wanted to argue for them to keep searching now, but she knew Jadeclaw was right. They dipped their snouts in farewell to the shopkeeper and proceeded to the one and only inn that existed in Frostfall. It wasn't far from the shop, and it was just as humble as the other establishments around. It was a three-storey wooden building with the usual sharply-slanting roof. It was the standard inn setup, with the ground floor serving as a restaurant and rooms for rent located upstairs. The restaurant space was dark, with some of the wooden benches and tables appearing as if they had been charred black in a fire at some point, and a general lack of torches or candles added to the gloom. There was however a hearty firepit in the center with a sweet-smelling stew slowly cooking in a large kettle hanging over the fire. Lavender's tummy growled.

"Welcome to "Last & Only Inn", said a cheery innkeeper.

"Hello, we'll need a few rooms if they are available," said Peacefinder.

"Of course, of course," said the innkeeper.

He was a surly dragon with dark green scales on his back and a light green tummy.

"But first, you'll need to eat!" he said.

"Oh you read my mind," said Bubbletail, who had already located some bowls and spoons for the stew.

The innkeeper served them all a heated carrot stew. Lavender didn't realize just how hungry she had been.

"What brings you to Frostfall?" asked the innkeeper, after they had eaten their fill.

"We're looking for a friend," said Lavender.

Peacefinder then took the opportunity to mention Nightfall and show the drawing to the innkeeper. He didn't have any new information.

"So what do we do next?" asked Bubbletail.

"Tomorrow, we're going to split up and search for clues around the town," said Peacefinder. "Bubbletail and Firesneezer, you poke around the market some more. See if you can find anyone who's seen him recently. Jadeclaw, you ask around the city watch, they will respect you as a Kingsguard and might give some answers," continued Peacefinder.

"I don't like this idea of splitting up," protested Jadeclaw. "My job is to protect you."

"Yes and your job is important but I don't think we're about to be attacked by wolves or trolls or grumpkins in the middle of Frostfall," countered Peacefinder. Jadeclaw reluctantly agreed.

"What about me?" asked Lavender.

"You and I will go down to the docks," replied Peacefinder. "The ferry operator told us there may have been a sighting of Daybringer there."

They then made their way up the rooms. They were crammed against the inner side of the slanting roof, and Jadeclaw found that she was just tall enough to hit her head on the ceiling if she stood straight.

"It'll do for a few days, until we find our next destination," said Peacefinder.

Lavender was just happy to be sleeping in a bed instead of outside under a tarp. The next morning, Lavender felt fresh and ready for some detective work. They all met up for breakfast and went over their plan. Firesneezer and Bubbletail managed to locate some silly hats to "blend in with the locals", while Jadeclaw was still uncomfortable with the splitting up part. They ate sweet rolls for breakfast and then headed out. The air was crisp, with a thin layer of frost covering the rooftops. The sun was just making its way over the mountains, and Lavender was happy to see it was shaping up to be a beautiful day. The street wasn't as empty as Lavender thought it would be this early in the morning. Dragons were making their way down to the docks to start their day fishing. Peacefinder and Lavender joined the crowd.

"Are these the descendants of the ancient Glasswing dragons?" asked Lavender, as she and Peacefinder made their way down to the docks.

Peacefinder took a look around at the dragons walking. They looked like normal dragons, without the telltale semi-transparent wings that the Glasswing dragons were famous for.

"I think most of these dragons moved here after the fall," said Peacefinder. "That lineage still exists today," she continued, "but they are rare." Lavender was disappointed as she was hoping to catch a glimpse of a Glasswing dragon. They arrived at the docks just as the fishing boats were departing.

"We need to find the dockmaster," said Peacefinder.

Lavender noticed a long, narrow building set on stilts above the water. There was a red sign above the entrance which read: Frostfall Dockyard.

"Maybe we should try there?" she asked, pointing towards the building.

"Good idea," said Peacefinder as they climbed the steps of the porch.

They knocked on the door and found an office with a large warehouse behind it.

"Hi, we'd like to ask about a dragon who was here trying to buy a boat some time ago," said Peacefinder to the secretary minding the desk.

146

The secretary took a long look at them without responding. She finally said, "you two some kind of police force or something?"

It was clear that she wasn't intending on being helpful.

"No," said Peacefinder. "We had a friend who disappeared some time ago, and we are trying to find him."

The secretary thought for a moment. "What was the name of this friend?" she asked. "Nightfall," replied Peacefinder.

The secretary's face took on a look of concern at this point. "Wait here," she said.

Peacefinder looked at Lavender. "Well this is strange," she said.

A few minutes later, the dragon emerged from the door with a blank look on her face. "Here you are ma'am," she said.

The dragon dropped a notebook onto the desk and pushed it towards Peacefinder.

"Here's a record of everyone who bought something over the past few months," she explained. "If he was in here, he's in there."

"Thank you," replied Peacefinder as she flipped open the book.

Lavender helped to scan each page carefully but quickly, but there was no record of Nightfall. She gave Peacefinder a look of concern and turned to the third page.

"If he bought this over a year ago, wouldn't his name be at the top?" Lavender whispered.

"Not necessarily," the cashier said, apparently eavesdropping on the two of them, "There's been around…only twenty dragons who have bought a boat the past year," she explained sadly, "and not all of them signed the ledger correctly," the dragon finished.

Lavender couldn't help feeling a little sympathy for her as she nodded and went back to reading. There, as the second name on the second page, was Nightfall, along with the date of purchase. Peacefinder beamed with satisfaction and Lavender smiled.

"Thank you so very much! Would you like anything in return?" Peacefinder asked as she scribbled down the day and time Nightfall, also known as Daybringer, wrote his name in a notebook.

The secretary gave them a strange look and said, "Unless you want to buy a boat, happy I could help. Now, if you don't mind…" she trailed off and they got the hint.

They left the dockyard office and stood at the end of the wharf.

"Now that we have the exact day and time, you can try using your sight again," said Peacefinder to Lavender. Lavender didn't hold much hope after she failed at the general store, but she would try. She fell deep into concentration and began to peer into the past. The sun rose and fell over and over again as she searched for the right day. Her vision became blurrier and blurrier the further back she went. The world became a murky haze, and she could barely make out the horizon. She counted the times the sun rotated above her. She thought she found it. The world slowed down again. It was a rainy day, and the wind threw rain droplets against the side of her face. As she turned, she saw what looked like a dockworker walking out of the dockyard office. Behind him came an old, bronze-colored dragon wearing a large hood that concealed his eyes. There he was- Daybringer. He had a look of somber sadness, and he walked with unease. The dock worker showed him to the boat he just purchased. It was a small sailboat made from the same dark wood that every boat in the dock was made out of. Its sail was furled, but Lavender could make out the color- a faded green. The dock worker explained a few things to Daybringer, who seemed to only be half-listening.

"Well, if you've really got your heart set on going to Stoney Shore, I'd definitely wait for better weather," said the dockworker to Daybringer.

Daybringer only replied that he was in a hurry. The dockworker clearly thought the old dragon was crazy, but was happy to take his sapphires for the boat, so he didn't ask any more questions. Daybringer then made his way slowly into the boat. He carried something- a large, rectangular wooden case. Lavender would try to use her sight to follow him as he sailed. She made to enter the boat herself, but then, something impossible happened. Daybringer looked directly at her and said in a booming voice, "I need to find it! Don't try to stop me!"

He then brought the heavy oar around and swung at Lavender so that she lost her balance and fell into the water. She returned from her vision with a yelp. She was back in real time. She was sweating and shaking.

"What happened?" asked Peacefinder, looking concerned.

Lavender needed a moment to catch her breath.

"I saw him...he was here," she said. "But...he saw me! He saw me and he told me he needed to find something, and that I shouldn't try to stop him. He looked directly at me. He pushed me into the water with his oar!" she cried, still distressed over the experience. "I thought that was impossible!" she yelled. "How could he interact with me if I wasn't really there?"

Peacefinder listened intently.

"Daybringer is a very special seer," she replied. "Since he can see into the future, it's possible that he saw that we would come for him. Did he actually touch you with that oar?" she asked.

Lavender gave it some thought. "No. I just lost my balance because I dodged it out of reflex." Peacefinder thought for a moment.

"Then he didn't really interact with you. He may have seen you, but he cannot interfere with your vision," concluded Peacefinder.

"Well, it was scary," said Lavender.

"I'm sure it was, and unexpected." Then Peacefinder turned quiet. "Even though you saw him, we are no closer to knowing where to look for him next."

Lavender smiled wrily. "Oh, but we are."

Peacefinder looked up with renewed hope. "We are?" she asked.

"Stoney Shore," said Lavender. "That's where the dockworker thought Daybringer was going." Peacefinder smiled.

"Let's find the others." They walked off the dock and started back up the hill towards the market. Then, Peacefinder stopped suddenly, her eyes closed and her body stiff.

"We have a problem," she said. Lavender looked at her with concern.

"Quickly, our friends are in trouble," she said, as she started running up the hill. Moments later, Lavender heard the sound of running and screaming. Up the road, two little dragons were running as fast as they could in their direction. It was Bubbletail and Firesneezer. Gaining on them were two big, burly, mean-looking dragons carrying short, stubby wooden clubs. Lavender looked to Peacefinder, who was already prepared, her bow unpacked.

"Help, help, run, run!" yelled Bubbletail as they ran past them and just kept going.

Upon seeing Peacefinder and Lavender, the two thugs stopped to catch their breath.

"Seems like we have more troublemakers than we thought," said one of the thugs in a hard, raspy voice.

Lavender curled her claws dangerously. "We're not the ones causing trouble," she said, "but I can't let you hurt our friends."

Upon seeing Peacefinder's shiny bow and sharp arrow, the thugs paused. Then one of them smiled and said, "There's two of us but you've only got one arrow. Seems to me like you're getting pummeled no matter what!"

Peacefinder didn't flinch. "Your math isn't quite right," she said. The two thugs looked at each other.

"What's math?" asked one.

At that moment, Lavender saw a streak of shiny metal fly through the air and hit against one of the thugs. It hit him in the leg and he fell over immediately, stunned. Just as the second thug looked over to see what had happened, Lavender heard a "whoosh" sound and the second thug was down. Standing behind the thugs was Jadeclaw. Peacfinder smiled.

"I had a feeling you'd arrive just in time," she said with a smile.

Jadeclaw looked over to the two thugs, still recovering from the impact of the spear against their legs. Jadeclaw then unwrapped the spear's deadly tip.

"That was just a tickle compared to what you'll experience if you don't tell us exactly why you're chasing them," she said to the thugs.

Bubbletail was cowering behind Peacefinder while Firesneezer had managed to run all the way down to the docks and was just now walking back, relieved. The two thugs took one look at Jadeclaw, with her shiny armor and Kingsguard spear, and knew they were beaten.

"Hey relax, we're just doing a job," said one of the thugs.

"A job?" asked Jadeclaw. "Who hired you?"

The thugs looked at each other with hesitation. Finally, one spoke. "It was this old dragon. He told us to chase off anyone who comes by looking for someone named Nightfall. He paid us twelve whole sapphires each!"

The thugs seemed very proud of how much they got paid for what seemed like an easy job. Lavender's mouth gaped open in shock. *Nightfall...Daybringer...he would do something like this? But why?*

Peacefinder thought for a moment.

"How would you like to make another twelve sapphires?" she asked. The thugs couldn't believe what they were hearing.

"Do you also need us to chase away some little dragons?" one of them asked- clearly the dumber of the two.

"No, I can see you're pretty useless at that. What we need from you is information. Namely- the location of the old dragon who hired you."

They considered this for a moment. "He never said where he was going, only that he needed to make sure nobody found him," said one of the thugs.

Peacefinder looked disappointed, then gave up on this idea and told the thugs to scatter. They didn't think twice and quickly ran off, thankful to have gotten away.

"Let's get back to the inn," said Jadeclaw, having noticed that in all of the commotion, they now had a crowd of onlookers around them.

Back at the inn, Peacefinder explained what they had learned.

"The local town watch wasn't very helpful," said Jadeclaw. "They don't keep records of who comes and goes, and a dragon who keeps a low profile can easily go unnoticed."

"Yeah, and we also didn't learn much," said Bubbletail. "Only that Firesneezer is a really good runner when being chased by some thugs." They all laughed.

"So Lavender's lead is all we have to go on." She then explained what Lavender saw in her vision. "This place- Stoney Shore, what can you tell us about it?" asked Peacefinder.

Bubbletail got up and sorted through a pile of rolled-up scrolls on the desk, finally finding what he was looking for and unraveling it.

"Here we are," he said.

The scroll was a map which showed Frostfall in the center, the lake, and the surrounding shoreline. A number of place markers were written on it. Bubbletail pointed to a wide inlet which opened up a gap between the surrounding cliffs. There was a structure there as well but it didn't look like a house.

"That's it," he said while pointing. "A long time ago, Stoney Shore was a rock quarry. That's where all of the stone was mined. But when Frosthall collapsed, the quarry was destroyed. It was never rebuilt, although some ruins still remain."

They all looked on thoughtfully. "Have you ever been there?" asked Jadeclaw.

"Are you kidding?" asked Firesneezer. "I wouldn't go there if you paid me. That place is haunted." Jadeclaw gave him a look of amusement.

"Let me guess- ghosts and goblins live there," she said.

"I don't know what lives there but I don't want to find out!" replied Firesneezer. "A couple of years ago, there was a bunch of robberies on the roads and even on the lake," he explained. "A group of bandits was making trade with Frostfall impossible. The town watch found out that they were hiding out at Stoney Shore."

154

Lavender was listening intently to the story.

"So one day, they went out in force to crush the bandits. Four long boats, nearly the entire town watch, fully armed for battle." Bubbletail looked sombre. "I remember the entire town was cheering them on as they departed on the boats," he said.

"Yes," said Firesneezer. "Everyone expected them back in time for dinner. It was just a bunch of bandits after all. They were never seen or heard from again."

Lavender was shocked by the story. What could have happened to all of them?

"Then the fisherman and the remaining town watch took a few boats out to search for them," continued Firesneezer. "Of those dragons, only two came back. One of them had gone completely silent, his dark purple scales turned a hazy white. And the other, well, he was just rambling on and on about a monster made of stone."

The room was eerily quiet. Finally, Peacefinder broke the silence.

"So what happened to the bandits?" she asked.

"Nobody knows," replied Firesneezer. "But there were no more bandit raids or attacks on trade caravans after that. This is why nobody would ever dare to go to Stoney Store."

Jadeclaw pondered for a moment, then said, "well, right now Stoney Shore is our only lead to finding Daybringer. So we will have to dare to go there," she said.

Firesneezer stuffed his face into his palms.

"I was afraid you'd say that," he said, looking completely deflated.

"There's a first for everything," she remarked.

"Whatever happened at Stoney Shore, one thing is for certain," said Peacefinder. "A place that everyone is afraid to go to is the perfect place to hide. Get some rest everyone. Tomorrow, we will see what that place is really about."

That night, as Lavender tried to sleep, visions of the past haunted her dreams again. A battle in the sky. Hundreds…thousands of dragons clawing at each other. The strange-looking creatures known as humans riding on some of them, screaming and urging them on. The shadow of a menacing black dragon with gleaming red eyes could be seen swooping down. A dark figure wearing a crimson robe and a hood sat on its back. He was human, and he was carrying something. It was a staff, with a gleaming white orb attached to one end. She recognized this orb. It was similar to the ones she saw in her previous vision. This orb was the key to everything. This was the reason why the great calamity was coming. The shadowy figure laughed and urged his dragon on. The smoke now covered her eyes. She awoke, coughing.

The next morning, Lavender found herself being pushed out of bed by Peacefinder.

"Hey, the sun isn't even up yet," she protested.

"No, but we are, and we have to be. Today is a very important day," said Peacefinder, while packing an assortment of dried fruit and bread into her pack.

Then Lavender remembered where they were going, and a jolt of fear ran down her spine. "Are you sure you want to do this?" she asked, already knowing the answer.

"Don't worry," said Peacefinder. "Whatever those bandits and town watch guards were up against, we can handle it."

Lavender appreciated the attempt at confidence, but it didn't help. Still, she knew that their mission was important and that she had to conquer her fears. She was an adventurer after all. Jadeclaw, Bubbletail and Firesneezer were waiting downstairs. Bubbletail was wearing what looked like a trash can, with the lid open and his head peeking through. Firesneezer was wearing some kind of pot on his head and carrying a small door in front of him. They looked ridiculous.

"What are you supposed to be?" asked Lavender through her giggles.

"This is the best we could do on short notice," replied Firesneezer. "You didn't expect us to walk into the jaws of death without any protection, did you?"

Jadeclaw chuckled. "Nothing like a pot and a trash can to strike fear into the hearts of monsters. And…is that a door?"

"We used what we had," commented Firesneezer, still clutching the wooden door he was determined to use as a shield. Lavender laughed. She was thankful for Bubbletail and Firesneezer. It was before dawn and the streets were dark and empty. They walked all the way down to the dock with not another dragon in sight. Peacefinder unfurled her Gliderwing.

"We fly in," she said. "That way we make the least amount of noise."

"That, and the fact that the ferry operator said you were completely bonkers when you asked him to take us there," said Bubbletail.

"Yes, well, that too," admitted Peacefinder.

"But how are we going to fly?" asked Firesneezer.

"Jadeclaw and I will carry you," replied Peacefinder.

"Oh," said Bubbletail. "This is going to be uncomfortable isn't it."

It took awhile for them to get their Gliderwings sorted out and all the gear loaded, plus Bubbletail and Firesneezer, who were sitting on Jadeclaw and Peacefinder's back.

"We are heavily loaded, so we are going to need a running start," said Peacefinder.

"Hang on," she said to Bubbletail, as she lined up on the longest dock.

She started running as fast as she could while flapping her wings with furious energy. Lavender looked on in amazement. But despite her effort, she was not getting off the ground, and the end of the dock was getting closer and closer. Then she leaped off the dock and at that very moment, unfurled her Gliderwing to catch the slightest breeze. Her wing tips glanced the surface of the icy lake, and she glided just above, her reflection clearly visible in the water. Then, with a few powerful flaps, she was flying. Above the sound of her wings, was the sound of joyous screaming.

"Woohoo, this is amazing!" yelled Bubbletail, who had never flown with a Gliderwing before.

Next it was Lavender's turn, and though she was carrying more gear than usual, she wasn't carrying a dragon on her back, so her takeoff was much less dramatic. When she was in the air, she circled back to watch Jadeclaw take off. Jadeclaw's powerful wings made her takeoff run shorter, but she wasn't as graceful with the Gliderwing as Peacefinder, and she ended up dipping so low that she got a mouthful of lakewater before managing to gain altitude. Firesneezer was laughing and crying at the same time, out of both joy and fear. They then turned east, and watched the sunrise as they flew over the lake. Lavender was happy to be in the air again. It gave her a feeling of peace and freedom. They flew for what felt like hours, mainly because the wind had picked up and Lavender felt very cold. Down below, a hazy mist had formed on the lake, making it difficult to navigate.

"You see those two cliffs ahead?" said Bubbletail. "That's it, we're close now."

A few minutes later, they were circling in the air around their destination. It was a rocky shoreline with a long strip of beach. Further inland, Lavender could just make out the ruins of some buildings. It was quiet, and the mist made it difficult to see anything. They then swooped down one last time below the mist and landed hard on the sand. Pebbles went flying and Jadeclaw tumbled over, with Firesneezer flying forward head-first onto the sand. The whole thing made so much noise that it echoed through the valley.

"Well, if they didn't know we were here, they certainly know now," commented Peacefinder.

They quickly packed their Gliderwings, then unpacked their trekking gear and made their way inland, where they were hidden by some large boulders. They stopped for a moment to listen. Nothing. Peacefinder focused her ability on the ground ahead.

"The buildings are abandoned, and there's no sign of...anything," she told the others. "Further ahead, I can just make out the entrance to the old underground mines."

"Let me see if I can learn more," said Lavender. She then focused her ability on what happened at this spot in the past. Time rolled backwards. It was dark, but there was light from a large bonfire. There was singing and laughing. The bandits were here. They were all having a good time, when suddenly, the ground shook. They all stopped to listen. A low rumble, and then a thumping noise. It continued, and got louder. The bandits all looked to the entrance of the mines. They gathered their bows and arrows, and some of them picked up spears and clubs. The thumping now became louder and faster and then Lavender saw a creature straight out of fairy tales. It was huge,  hulking, ash gray in color with spikes on it's back and massive horns on it's head. It held what looked like a tree trunk in one hand, which had been shaped into a club. The ogre had terrible fangs and dark, almost black eyes. It grunted and screamed as it ran at the terrified bandits. They shot the ogre with arrows and some threw their spears. The creature's skin was so thick that these things just bounced right off of it. It then started swinging it's club and sending the bandits flying. It was a scene of total panic and chaos. Then, just as quickly as it had started, it was over. The bandits that didn't flee were all dead, the campfire scene a gory mess. The ogre, having gotten rid of his unwanted guests, made its way back into the mine it emerged from. Lavender returned to reality, terrified.

"What did you see?" asked Bubbletail eagerly.

"You're not going to believe this," she replied, pale with fear.

"How are we supposed to take on an ogre?" asked Bubbletail, after Lavender explained to everyone what she saw.

"And besides, Daybringer is clearly not in that cave, just casually hanging out with an ogre!" added Firesneezer.

"That may be," said Jadeclaw. "But that creature poses a threat to every dragon that lives in these parts, and aside from finding Daybringer, we need to rid this land of the menace."

"She's serious," said Firesneezer. "She's going to go in there and fight an ogre five times bigger than a house!"

"It wasn't five times bigger," Lavender clarified. "Maybe three times bigger."

"We need a plan," said Peacefinder. She used her ability to scout around the area.

"Can you see inside the cave?" asked Jadeclaw. "If we can catch it while it's asleep, that would make this an easy job."

"I can't see inside," said Peacefinder. "It's just darkness and I don't know where to look. That cave system is enormous."

"If we cannot surprise it inside the cave," said Jadeclaw, "then we need to bring it out into the open."

"Are you mad?" asked Firesneezer. "Did you not hear what happened to the last group of dragons that took it on in the open?"

"I did," replied Jadeclaw. But they didn't know what they were facing. We do. So we can fight it the smart way."

"Oh, there's a smart way to fight a gigantic ogre, please, enlighten us!" said Firesneezer. Jadeclaw sneered.

"Yes, there is, and we'll need to work together," she said.

"What's your idea?" asked Peacefinder.

"You see those tall cliffs above us?" asked Jadeclaw. "Well, when we were circling to land, I noticed a bunch of loose boulders up there. If we can place those boulders so that they fall right as the orge emerges from the cave, we'll crush it."

Peacefinder gave this plan some thought.

"But the ogre is quick- how are we going to keep it standing in one place while we drop a rock on it's head?" asked Bubbletail.

"We build a trap," explained Jadeclaw. "We'll need to get as many of these stones as possible to build a wall around the entrance. Just big enough so that the ogre will need to stop for a moment to throw them out of the way. When it does, splat."

"This is all fine and good but what if the ogre decides to show up, like, right now?" asked Bubbletail.

"I can see a bit into the cave, to the first bend, before it gets too dark," said Peacefinder. "I'll keep my sight focused on the cave. If the ogre suddenly appears before we are ready, I'll sound the alert and we all run as fast as we can."

Lavender was scared, but also determined to help bring this ogre down.

"This can work," said Jadeclaw. "I'll fly up to the top of the cliff and prepare several boulders for dropping. The rest of you, start building the wall to surround the cave entrance. But do so quietly," she noted.

"Move a bunch of boulders heavier than we are…but quietly," said Firesneezer in a grumpy tone.

Jadeclaw continued, unphased. "When we are ready, you two start making noise and taunting the ogre to come out."

"You mean, we're the bait?" asked Bubbletail.

"Call yourselves the heroes," said Jadeclaw. Bubbletail and Firesneezer looked at each other with doubt.

"It's our best chance," said Lavender. "One last question before we get started," she asked. "What if it doesn't work?"

"If it doesn't work, then we're toast," said Bubbletail. Lavender looked to Peacefinder.

"Pretty much," she said. "Toast."

They spent the better part of the afternoon preparing their trap. Jadeclaw had dragged three massive boulders to the very edge of the cliff, ready to drop. They had to lug dozens of heavy boulders to the entrance to the cave, and then use extra energy to put them down gently so that the ogre didn't hear and come out too soon. But despite all of their efforts, the wall they had built was measly in comparison to how big Lavender said the ogre was.

"This isn't enough," said Peacefinder. They all looked dejected.

"There aren't many boulders left that are small enough for us to move," said Lavender.

163

"Yeah, and besides that, my arms feel like they are about to fall off," said Firesneezer.

Just then, Peacefinder sat up, startled.

"Everyone, I think this is as good as it's going to get."

Deep inside the cave, they heard a thumping noise. Everyone sprang to action. Peacefinder gave the signal to Jadeclaw to be ready. She had to time this perfectly. She couldn't see the ogre yet, but it was coming. Lavender hid behind the large boulders with Bubbletail and Firesneezer. Then, they started to hear the thumping as well. It got louder and faster, and then Peacefinder could make out the shadowy form inside the cave. She gasped. She'd never seen a creature like this before. It was about to emerge from the cave so Peacefinder gave the signal to Jadeclaw to drop the boulder. She heaved all of her weight against it and it made a grinding sound before sailing off the side of the cliff. The ogre emerged from the cave and fixed its gaze on Peacefinder. It moved with incredible speed, leaping towards her and getting tripped up by the wall they had built. The loose rocks made the heavy ogre slip back towards the cave's entrance. Just then they all heard a deafening sound of rock smashing against rock and dust exploded in all directions. Peacefinder couldn't see anything, but she could hear a furious scream. The ogre wasn't dead. She could hear rocks being thrown aside as it tried to crawl over the rock wall.

"Quickly Jadeclaw, drop the rest!" She screamed.

Jadeclaw wasted no time in sending one, and then another boulder down the cliff face. These last two were smaller and when they hit the earth, it made a shattering sound but not as intense as the first. *Was it enough?* wondered Peacefinder, as she hid behind a boulder while the dust settled. It took awhile for all of the rocks to finally stop falling and for the dust to settle enough to be able to see again. Peacefinder could see that the ogre had been buried in an avalanche of falling rocks that was brought down together with the big boulders. She listened intently and watched for any motion coming from the rock pile. Jadeclaw flew down to support them in case the ogre emerged. Lavender and the two little dragons also came out of hiding.

"Is it…dead?" asked Bubbletail.

Peacefinder approached the boulder pile carefully, expecting the massive ogre to emerge at any moment and start attacking them. But then she decided that nothing could have survived that.

"I think we got it," said Peacefinder.

"YAAAAS," screamed Firesneezer. "Did you see that first rock come down, that smelly ogre had no idea what was coming," he continued, doing a little victory dance. Bubbletail smiled, and then his eyes grew wide.

"Does that mean that we are….ogre slayers?" he asked.

"Sure," replied Jadeclaw. "But let's be honest, nobody is going to believe you. Ogres are a myth, and slaying one the size of…what was it now, seven houses…well, that's just nonsense," she said while smiling.

Peacefinder finally felt relief. Their plan had worked.

"With this ogre menace out of the way, we can explore this old mine," she said, wasting no time.

"But be on your guard. Just because the ogre is gone doesn't mean there aren't other dangers lurking in there."

Bubbletail and Firesneezer were a little annoyed that their celebration was being cut short, but the sun was rapidly setting and they wanted to get out of there as soon as possible. They took a few torches from their packs and made their way over the rock avalanche and into the mine. After descending for several minutes down an ever-darkening passage, they reached a large cavern with several tunnels branching off in different directions. The light from the torches danced off the irregular rock walls, making shapes that eerily resembled ogres.

"Let's check each one," said Peacefinder.

The first tunnel was wide and contained several broken carts.

"They must have used these to transport the stone," commented Lavender.

"This tunnel is a dead end," said Jadeclaw, coming to a cave-in.

"Let's check the rest."

The second tunnel led them down a long corridor which gradually became narrower. It eventually ended in a dead end as well, but Lavender noticed something odd.

"Look at this smashed boulder," she said, pointing to an oddly-shaped pile of rocks leaning against the wall. Peacefinder looked over the boulder.

"Look here, these marks look like something was smashed into this rock," she observed.

They all began to move the larger of the rocks to the side. Behind the pile of rocks was a secret passage that led into a large room. Inside, they found a small waterfall and they could see

166

sunlight pouring into the eerie clearing from a hole high up above. The room had a series of torches placed all around on the walls. They lit each one. The room became bright with torchlight and they could now see what it was.

"A hideout," said Lavender.

"Yes, but for who?" wondered Peacefinder.

The room was full of various objects, including a wooden table, desk, and bookshelf. It contained several crates of dried fish and fruit, and in the corner stood a straw bed. Several of the books were thrown about the room. Lavender picked up a few.

"These are all old books about the mages of Frosthall," she said, skimming through a few of the ancient books.

Jadeclaw looked up. "Not exactly on the top of bandit reading lists," she commented.

"Look at this," said Peacefinder.

She took an old cloak out from a wooden cabinet. It was elegantly embroidered with the letters KS.

"What does KS stand for?" asked Bubbletail.

Peacefinder was smiling now, and said "King's Seer. This was Daybringer's cloak!"

"Why would he leave it here?" wondered Firesneezer.

"It seems he left in a hurry," observed Jadeclaw. "All of his things are thrown around as if he was under pressure to get out of here and fast."

"Could it have been the ogre?" asked Peacefinder.

"Only one way to find out," said Lavender. She sat down on the straw bed and focused her ability on the past again. The room was dark. Dark and dark and dark and then suddenly, the torches were lit again. There he was again, Daybringer, frantically running around the room, stuffing items into a sack. Outside, she could hear fierce pounding. The fierceness and anger coming from the other side of that boulder meant it could only have been the ogre. Then Daybringer pulled a lever on a wooden mechanism that released a ladder hanging from the ceiling. He climbed his way up just as the ogre smashed through the wall. She watched him escape through the hole at the top of the room and vanish.

"He was here," she said to the others, after coming out of her vision. "But he left when the ogre arrived."

She pointed up at the ceiling.

"Then we are once again at a dead end in our search," said Peacefinder, dejected.

She looked around the cave and felt sad. Daybringer was one of the wisest and kindest dragons she had ever known. And now he was living in caves and being hunted by ogres. She had to find him to help him, save him, or at least understand why he chose to do this.

"We're not exactly back where we started," said Bubbletail. He was holding a large scroll. It was printed with another map, but this one was different from maps Lavender had seen before. It was full of marks and lines in various colors. There were also notes written on the side.

"What is this?" she asked.

"This is what Daybringer has been doing over the past ten years," said Bubbletail.

"What?" exclaimed Peacefinder. "How can you know that simply by looking at a map?" she asked.

"Because any local explorer knows these places, and it seems Daybringer has been to most of them. This map shows all of the possible locations of the treasure of Frosthall."

They were all sitting around him now, listening intently. He continued.

"As you may know, the mages of Frosthall were famous for creating orbs of power. These orbs were magical, and they could be used to make fantastic things happen. It was this power that led to Frosthall's end. But before all was lost, several mages took some of these orbs and escaped the city with them. Some of these orbs have been found, smashed or ruined, but the majority are still lost. Many treasure hunters come to these parts to search for them because their value is beyond measure. The markings and notes on this map make it look like Daybringer is doing the same thing. He's looking for the ancient orbs."

Peacefinder was dumbfounded. "Why would the king's own Seer, a dragon who is revered and loved and whose insights help the king make good decisions, suddenly go off on a ten year long treasure hunt?"

"You did mention that he was acting crazy before he left," Jadeclaw said under her breath.

"I don't believe he was crazy," replied Peacefinder. "I believe Daybringer saw something that sent him on this mission, something so important that he was willing to give up his comfortable life and not even tell any of his friends. Maybe it's something dangerous. Maybe that's why he's trying so hard to not be found. Maybe he doesn't want to put others in danger." Peacefinder looked sad, and then hopeful. "I believe he is still out there, searching. And with our help, maybe he can find what he's looking for."

They decided to spend the night inside Daybringer's hideout, with Jadeclaw and Peacefinder taking turns on watch. The next morning, they climbed their way out of the cave, re-tracing Daybringer's path. The mist and fog had cleared and it was looking to be a beautiful day. The air was cold and crisp, and frost crunched under their feet. The cave exit put them on top of one of the cliffs overlooking the lake. The view was spectacular.

"I can see he flew north from here," said Lavender, while again focusing her sight on the past. "But I can't see anything beyond that."

"He's crossed out all of the places he's already been to on this map," said Bubbletail. There are only a few left. And if we look north we find…" he ran his claw up the map. "There," he read the wording on the map and turned pale. "The Icelava fields of Kedrona," he read, and then sighed. "This really is becoming the world's most dangerous places tour," he said.

"Your friend isn't very good at this whole tourism for fun thing," added Firesneezer.

"Why, what's the Icelava fields of Kedrona?" asked Lavender.

"Only the most dangerous place you can imagine," replied Bubbletail.

Lavender was already regretting her question.

"Volcanoes spewing poisonous ash into the air and throwing chunks of hot lava combine with a frozen wasteland of glaciers. You can be set on fire one minute and freeze to death in the next," explained Bubbletail.

"Plus, there's no food or shelter for hundreds of leagues in any direction," added Firesneezer.

"Have you seen it?" asked Jadeclaw.

Bubbletail looked to Firesneezer. "I'll be honest; we're not that determined to find treasure."

"Yeah, we like to stick to the easier spots, you know, the ones without mountain-sized ogres or fields of lava."

"But you are ogre slayers," Lavender pointed out. "AND, you'll be the legendary heroes that conquered the Icelava fields of Kedrona!"

Bubbletail wasn't fully convinced, but he did like the sound of it.

"How sure are we that he's going there?" asked Jadeclaw.

"You said there were several locations that he hasn't visited yet."

Bubbletail looked at the map again.

"If he flew north to continue searching, then this is the only logical destination."

"Then north it is," declared Peacefinder.

## CHAPTER FOURTEEN: THE BATTLE OF GRAPEFINE

The city of Grapefine was known as a very fun place. Almost everyone worked in the grape industry, which was all about making grape-based products, like juices, jams, and wines. The grape vines surrounded the city in all directions, and everyone who lived there enjoyed the various festivals, holidays, and activities that the city had to offer. Many tourists came to Grapefine to try the various grapes and enjoy the relaxing atmosphere. But now, nobody was happy or relaxing in Grapefine. The city was surrounded by an army of barbarians, who somehow took dragons straight out of fairy tales and made them real. The dragons circled overhead sometimes at night, and the people inside could hear their screeches. The Blood-Red Army made noise all night outside of the city walls, making it impossible for anyone inside to get any sleep. The northern division of the royal army had entered the city right before it was surrounded, and the soldiers were the only thing stopping an

172

attack now. But the defenders on the walls were exhausted, and the hot weather made it worse. Grapefine had several deep wells, so they still had plenty of water, but aside from grapes, the food was starting to run out. The mayor was told that they could hold out for another three days before they would be forced to surrender the city or fight. But everyone inside feared what would happen to them either way. The soldiers weren't really afraid of the human army they faced, but they were very afraid of the dragons.

Malon kept the fear level high by never flying the dragons over the city during the daytime, so that soldiers only caught glimpses of them at night. *The rumor is always bigger than the truth*, thought Malon to himself. But while everyone agreed that Malon was creating terror inside the city, none of his soldiers understood why he never flew Doomswing over the city, or why he didn't just destroy the gates with dragonfire and end the suspense. But Malon was setting a trap. He was waiting for the soldiers from the southern army to arrive, and his scouts had told him exactly where they were. They would arrive in two days, and then Malon would wipe them out and take the city as well.

On the morning of the next day, Malon woke to find a thick fog had moved into the valley. Thick fogs were bad for him, because it made it difficult for his dragons to fly and see where they were going. But this didn't really matter, as the southern army was still one day away, and the food inside the city would run out tomorrow. Today was just a lazy day of sitting around, waiting. If the soldiers inside the city decided to fight, Malon's army was waiting for them at every gate, dug in and ready. There was no way out. But then, he felt the earth tremble, and heard an endless thumping sound. He ran out of his tent to see what was happening. Then, for the first time since he gazed upon Doomswing, he felt a bolt of terror run down his spine. The sound he heard came from galloping horses, hundreds of them. The cavalry of the southern army had arrived. They marched all night and managed to sneak up on him. Not only that, but instead of coming from the south, which is where he had his troops ready, they came from the north. They must have circled around at night. His army was totally unprepared to face an attack from the opposite side. His soldiers also had very few horses, or long spears that could stop them. As soon as he saw the cavalry emerge from the thick fog, he knew he made a mistake. The cavalry charged straight into the army that was surrounding the city, and the battle had begun. But for the first several moments, it wasn't a battle at all. The cavalry cut through the lines of Malon's soldiers as if they weren't even there. Wave after wave of heavily-armored troops on heavily-armored horses pierced their way through his army with their shiny lances. Many of his soldiers didn't even know what was happening before they were struck down. His generals attempted to counter-attack, but his soldiers were so shocked by the sudden violence that many of the survivors turned and ran. Malon had only one option now- his dragons. He quickly got to Doomswing, and ordered the dragon to take off. The other dragons followed. Malon was angry, and he would now unleash the full fury of Doomswing on the cavalry soldiers.

He swooped back around and pushed an order into the dragon's mind- dive. A formation of over twenty dragons now dove all at once. The cavalry were chasing after Malon's bandits when the attack from above came. They weren't expecting it at all, and the fog made the dragons invisible. They swooped down with the sharp talons and cut through the light armor of the cavalry troops. The dragons couldn't fly at full speed through the fog, and their accuracy was off, but they made up for it in brute force. Again and again they swooped down, each time taking out two or three soldiers. Doomswing was the most deadly of all, using white-hot dragonfire to scorch everything below him. Surprised and shaken, the cavalry ordered a retreat. Seeing this, Malon pressed his advantage. He now ordered the dragons to fly low, attacking the king's ground troops that were just coming out of the forest to attack. The troops saw the dragons coming and began to run, but it was too late. The dragons tore through the soldiers, their spears and shields flying.

Commander Veralus had planned this sneak attack, and risked his entire army being discovered at night to get there sooner. Now, he heard the terrible sound of talons clashing on steel and soldiers shrieking in agony, crashing into the ground and each other. Although he was still far from the fight, the sounds were so loud that he could hear it all clearly. He had fought in many battles, but never had he seen a dragon before, and he was just as shocked as all the other soldiers. Seeing Malon's destructive force, Veralus ordered his soldiers to retreat. But he still had one card to play; the ancient weapon he brought to use against the dragons. It was a contraption that was originally built a thousand years ago. He had it brought out of a museum, cleaned up and transported to the battle. Nobody knew what it was actually called, but the soldiers began to call it the Dragonspoon because of how it looked. The contraption now sat behind him, covered in a tarp. When the soldiers removed the tarp, the machine gleamed in the daylight. It was indeed shaped like a giant spoon, with a triangular base in the center. The entire machine was made out of bronze, and was very heavy and hard to move. The spoon end was now being loaded with what looked like sparkling rocks, each about the size of a ball. The rocks were jagged and the edges were sharp. On the opposite end, a huge, square-shaped block was being hoisted up with several chains. The chains were being pulled by four huge oxes. Veralus had similar, modern machines called catapults, which were used in breaking walls, but those had also not been used in a very long time. He had to ask the keepers of the library at Ravensthorn to consult ancient texts in order to understand how it worked. At the time, he was criticized for his decision to bring the machine. But he knew that this was the only weapon they had which had been built especially for fighting dragons. Now, as it was being prepared, Veralus wondered if his gamble would pay off. He had nothing to lose. It took quite some time to get the machine ready, but eventually Veralus was told that it was ready to fire. The dragons continued to terrorize the royal army, and as the soldiers were now retreating, they were coming closer and closer. When the dragons were so close that Veralus could see them swooping between his troops, he realized that he couldn't fire without risking the lives of more soldiers. On the other hand, nothing any of them was doing was slowing down the attack. It was then that Veralus saw Doomswing emerge from the fog, his black wings fully extended. The dragon was immense, and the entire army gasped. Doomswing then let off a burst of flame so hot, that the wind from it could be felt even where they stood, which was still very far away. The flames melted the earth and everything on it. Veralus knew then that they were facing an enemy much, much stronger than they were. At this rate, just that one dragon would wipe out his entire army. He had to make a terrible decision. He told his soldiers to target that huge dragon, raised his hand up, and in a powerful voice yelled: "FIRE!"

Malon was used to the sounds of air rushing by and the slams of soldiers against the dragon's talons by now. But then he heard a new sound; a loud whoosh coming from the back of the army. He swung his head around to see, and could make out a strange-looking contraption, which suddenly got much taller. Then he saw hundreds of shiny objects flying through the air at great speed. They were flying directly at him. They weren't arrows…what were they? He ordered Doomswing to stop the attack and fly high to avoid the objects. But by then, the objects were already on them. The shiny objects exploded into millions of sharp pieces of glass. The sound of the explosions was immense. Malon felt a searing hot pain enter his leg. The glass bounced off Doomswing, doing no damage, but the dragon sensed the immense pain from Malon and banked out of the way and high into the sky. Malon was in bad shape. He could barely see through his watering eyes. But he knew that if he passed out, Doomswing might just drop him off his back. He did all he could to stay focused on flying and keep the dragon in the air. He flew away from the battle, trying to find safety anywhere he could. He had no idea where the other dragons were or if they even survived. All he could think about was escape. After what felt like an eternity, Malon managed to get away and finally landed in a field surrounded by forest, far from the battle. He fell from the dragon and looked down on his leg. Shards of glass had destroyed it. He couldn't walk, but more importantly, if he couldn't get himself to a doctor to stitch the wounds closed, he would bleed to death. Doomswing just casually looked at the wounded human.

"My, what fragile creatures," he commented.

Malon pushed a thought to the dragon.

"I need a doctor, fly me to the nearest friendly town."

Doomswing thought about this for a moment, and then agreed to do so. They had already conquered several small towns along the way, so he was likely to find help in one of those. And so the dragon casually lifted off the ground, while his rider continued to slowly die.

Veralus watched as the huge black dragon banked hard after the attack. The dragon flew gracefully, but it clearly had some effect as it was no longer attacking. Seeing this, the other dragons began to fly around in confusion. Veralus ordered another shot at them, but by the time the machine re-loaded, the smaller dragons had also broken off their attack. The rest of the southern army now chased after Malon's remaining human soldiers, and either chased them all away or captured them. They had done it; they had defeated the Blood-Red Army.

In the aftermath of the battle, the royal army re-grouped together with the defenders inside Grapefine. Although the battle was a victory for the royal army, the vicious dragon attacks had claimed many lives. Soldiers were running around trying to find care for the wounded, while others helped to carry away those who had been killed. Veralus looked over the blood-stained field where it all had happened. He took no joy in this victory. All of the dragons had escaped, and he refused to believe that the big dragon was hurt by the attack. He didn't know how he had won, and that made him very uneasy. Still, he was thankful to be alive. If not for the Dragonspoon, they might all be dead now and Malon would have won. And what of Malon? Veralus never saw him during the battle, although he did wonder if Malon was riding that dragon. It all happened too fast, and the dragon was too far away to see if anyone was riding it. Veralus ordered that scouts ride out in all directions to look for the dragons. But when they returned, they reported no sign of Malon or the dragons. This made the commander uneasy, and he decided that he would personally lead a scouting team out to look for them as soon as the fog had cleared. It would not clear all day.

The next morning, Veralus was busy sending messages and dealing with a thousand other matters that needed his attention. It wasn't until noon that he put on his armor and mounted his horse. Just as he was about to ride out of the city gate together with a hundred of his cavalry soldiers, a messenger rode up at full speed and stopped in front of him.

"Commander," said the messenger, clearly out of breath. "A message from the king," he said, handing Veralus a rolled-up paper with a golden seal in the center.

Annoyed, Veralus snatched the paper out of his hands, broke the seal, and read it on the spot.

"What does it say?" asked one of his lieutenants.

Veralus turned to his officer and with a look of annoyance said, "we've been ordered to return to Ravensthorn."

The commander looked out past the gate at the distant forests. "The king wants to honor our victory with a feast," continued Veralus.

At that moment, Veralus felt the weight of this decision even more than the one he had to make the day before on the battlefield. This victory was not complete. He thought of disobeying the king's order and riding out to search for Malon and the dragons. But disobeying a king's order in front of his army would be bad.

He sighed, and said, "Prepare the troops. We ride for Ravensthorn."

When word of the victory reached Ravensthorn, the entire city rejoiced and the king declared the biggest feast ever to be held to honor the royal army. Now that his city was safe, he also gladly shared the rations with the thousands of refugees who had crowded outside of the city walls. Ravensthorn wasn't interested in helping them when the threat of war was still real. Or rather, the king hadn't welcomed them in. But that was all in the past now, and all was well again. The king even declared it a national holiday- the Defeat of Evil Malon Day. But the king, in all his arrogance, didn't have any proof that Malon was defeated. And so began the king's biggest feast - and biggest mistake.

## CHAPTER FIFTEEN: DAYBRINGER

They had gathered up all of Daybringer's rations from the cave.

"Together with what we brought from Frostfall, it should be enough to last us for two weeks," said Peacefinder.

"That should be more than enough time," said Bubbletail.

"But we are seriously overloaded now," Jadeclaw commented as she stuffed the last of the rations into her sack.

"Taking off with all of this gear won't be a problem since we have a cliff here to jump off from, but we have to be mindful of where we land."

"Did you say- jumping off this cliff?" asked Firesneezer. "We go from slaying ogres to exploring hidden hideouts to jumping off cliffs...all within twenty-four hours!"

"And don't forget the Icelava is next on our agenda," Lavender peeped up from reading one of Daybringers books. "How does ice exist next to lava anyway?"

"You'll rarely see the lava part," explained Peacefinder. "It's mostly just ice."

"Oh, that's reassuring then," Firesneeer retorted. "I was worried about getting roasted and frozen but now it's mostly just frozen."

They ate a breakfast of dried fish and fresh apples- the last of the apples they brought from Frostfall.

"I was wondering about something," said Lavender, while still chewing on her apple.

"If Daybringer can see the future, why was he caught off guard by the ogre? And why is he having trouble finding whatever he's looking for? Shouldn't he be able to just look into the future and know exactly what to do?"

"Yeah what's with him," added Firesneezer, quickly realizing it was totally unnecessary.

"It's the same reason I cannot see where Daybringer is now and take us straight there, or you cannot retrace his steps once he took off from this cliff," replied Peacefinder. "The gift of being a Seer is a wonderful gift, but it has its limits. Sometimes we can get a glimpse of far away places or times, but those come as dreams which are murky, confusing and easily forgotten." They were all sitting around Peacefinder as she spoke. "But it's even more so for the Future Seer," she continued. "Seeing into the future is like trying to see into a dark room. Sometimes you think you see things which are not there, and sometimes you cannot see things which are there. You see one possible future, but if things change in the present, that vision of the future also changes. At least that's how Daybringer explained it, a long time ago." Everyone was quiet now.

"We'll find him," said Lavender.

Peacefinder smiled at her. "Yes, together we will," she replied.

With breakfast finished and their Gliderwings unfurled, Jadeclaw, Peacefinder and Lavender decided to make the jump together. Bubbletail and Firesneezer were just holding on for dear life.

"On the count of three," said Lavender.

"One, two," Jadeclaw started running.

"Hey!" yelled Lavender, as she sprinted forward to try to catch up.

In her eagerness to catch Jadeclaw, she forgot her fear of jumping off this cliff, which was now directly in front of her. It was too late to turn back now. She glanced over at Jadeclaw, who had just plunged down. She jumped. She felt the panic of falling, and let out a yelp, but the feeling only lasted a few seconds as her Gliderwing caught the wind and lifted her into the air. What a feeling it was. Firesneezer was doing his usual laughing and crying routine, while she could hear Bubbletail whooping behind her. After they regrouped at a higher elevation, they turned north. With a brisk wind pushing them along and the Gliderwing stable, Lavender pulled out another book. She had become an expert at fly-reading by now. "The Tales of Blizzardtail, Great Explorer of the North" was the title. *Perfect*, she thought. She browsed through the book. Unlike the others, this one was full of not just text, but also illustrations. There were wonderfully sketched landscapes and animals, along with notations to explain. *It seems Blizzardtail was also an artist*, she thought. As she read, she learned that Blizzardtail was the first dragon to explore the wild territory north of Frostfall. He climbed Skytop peak- the tallest mountain in the known world, explored the darkest caves, and is responsible for most of the maps they had of the area, including the one Daybringer was using. The stories of his travels were fantastic. Avalanches, icefalls, cave-ins, encounters with bears and ogres and trolls and even a grumpkin. Lavender dived into the book and forgot completely about where she was.

*The Icelava fields are one of the most unique landscapes I have ever seen. The ice is fractured into patterns, as if some giant dropped a mirror on the world, and it shattered into a million pieces. In between the ice, you can see the rising slopes of volcanoes. Most of them are small and barely peek out from above the ice, but a few are large enough to be considered mountains. Some of these volcanoes spew a constant stream of slow-moving lava down their sides, which melts the ice in a cloud of steam. Others spew black soot and smoke into the air, making the entire place smell of sulfur. Still others lay dormant for years or decades, waiting for the right moment to erupt, sending lava high into the air which then comes down like meteors onto the ice, cracking it and melting it. The sight and sound of this kind of eruption is both beautiful and terrible at the same time. Few dragons have ever seen this place.*

Lavender read that last line again and felt very special. She would soon be one of the few. She continued reading.

*It was in the Icelava fields that I first encountered the creatures known as ash-claws. They are roughly the size of bears,*

184

*but without the fur and with thick, midnight-black skin. They have large claws, and are very dangerous. Ash-claws live in burrows around volcanoes, where the melting ice forms lakes and rivers. They use their long claws as spears to catch fish. Incredibly, they seem to be completely immune to fire, as I have seen one walk through a lava stream without being burned. I observed an ash-claw burrow for several days before one of them noticed me. The creature made a high-pitched shriek, and almost immediately, a hundred of them emerged from the earth and started chasing me. I was high up on a cliff but had to gather up my things and put on my Gliderwing. I got away just in time.*

Lavender gulped. *As if the landscape wasn't trying hard enough to kill you, now we also have ash-claws to deal with,* she thought to herself. She then noticed that the landscape below her changed from mountainous forests to endless plains with ice-covered lakes and rivers. The wind had picked up and started shaking her Gliderwing. She realized that the sun was much lower on the horizon. They had flown all day! Suddenly a gust of wind hammered into her side, pushing the Gliderwing sideways. Lavender wasn't a master flyer yet, but all of the hours she had spent flying had taught her to be calm and not overreact. She gently pulled on the control strings and gradually brought herself back to level. She had lost some altitude, and she could see Jadeclaw making her way down to her.

"It's getting rough and it'll be dark soon, there's a cliff up ahead we can land on," yelled Jadeclaw over the wind.

Lavender looked ahead. She could see a sharp cliff emerging from the ground below, angled towards the sky and with a perfectly smooth top edge. It looked like a shard of ice. Then she realized- it was ice! She'd never seen such a large piece of ice before. A few minutes later, they made their approach and landed without any trouble. The smooth ice made for a very easy landing. The air was cold and the lack of any trees or bushes meant they were totally exposed to the wind. Although dragon scales allowed dragons to put up with very hot and cold temperatures, she was already feeling the cold. Bubbletail and Firesneezer wasted no time setting up a canopy that would shield them from the wind. Jadeclaw started digging into the ice, creating a hole.

"What's that for?" asked Lavender.

"This is our fire pit. We'll have to sleep close to the fire tonight, as we will every night in these cold temperatures. The pit is there so that the flames don't leap out and light our tarp on fire."

"Or our tails," added Bubbletail.

Lighting a fire on a huge slab of ice was challenging. They tried using the torches which were designed to be easy to light, but the fire just went out a few moments later.

"Maybe the wood we have is wet," said Bubbletail.

"I think it's just the cold," said Peacefinder.

"I am feeling a bit cold," said Firesneezer.

"In fact, I think I'm going to….quick, Bubbletail, get the wood ready," he said as he moved his snout closer to the fire pit.

Lavender didn't know what was going on. Then he drew back his snout and let out a huge sneeze. It was the loudest, most powerful sneeze Lavender had ever heard. But it wasn't just a sneeze.

"Holy cow!" said Jadeclaw.

Firesneezer lived up to his name. In front of them, the fire pit roared to life and the warmth from the blaze instantly felt good.

"I can't believe you did that!" exclaimed Lavender. "You literally…"

"Sneezed fire? Yeah, it's in the name." said Firesneezer casually.

"This is an amazing ability," said Jadeclaw. "You could use this to become a formidable warrior!"

"You're like the legendary dragons of ancient times," said Peacefinder through a smile.

"See, now you all believe me and think I'm useful and cool. I only have to sneeze fire out of my nose to prove myself!" said Firesneezer.

They all laughed. As they ate their dinner, Lavender told them about the book she had read. Bubbetail's eyes grew wide when he heard the story of the ash-claws.

"Although Blizzardtail's maps and explorations are legendary and true, some of his more wild stories are considered to be too fantastic to be real," said Peacefinder. "Still," she continued, "there really haven't been many dragons out this way, and just because they didn't see ash-claws doesn't mean that Blizzardtail was making it up."

"I guess we'll see for ourselves," said Jadeclaw. "We'll have to be ready for anything."

"How much further?" asked Lavender.

Bubbletail looked at the map and said, "we flew far today, thanks to the wind. We're right on the edge of the Icelava fields. But our destination is further east- to a cavern known as the Icelava Temple."

Lavender was fascinated. She hadn't seen anything in the book about that.

"What's the Icelava Temple?" she asked, her curiosity peaking.

"I think it was discovered by one of the later explorers who came after Blizzardtail. It's a deep cave inside the ice. It's a natural ice formation but because the ice is lined up so perfectly, it's supposed to look like a huge temple," explained Bubbletail. "There are rumors that the ancient mage dragons of Frosthall escaped to that cave right after the destruction of their city. Although no dragon who explored it ever found any artifacts, the number of dragons who actually tried is very small. In fact, we don't even know if the cave still exists."

"Why would it not exist? Lavender asked.

"Because the Icelava fields are unstable," answered Peacefinder. "The ice is melted by the lava and re-frozen, making a landscape that is constantly shifting. The cave might have been crushed or melted away by now. We won't know until we see it for ourselves."

They eventually finished dinner and huddled by the fire to sleep. Lavender had a restless sleep. She was awoken by the howling wind a few times, and when she did sleep, her dream took her back to the moment she saw Daybringer in the boat. She felt uneasy about the vision all over again. The next morning was cold and the sky remained dark for much longer than it normally would. Lavender didn't feel like getting up, but she forced herself to. The fire was nearly gone and the others were packing up to leave. Everyone looked like they hadn't gotten much sleep. Lavender chewed on a fruit bar before slowly attaching herself to the Gliderwing again. Peacefinder noticed that everyone was in a down mood.

"Come on everyone, we're almost there. The cave will be warmer and we'll find Daybringer there. I just know it."

They all nodded and remembered how important their mission was. Lavender took a moment to peer into the past in case she might catch a glimpse of Daybringer again. She sorted through days and days of nothing but ice and wind and snow…until she saw something in the sky above the ice cliff. It was a pale shadow against a dark sky, but the shape was certain. It was a dragon, flying high above using a Gliderwing.

"He was here!" she shouted, coming back to reality.

"When?" said Peacefinder, excitement returning to her voice.

"Um, maybe a week ago. Not long at all!"

When she heard this, Peacefinder leapt into her Gliderwing. "Come on everyone, we're closing in on him!"

She didn't wait for a reply, instead threw Bubbletail onto her back, got a running start and lept from the tall edge of the ice cliff. The rest of them followed, energized by the news. The flight to Icelava Temple allowed Lavender to see the Icelava fields from above. They were exactly as Blizzardtail had described. Large, flat sheets of ice, broken and cracked in places, with volcanoes visible in the distance. They flew over one small volcano and

Lavender could see the ice melting and forming a river. Further east, she could see how a similar volcano had formed a small lake around itself, with the lava creating steam all around it. The wind had calmed down and although they were high up, she could catch the faint smell of sulfur. They flew like this for many hours with the landscape looking the same the entire time. Finally, they came to a large ice shelf that jutted straight up into the air. It was similar to the ice cliff they landed on, but much bigger and much longer. It was like an entire continent of ice had lifted itself up. Far in the distance, Lavender could see the peak of a huge volcano, covered in black smoke. She saw Peacefinder and Jadeclaw start to circle around. They had arrived. They landed at the bottom of the huge ice wall. Her talons slid as she touched down. Landing on ice was fun, but this ice was covered in a thin layer of black ash which went flying into the air as she landed. It made her cough. The others were also coughing, as landing threw up a cloud of ash.

"I'm not sure where exactly the entrance is," said Bubbletail, "but according to the map, it has to be somewhere along this ice wall."

They looked left and right. The ice wall stretched for what seemed like forever in each direction.

"We could be here awhile," said Jadeclaw.

"Maybe Daybringer could help," said Lavender.

She came close to the ice wall. It was towering over her and she could feel the coldness from the ice itself. She closed her eyes and looked into the past. She saw the same scenery day after day, but eventually she noticed a figure walking along the wall, far away from where she stood. She ran in that direction, but by the time she got there, the figure was gone. She looked to the wall and noticed a large crack in the ice. *This must be it*, she thought, as she returned to reality.

"It's not far from here," she told everyone, "and I saw Daybringer go in. We're on the right track."

"Good navigation," Jadeclaw said to Bubbletail. "We could have spent days looking for the entrance."

Bubbletail beamed with pride. "What can I say, I know maps!" he said in reply.

They gathered up their gear and made their way to the entrance. When they arrived, they could see a large gash in the ice wall which led to a cavern inside.

"This doesn't look like some grand temple," commented Firesneezer.

"Maybe it gets better when we go inside," Lavender remarked.

They cautiously made their way through the gash in the ice wall. The corridor that led them deeper into the ice was tall and narrow, with the light from outside still bright enough to see ahead. Eventually they came to a larger opening, where they had to light torches to be able to see. They were in a large, circular room with a very tall ceiling and a spiral staircase made out of ice.

"Woah," said Bubbltail. "This isn't a natural ice formation at all."

The spiral staircase was cut perfectly out of ice, but the ice was different from what the walls were made out of. It was smooth and not slippery. It didn't seem to melt when Lavender brought her torch close to it.

"That's because this isn't ice," said Peacefinder. "It's glass."

Lavender stood in awe. "What dragons could forge glass in this way, and why would they build such a wonder in a dark, frozen cave?"

Peacefinder looked up the staircase, which went up the shaft for a very long way. "I don't know, but we're going to find out," she said, as she began climbing the stairs.

The group made their way up the glass stairs. As they climbed higher, they saw that there was a light source far above them. It looked like a glass ceiling had been created to allow the light from outside to come in. Lavender still couldn't believe that this existed here. But what she was about to see next would be even more amazing. When they got to the top of the stairs, they found themselves in a large, dome-shaped room. The top was the glass ceiling, and inside was the entrance to what looked like a grand, ancient temple. The entire structure was made out of a white, pearl marble stone. The glass-topped dome allowed plenty of light in, which warmed the room. They strolled around, admiring the amazing sight in front of them. There were two statues on each side of the room. They weren't like anything they had seen before. They looked like narrow pillars with half-circle shaped glass mirrors at the top. There were large columns on both sides of the entrance, and the entrance itself was a grand, metal door made out of a silver-colored metal. Above the door, there was an inscription written in old text. It read: *In Darkness, We Seek the Light*.

"What could this mean?" asked Lavender.

Peacefinder pondered for a moment. Then, she tried to open the door. It wouldn't budge.

"I think this is a riddle of some kind. We need to solve it in order to get the door to open."

"Maybe Daybringer has been through here and I could see what he did," said Lavender.

Lavender took a moment to sit down and then started peering into the past again. She saw Daybringer in the room with her. He was examining the door and mumbling something to himself. Suddenly, he stopped and turned to face her. Lavender again felt the fear wash over her, but this time she stood her ground, knowing that this was all happening in her mind.

"I've seen you before," he said. Then he became frustrated. "You're close! Too close….you're here to steal it, you bandit! I need to find it! My visions of the future….they must not come true…I must find it! Leave me!" he roared the last sentence at Lavender and in her shock, she lost her concentration and returned to reality.

"Well? Did you see anything?" asked Peacefinder.

Lavender pried her eyes open and realized she had broken into a cold sweat. She saw Firesneezer bouncing up and down, bubbling with excitement, and it brought her back to the moment. The others now gathered around her, realizing that she had just experienced something powerful.

"He saw me again. Even though I know he isn't really seeing me, it's still very scary," she explained. "He thinks I'm a bandit," she said.

Peacefinder pondered on this. "What did he say exactly?" she asked.

Lavender thought for a moment, recalling his exact words. "He said he needed more time to find something....and that the visions he had of the future must not come true."

A look of shock and worry crossed Peacefinder's face.

"So he thinks we're bandits trying to steal the same treasure he is after?" asked Bubbletail.

"That would make sense," explained Peacefinder. "He has only seen Lavender, and he doesn't know her."

"But surely he can see the future now, and know that you are here as well?" pressed Bubbletail.

"Yes, that is odd," said Peacefinder. "Unless…" she trailed off, regretting that last thought.

"Unless what?" asked Firesneezer.

Peacefinder looked down. "Unless he doesn't know because we will never get to him alive," she concluded.

They all looked dismayed.

"Can you try again?" asked Firesneezer, looking at Lavender.

"He will just continue to block her visions," replied Peacefinder. "It's no use."

Lavender felt her heart sink. Had they come so far only to fail? Over the past few weeks, Lavender had felt the one thing she craved for so long: meaning. But now, it felt like the odds of success were next to zero, and her special ability was useless.

Peacefinder must have sensed her sadness because she took her talons and said.

"Tomorrow we shall figure it out, but right now we need rest. We cannot think with tired minds."

Lavender nodded and looked up through the glass dome. Peacefinder was right. The shadows were growing longer along the sides of the temple, washing the sky in a sunset orange.

*Tomorrow*, she thought, *tomorrow*.

As much as she tried, Lavender could not fall asleep. She was so caught up in her frenzy of thoughts that sleep couldn't set in. The sky was now an inky black with stars winking at her every now and then. She rolled onto her back and stared at where the moon took its place right above her. The silver moonlight illuminated her snout and seemed to comfort her. Lavender stared at the inscription which was the same dark shade as the sky. The entire room seemed a lot more ominous at night. Aside from Firesneezer's gentle snoring, it was absolutely silent. She looked around and noticed Jadeclaw standing watch. She was patrolling the entrance to the room with her eyes, spear in hand. Lavender couldn't bring herself to leave the puzzle unsolved, so she got up and reread the text. *In darkness, we seek light. What could that mean?* She pondered to herself. Lavender looked up at the sky again. *Maybe it means when there is darkness, like as in when it is night, we seek light, like the sun or stars.* She thought about the possibilities, but there were too many to count. Lavender wringed her claws in frustration. *What happens if I get this wrong? Will all of this be for nothing?* she thought. *Just calm down, Lavender. Calm down.* She peered out of the dome again, but nothing new came to mind, so she just crawled back to her sleeping place on the marble floor and flopped onto her belly.

Just as she was forcing herself back to sleep, something caught her eye. High up on the door were two small, midnight black gems embedded into the metal. She immediately jumped to her feet and bolted over to the door, fully awake now. Jadeclaw tracked her movement, immediately scanning for danger, but Lavender gestured to her that everything was fine. She touched the cold metal door and looked up at the black gems, which were much too high up to touch. They didn't seem to radiate any danger, but did look out of place. She realized that the gems were perfectly round, and resembled the sun when it is being eclipsed by the moon, but neither gem gave off the slightest bit of light. She noted that the gems were the same, perfectly round shape as the glass mirrors that stood on top of the tall pillars, but the material they were made from made them also look different in every way. *In the darkness, we seek light*, Lavender repeated. The words were now etched into her brain and she could recite them thoughtlessly. She spent the next hours repeating the words to herself over and over, allowing various ideas and possibilities emerge into her mind, then be crushed down again, only to re-emerge over and over. The black jewels were the darkness, the dome above brought the light. And then, there are the mirrors. Then everything became clearer; the mirrors can be used to reflect the light onto the black gems!

She was pleased with this idea, but there was still a question nagging at her. How to do this? It was one of Lavender's most hated questions. Moving the pillars was obvious, and they had tried to do this earlier that day. The pillars were fixed solid and were super heavy. They weren't budging. *Ideas are a dime a dozen*, she heard the voice of Miss Pepperwing say, *but what it's the doers that get things done.* Lavender disliked that quote, even though it rang truer than ever in her current situation. She lay down on her stomach with her snout propped up by her talons and thought. *Maybe if I somehow drain the light and transfer it to the gems. No, that's a little creepy. What if I'm completely off track. Maybe they can share the light somehow*, she suggested to herself. Her eyes narrowed and she clenched her talons tightly. She looked up and noticed that the morning light was returning to the cave, and soon the bright sunshine would come peering through. Lavender felt frustration build up inside her. Out of this frustration, she yelled out and smacked her tail against a pillar. It made a bone-chilling screech. Bubbletail jumped up and out of his slumber.

"What was that?" he yelped.

Peacefinder was also quickly awoken by the sound, while Jadeclaw, who was awake all this time, raised her spear in surprise. The only one who continued to snore was Firesneezer.

"I don't know," Lavender replied, still in a daze.

Jadeclaw was again searching for danger with her spear in hand, in case the loud noise woke up anything else that might be living in the cave. Peacefinder approached the pillar cautiously.

"I think the sound came from here," she said.

"But why would a pillar screech like that? Did we hurt its feelings?" Bubbletail asked.

Suddenly, Firesneezer sat bolt upright.

"Have you ever tried to rotate a wagon wheel that's really old?" he said. The others stared at him in total shock.

"What now?" Bubbletail said, but Firesneezer continued on.

"It squeaks and groans just like the pillar did."

Peacefinder caught onto his meaning. "I bet this pillar is really old, and whatever is inside it has worn down," Peacefinder commented.

"But we tried moving both of these pillars hours ago and they wouldn't budge," said Bubbletail.

"We tried moving them," said Lavender, a sly smile coming across her face. "But we never tried rotating them."

At that moment a lightbulb went off in Lavender's mind. The question that had been nagging at her this whole time was finally answered.

Lavender yelled, "I finally know the answer!"

"The answer to what?" they all said in unison.

"How to bring light to the darkness," she replied. "Just help me try to rotate  this pillar more," she said as she braced her talons against the pillar and started pushing.

A look of understanding crossed Peacefinders face and she exclaimed "Come on everyone, help her!"

They all rushed over to the pillar and began to push. The pillar creaked and crunched and ever so slowly began to rotate. The thin sheet of mirrored glass began to flicker. Just then, the morning sun lit up the room, and a beam of light began to move across the entrance. They were all amazed at the sight. Lavender's gaze followed the beam, transfixed by its bright glow. She tore her eyes away from the magnificent scene and focused on the two pillars in front of her.

"Push harder!" she exclaimed as the others pressed their talons on the cold marble.

A towering shadow below them inched across the floor and Lavender looked up to see the half of the obsidian gem being illuminated.

"We're doing it!" Bubbletail yelped with joy. "We're doing it! Wait, what are we doing?" he asked in confusion.

Lavender then realized that she was the only one who discovered the black gems. She now savoured a moment, completely believing in herself and that she was right about this. Not even Peacefinder figured it out.

"This," she said, a huge smile rushing across her face.

The final push aligned the mirror with the first black gem, and suddenly a bright glow began to emerge from the edges of the gem.

"Just like a solar eclipse," whispered Lavender.

She looked over at her friends. They are all staring at the gem in awe. Peacefinder then looked at Lavender, also smiling.

"You stayed up all night to figure this out, didn't you?" she asked. "I thought I said something about tired minds," she added.

"My mind was tired....tired of getting beat by this door!" exclaimed Lavender.

"Well, let's finish the job," said Jadeclaw, returning to the group after checking for danger.

Together with her help, they all dashed over to the twin pillar on the opposite side and pushed. This one rotated much more easily than the first, and pretty soon they had the second gem aligned and giving off the same glow. Then, a deep rumble shook the entire room, and the massive metal doors began to swing open.

"My goodness," exclaimed Peacefinder. "You did it my dear, all by yourself and even without your ability." Lavender beamed with pride. She was more than just a dragon with a gift.

None of them could imagine what they would find behind the door. That's why they proceeded inside with great caution. Jadeclaw led the way, a torch in one hand, her deadly spear in the other. Peacefinder followed, her bow at the ready. Then came Lavender and Bubbletail, and finally Firesneezer- ready to sneeze at any enemies they might encounter. Upon entering the room beyond the door, Jadeclaw quickly realized that her torch was not needed. The light that they shined on the black gems was being reflected by dozens of large glass mirrors hanging high above them. The room was large, with many towering pillars propping up the ceiling. Inside, they spotted a jumbled mess of broken wagons, shields, spears, and various wooden crates. It was all scattered around the large room. There was no sign of any living thing.

"Look there," said Bubbletail, pointing to one side as they walked down the center section of the room.

Two of the massive pillars had collapsed, leaving the ceiling to partially cave in. The rocks and dirt from the cave-in wasn't enough to block their path, but they had to climb over several large boulders to continue on.

"This place is old," Firesneezer stated.

"Hundreds…maybe even thousands of years old," added Peacefinder.

The walls were etched with elaborate carvings. They showed dragons with spears and shields, battling what seemed to be huge ogres and other beasts that seemed like they only belonged in fairy tales. The carvings were both beautiful and terrible. At the end of the room was another entrance, equally fancy and decorated with more carvings. Once again, they saw writing above the entrance. *Our past is your future, your future is our past.* While Peacefinder and Lavender took a moment to ponder on this statement, Firesneezer just kept walking forward. He jumped up onto what looked like a giant, metal bridge.

"No need for magic tricks or high-level puzzle-solving skills on this one team," he said. "Someone already did us a favor this time," he said, gesturing to the structure that he was standing on.

They quickly realized what he meant. He was standing on the metal door, which had fallen right off and was laying in front of them.

"Woah," said Bubbletail, taking in the sight.

"It must have been an earthquake," said Firesneezer.

"Lucky for us," he added, proceeding cheerfully.

"Or not," said Jadeclaw, taking a closer look at the fallen door.

"Look at these marks and dents," she said. "This metal looks as if it was struck by something very large, and then melted by the impact," she said, looking amazed.

Lavender felt a shiver run down her spine. "Could hot lava do something like that?" she asked.

"This steel door must weigh more than anything I've ever seen," said Jadeclaw. "For it to collapse like this and be blown away....that would require an explosion. "But the rest of the entrance is undamaged," noticed Peacefinder. "If a volcanic explosion ripped through this chamber, the entire room would have collapsed."

Jadeclaw gave Peacefinder a look of concern. "Whatever happened here, it wasn't natural," she concluded. "Could it have been magic?" asked Jadeclaw.

Peacfinder began to say, "well, magic is generally..."

"Um, excuse me", interrupted Bubbletail.

"I hate to break up this doomsday planning meeting but...Firesneezer is already through the gate."

They all looked up at once. "He's what?!" exclaimed Jadeclaw. "Silly little dragon is going to get us all killed!" she said, holding back her anger.

She then marched towards the entrance to the next room. The rest of the group followed her. But what they saw on the other side of the entrance wasn't a room at all; it was a long, wide shaft heading straight down. The first thing they noticed was the heat. While the previous rooms were chilly, this room was uncomfortably hot. There was a narrow, stone bridge that connected the two ends of the shaft. The entrance on the other end had completely collapsed, and the stone bridge was hanging precariously on three long chains suspended from the ceiling. In the center of the shaft was another spiral glass staircase, but this one was unlike the first. While it was also made of glass, it wasn't beautiful and perfect like the first. This glass was sagging and uneven, and the stairs themselves seemed to merge into one another.

"What happened here?" said Peacefinder.

"Oh, hi everyone," yelled Firesneezer, who had made it about halfway across the stone bridge before losing his composure and getting scared. "I'm glad you're all here. I was just checking the sturdiness of this bridge for you," he said, trying to keep the fear out of his voice. "And, um…it's not super sturdy."

He was hanging onto one of the chains that was supporting the bridge. The bridge rocked back and forth as he trembled, and the chains made a terrible creaking noise.

"Stay right there and don't move," said Jadeclaw.

"Sure, that's fine," replied Firesneezer with a squeaky voice. "Just hurry. I need to pee," he added.

Jadeclaw looked over the edge of the shaft. She picked up a rock and threw it down the shaft. They all listened for the thump. Jadeclaw was counting seconds in her head. Finally, after what seemed like way too long, the sound of the rock hitting the bottom came.

"What do you think?" asked Peacefinder.

"It's far," was Jadeclaw's only reply.

"We have no choice," replied Peacefinder.

"Then let me go first," said Jadeclaw. "But I'm not about to trust that glass staircase to get us down," she added. "That entire structure could come down at any moment."

Lavender looked over to the strangely damaged staircase again.

"Why is it like that?" Lavender asked.

"It's been melted," replied Peacefinder. "And now we know for sure," added Jadeclaw.

"What do we know for sure?" asked Bubbletail, who up until this moment had been cowering against the nearest wall.

"That whatever did this wasn't natural," replied Jadeclaw.

"Glass melts at an extremely high temperature," explained Peacefinder.

Jadeclaw was busy unraveling a long rope from her pack and creating a complex knot. When she was done, she threw both ends of the rope down the shaft, while the center of the rope was wrapped loosely around several rock pillars. She tied her pack to the rope, and lowered it down. The complex knot she had tied allowed the pack to move down the rope at a quick but safe speed. It took awhile for the rope to finally become loose in her talon, indicating that the pack had made it to the bottom. Then she tied her spear to the rope in a similar knot. She then looked up at all of them.

"When I'm down, I'll send the spear back up for each of you. Grab onto it, the same way I am doing now, and hold on no matter what. I'll then lower you down as slowly as possible."

Lavender then had a thought. "But, then you'll be without your spear," she said.

Jadeclaw looked at her, smiled and said, "Fortunately I've still got my talons, teeth, and my wicked sense of humor," she said with a smile. "I'll see you at the bottom," she added, as she gripped the spear in her hand and leaped from the edge.

She descended down the rope so quickly that she was out of their sight within seconds. Bubbletail's mouth gaped open.

"Are we…are we all doing that?" he asked, voice full of fear.

"And since we're talking about imminent death," came Firesneezer's voice from the bridge, "would someone mind coming to get me?"

In all the excitement, they forgot about the little dragon stuck on the bridge. Peacefinder took out another rope from her own pack and tied one end around a rocky pillar, and the other around herself. She then climbed out onto the stone bridge to fetch Firesneezer. The bridge swayed and the chains creaked, but she eventually made it to him and escorted him off the bridge.

"I wonder how Daybringer got down this shaft," wondered Lavender, as she helped Peacefinder untie the rope.

"Best not to even bother looking now," said Peacefinder.

"We're sitting very high up on a very narrow ledge. If anything you see scares you, you risk falling."

Lavender definitely didn't want to risk falling. "I guess you haven't seen Daybringer anywhere around here?" she asked Peacefinder.

"I haven't, but below us is nothing but darkness, so my ability isn't of much use," replied Peacefinder.

Just then, the spear emerged from the darkness below. Relieved, Peacefinder grabbed it and handed it to Lavender.

"You go next," she said.

Lavender took a big gulp, and grabbed the spear the way Jadeclaw had instructed.

"You'll have to leap off the edge, to make sure you don't hit yourself on the rock wall on the way down," instructed Peacefinder.

That was easier said than done. Leaping off of a cliff with a Gliderwing was scary, but there was some assurance that this machine, which was built for flying, would do what it was supposed to. Here, she was expected to leap into a hot, dark, super deep shaft with only a rope keeping her alive. Bubbletail and Firesneezer looked on, a look of dread on each of their faces. Even Peacefinder had a look that seemed to say "it'll be fine...probably." But what could she do- stay up here alone? That was an even scarier thought.

Without another moment to allow herself to hesitate, Lavender leaped off the ledge. The moment of utter fear as the feeling of falling hit her again, but much like when she took off with the Gliderwing, the moment passed. She was now zipping down the rope at an impressive, but not quite scary, speed. Moments later, the entire space around her became completely black. She could see nothing...not the rock wall, not the rope, not even her own talons gripping the spear. The only sound was the spear zipping against the rope, and her heartbeat, which felt like it was about to

206

jump out of her chest. The shock of being in total darkness went away eventually, and she calmed down. However, she now had a new problem. She was gripping the spear and hanging her entire weight on her arms, which were quickly becoming tired. As more time went by, her arms started screaming with muscle pain. She wanted to let go, to let her muscles relax even for just one moment, but she knew she couldn't. Then, to her great relief, the light at the end of the tunnel appeared. But the light was below her. It was the gentle red and yellow color of torchlight. She couldn't make out anything else below her, but after another moment she felt her speed decreasing, and another moment later, her tail hit the ground. She fell off the spear with a thump, and her burning muscles finally got relief. It was even hotter down here, and she was drenched in sweat.

"I'm glad you could join my little party," said Jadeclaw, who was already hauling the spear back up the shaft. At this moment, Lavender realized why she wasn't falling at full speed down the shaft. It was because Jadeclaw was taking on some of her weight with her rope pulley system. This meant that, not only did Jadeclaw need to get down the shaft herself as Lavender just did, she also had to haul the spear back up the shaft, and then take on some of the weight of the next dragon coming down … .over and over. Jadeclaw was also drenched in sweat, but her powerful muscles worked tirelessly. As Lavender lay on the ground in a wrecked heap, she was in awe at the strength of this incredible warrior dragon before her.

Eventually, it was Bubbletail and Firesneezer's turn.

"I can take the stairs. Really. This elevator is nice and all, but those stairs…they look totally sturdy to me," said Bubbletail, as Peacefinder secured his talons to the rope.

"You two are lighter than we are, so you can go down together," said Peacefinder. "But to make sure you don't end up falling on our friends down there, I'm tying you to the spear."

"Oh...thanks, I guess," said Firesneezer. "I wouldn't want my screaming death to interrupt their tea time down there," he added with a hint of sarcasm.

Although Firesneezer did scream for the first moments of his journey down the shaft, neither of them died. In fact, the method worked very well. Finally, Peacefinder made her way down, and as soon as her talons touched the ground, Jadeclaw collapsed. Lavender had been trying to help her, but the pulley system was really only suitable for one dragon to handle. Now, Lavender gave Jadeclaw more water, and let her lie down. Peacefinder came over to Jadeclaw.

"Once again, you've proven yourself a true dragon of the Kingsguard," she said. "Few could have done what you just did."

They spent some time resting at the bottom of the shaft, which had three corridors exiting in three different directions.

"I've already walked into each of those corridors," said Jadeclaw, still lying on the ground. "The one in the center is the largest, much larger than the other two. But it's also full of huge boulders and debris, and looks like it has collapsed further in. The one on the right is passable but ends with another shaft which goes even further down. And the one on the left leads to an iron door."

"Great," said Firesneezer. "Another shaft, another door, or a wall of rubble."

"I'll take 'wall of rubble', thanks," said Bubbletail.

"I guess we try the door first," said Peacfinder.

"I agree," said Jadeclaw. "If the shaft doesn't go anywhere, getting back up would be much harder than coming down," she added.

After they gathered their strength, they proceeded down the left corridor. Compared to the grand rooms they had gone through earlier, this corridor looked as if it had been built by someone else. It was narrow, with a low ceiling. The walls were jagged and rough, as if they had been carved out with primitive tools. There were no light or decorative carvings. They made their way through with the help of their torches. The heat inside this corridor was stifling, and they were all sweating and breathing hard.

"How far down do you think we are?" asked Bubbletail.

"Not that far, but we are probably close to a lava river," replied Peacefinder.

"That's good to know," said Firesneezer. "I was getting kind of bored with the bridge of swinging doom and shaft of endless horror. I can't wait for the jump across the lava river challenge," he said.

"I thought you'd be perfectly at home down here," said Jadeclaw. "After all- you are a legendary fire dragon," she said with a smirk.

Before Firesneezer could open his mouth, they reached the iron door that Jadeclaw told them about. Unlike the massive, imposing door they encountered before, this was a simple, rusty iron door that looked like it was ready to fall over. There was no lock, and it seemed like they could easily pull the door open and walk through. Firesneezer was about to pull on the handle when Jadeclaw stopped him.

"Wait," she said. "Everyone be quiet," she instructed.

She then looked carefully at the walls of the corridor. The stone here was no longer jagged and uneven; it was smooth and lumpy, and completely black.

"This stone has been melted," she whispered. Peacefinder took a closer look as well.

"You're right," she agreed.

"First the door puzzle, then the shaft, and as a final challenge we are hit with this flimsy door…it's too easy," said Jadeclaw.

"Do you think it's a trap?" whispered Bubbltail.

"That's exactly what I think," replied Jadeclaw.

"So what do we do now?" asked Lavender.

Peacefinder closed her eyes and used her ability to see what was waiting for them behind the door.

"I see nothing," said Peacefinder. "It's totally dark in there and nothing is moving."

"Wait, let me try," said Lavender. She closed her eyes and within moments, the flickering torchlight disappeared and she was in total darkness. Remaining calm, she peered back in time. Then, she saw another torchlight, and the familiar old wizard dragon appeared before her. But this time he didn't notice her. Instead, he silently opened the door and walked right in. *Huh*, she thought, *nothing to it*. Moments later though, she heard a terrible roar and a scream. She then saw the door flung open by a wall of white-hot flame. She startled herself back to reality. Panting, she told the others what she just saw. Peacefinder looked worried.

"You heard a scream ... .I hope he's not..." she trailed off.

"More importantly, you heard the roar and saw the flame. This explains everything. We must face this creature if we want to know what happened to Daybringer," said Jadeclaw, her spear at the ready.

"But we can't even see in there, it's completely dark," said Lavender.

"We can throw our torches in different directions after we enter, and then prepare for a fight," said Peacefinder.

"A fight...a fight with what?" asked Bubbletail. "It seems to me that we are facing a creature that can melt glass by simply breathing on it."

But Peacefinder wasn't listening. She was already committed to the task at hand. She drew her bow, lit an arrow on fire, grabbed the door handle and...

"STOP," a unfamiliar voice came from behind them. They all turned to look. There, in the dim torchlight, stood the entire reason for their mission. It was Daybringer.

## CHAPTER SIXTEEN: MALON'S REVENGE

Malon awoke. Everything felt strange, as if he was walking through a dream. It was dark, but he could see he was inside a room, and lying on a bed. His body felt heavy and he could barely move. When he tried to stand up, he fell back down with a thump. *Wait a moment*, he thought to himself. *My leg was destroyed*, he remembered. He looked down, and was horrified by what he saw. The bottom half of his leg was gone. All he had was a bandaged-up stump. He couldn't believe it. He had lost his leg. A medic came in and told him what had happened and how they fought to save his life. The words just washed over Malon, as if he was in a dream; or a nightmare.

He spent the next few weeks dealing with pain and trying to learn how to walk with crutches. The medics in the village clinic were trying to be helpful, but he knew they were all just afraid of him. And they had every reason to be. Malon was now angrier at the world than ever before. He wanted to punish the people that did this to him. He wanted revenge. And he would begin where it all happened- at the city of Grapefine.

Grapefine was shaken by the sudden appearance of dragons and an army of criminals. But once the danger had passed, life began returning to normal. There were additional soldiers around to help with rebuilding some of the parts of the city that were damaged, but other than that, the people who lived there were back to living their lives. But that would all change on a dark, moonless night several weeks after the battle. Malon had chosen this night to take his revenge on the city. As the townspeople slept, a shadow flew overhead. Then, several houses in the city center began to burn furiously. Moments later, the fire had spread to the market, and then to the wineries. The people ran out of their homes, stunned by the heat of the fires and how quickly they spread. Firefighters tried to stop them, but they were overwhelmed. The fires were so hot that they even melted the stone walls. Between the smoke and flames, some people thought they saw the shadow of a massive dragon swooping down. As the people tried to flee the city, they realized the metal gates had been melted shut and wouldn't budge. The fires burned all night. Few survived.

The next morning, a messenger from Ravensthorn was making his way to Grapefine to make his usual deliveries. As he approached the city, he was shocked to see huge, black pillars of smoke. He rode faster, and when he approached the city, he saw the horrible sight. Grapevine had been completely burned to the ground. All that was left was the melted stone walls and towers, and a handful of half-burned stone buildings inside. The messenger gasped, and quickly turned around to flee. But as he did, a shadow passed over him. Malon knew this messenger would come, and he was waiting for him. A moment later, the messenger was thrown from his horse as a huge dragon landed right in front of him. The messenger, like most humans, had never seen a dragon before, and the sight made him turn pale and scream in terror. Then, something even more amazing happened; a small, crippled boy sitting on the dragon's back began to speak to him.

"You are a messenger from the capital, are you not?" said the boy in a deep, raspy voice.

The messenger was so shocked that he couldn't make himself stop shaking. The dragon stared at him with gleaming red eyes, waiting for his answer. The messenger finally replied, "Y-y-y-yes."

"Then I have a message for you to deliver to the king," said the boy. "Tell him that the Blood-Red Army has not been defeated, and we will destroy every human city and town including the capital unless he gives up his kingdom to me."

The messenger, still trembling, managed to ask one question.

"Who are you?"

Malon made a wicked smile, "I am Malon, and this is my revenge."

Far away from the ruins of Grapefine, King Steadfast the 25th was having the formal celebration for the royal army, which had arrived in the capital about a week ago. He held a parade and brought in fancy food from every corner of the kingdom for the feast. Commander Veralus was sitting at the king's table, dressed in fine robes that the king had given all of his commanders. He was clearly uncomfortable. Earlier that week, he had spoken to the king and tried to explain how the threat from the dragons wasn't over. Veralus requested that the king triple his guard, build more Dragonspoons, and prepare the entire kingdom for more attacks. But the king was too busy enjoying his victory and his celebrations. As his top commander, Veralus had a lot of power within the king's army and the soldiers respected him. But in the end, the king made all of the important decisions.

Veralus didn't like the king. He thought that he was too soft, too weak, and too spoiled to rule the kingdom the way it should be ruled. In fact, Veralus himself had dreams of being king, and conquering the lands far to the west, where he heard rumors of a dragon kingdom full of riches. But Veralus knew that, as long as the council supported the king, he would remain in power. And so he sat in his fancy chair, dressed in his fancy robe, eating the king's fancy food, while secretly hoping for the king to fail. Little did he know, the moment he had been waiting for was about to arrive. While the king was enjoying a show and eating more food, the messenger from Grapefine barged into the courtyard. He looked miserable, and it was clear he had been through an ordeal.

"Your Highness," he screamed, "I have news- terrible news!" he continued.

The music cut off suddenly. The king was annoyed that his feast was being interrupted.

"Surely this can wait until after the show," said the king.

But Veralus saw the look of fear in the messenger's face and said, "tell us."

The king was once again annoyed that his show would not continue immediately, but he nodded in agreement, if only to get rid of this pesky messenger. The messenger stopped for a moment to catch his breath.

"I've come from Grapefine," he said. "Or what's left of it."

The room now became completely silent. Even the king put down his fish pie to listen.

"The city…the city has been destroyed!" said the messenger.

Some people gasped when hearing this. The king, however, chuckled and said, "what do you mean it's been destroyed? Our army was there just a few weeks ago. Malon and his band of misfits only did minor damage to the city before they were beaten. I think that a few knocked-over chicken coops doesn't count as destruction," he continued.

A few people laughed at this, and the mood in the room became calm again. But the messenger had more to say.

"No, Your Majesty, what I saw with my own eyes was the total destruction of the city. It must have happened right before I arrived because some of the fires were still burning. The entire city has been burned to the ground. Only ashes remain!"

The guests in the room once again began to gasp in fear as they heard this. The king also became uncomfortable.

"But there's more," continued the messenger. "I've come here with a message for the king. The message is from a boy. He was riding a terrible dragon that met me outside of the ruined city. He said that the Blood-Red Army wasn't defeated, and that if you didn't surrender your kingdom to him, he would come and destroy every human city and town, including the capital!"

More gasps, and now everyone turned to the king to see what he would say in response. The king took a moment to compose himself, then let out a weak laugh.

"Surely you must have dreamt all of this," he said to the messenger. "What was this boy's name?"

"Malon!" said the messenger.

Some of his guests were now openly wailing in fear, while others sat without moving at all.

"Calm down everyone," said the king, although he felt the opposite of calm himself. "I'll send my messenger raven to Grapefine tomorrow morning, and ask that the mayor of the city report back to me. Now, everyone, let's get back to the feast."

Shocked at the king's answer, the messenger lost his nerve and yelled, "you don't get it- there is no mayor! There is no city! It's all ashes!"

Everyone was shaken by what the messenger had to say and started leaving the party. Veralus saw this coming. He always thought that their first battle against the dragons could have been just the beginning, and that the real threat was still waiting for them. He made his way out of the king's banquet hall and went to speak to his troops. He told them what had happened, and got them ready to move.

The next day, the king called on his council to come together and decide what to do. All of his council members showed up, except Veralus.

"Where is he?" asked the king, to no one in particular.

"Your Majesty, commander Veralus asked me to bring you this message," said a voice from the back of the room. It was a messenger from the army.

"Well, what is it?" asked the king impatiently.

The messenger became uncomfortable. "The commander says…..that this meeting is a waste of time and he is busy preparing the army to defend the city."

The king was angry and annoyed. How dare one of his commanders disobey his order to come to council? But King Steadfast the Twenty-Fifth didn't have the respect of his army, and so there wasn't much he could do about the commander. In the meantime, Veralus was giving orders all over the city: reinforcing the walls, digging trenches, creating more shelters inside the solid stone of the mountainside, and building more weapons to defend against the dragons. But while he did all of this, Veralus knew deep down that they had no chance to defend the city against the dragons. So in order to survive himself, he created a secret plan: he would join Malon and help him take down the capital, and bring as much of the king's army as he could with him.

## CHAPTER SEVENTEEN: THE ORB OF

## UNDERSTANDING

The sudden sound of Daybringer's voice made Peacefinder raise her flaming arrow, ready to shoot. Seeing the stunned look on their faces, and the arrow pointing at him, Daybringer now spoke quietly.

"You went the wrong way, now put that arrow away and follow me before we all get killed," he said, gesturing urgently for them to come back down the corridor.

Without another word, they all followed him back the way they came. Just then, they heard a thumping sound from behind the door. Thump. Thump. Thump. The sound became louder and the entire corridor began to shake.

"Quickly now," said Daybringer, as he began to trot down the corridor.

The thumping stopped, and the sound of crashing rock came next. It was very loud and made them all break into a run. They reached the shaft that they had come down before, and now Daybringer brought them to the center corridor.

"This is the right way, if there can be a right way," he said.

Peacefinder had so much to say, so many questions.

"I know," he simply said, with a knowing glance. "But our catch-up chat will have to wait," he continued. "For now, we have a monster to deal with."

He led them over huge boulders and caved-in sections, and just when it seemed there was no way to continue, he showed them a section that was just big enough to squeeze through. Lavender looked distrustingly at the old dragon. He had intimidated her many times before in her visions, and now here he was. She wasn't sure what to think of that, but for now she was pushed on by the threat that they had to face. Daybringer now spoke in a slightly louder, but still hushed voice.

"I've been down here observing this creature for days...maybe weeks. At first I thought it was just some unknown species, some beast that no dragon has ever seen before," he said. "But now I know, it's worse than that," he continued. "This creature doesn't eat or sleep, it doesn't get tired or ever leave its lair. It's powered by magic; a terrible, ancient magic. And it has one purpose- to guard the object that I have been searching for. The object that I need to save the world from a terrible future."

They all looked astonished and scared. All except Jadeclaw.

"So how do we beat it?" she asked, unphased.

Daybringer looked at her, having noticed her spear and shield.

"You brought a Kingsguard," he commented. "Your bravery is well respected, but your spear cannot pierce this monster," he replied. "This creature was formed with magic, and it's only with magic that it can be defeated. Somewhere in that room is an orb. That orb is what gives the creature it's strength. It's what has kept it alive all of these centuries. The creature is a distraction. We must destroy the orb."

"That, we can accomplish," said Peacefinder.

"Yes," said Daybringer. "But we need a plan to distract the creature while we find and destroy the orb," he continued.

"Wait," said Lavender, finally getting the courage to speak up. "If you're the Future-Seer, can't you just tell us how this will happen so that we win, and then we just follow your instructions?"

A nervous smile crossed Daybringer's face. "There are many versions of the future," he replied. "In some versions, we succeed. In others, we fail. And in some versions, some of us don't make it out of here alive," he replied. "But I do have a plan," he concluded.

Lavender wasn't feeling very confident with this answer. She thought the great Future Seer would be able to actually see the future. Bubbletail and Firesneezer huddled close to her.

"So…if the version of the future that we don't want to happen…let's call it version B for Bad…if that does happen, how will we get out of here?" asked Bubbletail.

Lavender looked at him and sighed.

"Something tells me there is no version B in which anyone walks out of here alive," she replied.

"Thanks, very comforting. Good talk," said Firesneezer.

Some time later, Peacfinder came over to them.

"We're ready," she said. "And all of you have a role to play in this plan," she continued.

They all looked at her with wide eyes.

"I'm the bait aren't I," said Firesneezer. "Always the little dragon with the funny sneeze that ends up being the bait," he continued.

"You're not the bait," said Peacefinder. "But you are the main distraction."

"Oh, that sounds so much better than bait," replied Firesneezer. They then joined with the others while Daybringer explained the plan.

"Firesneezer, you're about to become as fearsome as your ancestors," said Daybringer.

He then explained the plan. It took some time, but eventually they were ready to move on the monster. They crept deeper into the ruined corridor that opened up into a huge room. It was dark and silent inside. The Jadeclaw and Firesneezer crept along one of the walls, as silently as possible. Firesneezer held a feather in his hand. Jadeclaw carried a flare and a glass mirror that Daybringer gave her. On the opposite side of the entrance, Daybringer and Peacefinder made their way along the wall as well. Bubbletail was with Lavender at the entrance. Lavender had several torches ready to light. The monster hunt was about to begin.

When they were far enough away, Bubbletail began to pound his tail against the floor. Thump. Thump. Thump. The reaction came quickly, as the monster could be heard roaring and moving towards the sound, but they still couldn't see it in the darkness. At that moment, a huge shadow appeared on the far wall, along with a roar. The monster turned to look, and saw a wall of flame come from the unknown creature's mouth. In fact, it was Firesneezer who used a feather to tickle his nose and make himself sneeze. When he did, Jadeclaw used the flare and the glass mirror to create an oversized shadow of Firesneezer onto the wall. In this way, the monster would think that a large, fire-breathing dragon had suddenly appeared in its cave. Confused, the monster began to run at this new threat, its huge claws pounding on the ground. But the thumping sounds continued from the opposite side and now the monster saw flames flying in all directions. This was Lavender, lighting and throwing the torches all over the cave. The entire room was lit up by the flames, and the monster was momentarily blinded by the brightness. At this moment, Lavender was able to finally see the monster. It looked like a dragon, but very large and with dull, black scales. It had blood red eyes and spikes sticking out of its back where its wings were supposed to be. Some of the spikes were broken, others stuck out in awkward directions. It's tail was very long but the last half of it looked like it was made out of stone. It had very large talons that seemed to gleam in the torchlight. The scariest part about it was its mouth. When it opened, two white-hot flames could be seen burning inside. Lavender shivered in fear, while Bubbletail stopped thumping and started running to the exit. Just as the monster was recovering from the shock of the sudden torchlight all around, it felt an explosion shake the room, and rocks began to tumble down onto its head. This was Peacefinder, who had fired one of her explosive arrows at the roof of the cave, right above where the

223

creature was standing. Covered in an avalanche of rocks, the creature felt a moment of doubt. After all of these years, could it be beaten? But then it pulled more power from the magic orb, and began to smash through the rubble.

In the moment when the creature needed more strength to get itself free, the orb that gave it power began to glow. Daybringer saw it first. "There!" he yelled, pointing to a sphere perched on top of a pillar near the very back of the room. Peacefinder loaded another explosive arrow, but the target was too far away. She began to run towards it. By now, the creature had freed itself and was very, very angry. It began shooting white-hot flames at the wall and entrance, sending a wall of heat across the entire room. Fortunately, they had all moved to a new spot by then, and the monster's flames hit nothing but rock. It looked around the room, searching for a new target. Then it saw Peacefinder. She was running towards the orb. The creature moved incredibly fast, and soon would be upon her. Then a booming sound and a powerful burst of wind pushed the creature against a nearby pillar, sending it crashing down. This was Daybringer, who used some kind of strange potion to create that wall of wind. But that little trick only threw the creature off for a second. Now it lined up a lance of flame that would stop the intruders. Then it felt something against its rear leg, like a bee sting. It momentarily lost concentration and looked down to see a dragon covered in shiny metal armor, holding a spear and a shield, poking at him. It had been ages since the monster had seen such a thing, but it didn't matter. This threat was insignificant. A quick swipe with his massive talon and this one would be dealt with. But as he swung at the dragon, he missed. This dragon was surprisingly nimble. He tried again, this time bringing his tail around from behind, swiping at the dragon. She anticipated the attack and jumped over the tail. Annoyed and thrown off his concentration, he simply ignored her and returned to the task at hand. He breathed in and prepared to release the flames. But just as he lined up his snout with Peacefinder, he heard an explosion. And then, with complete surprise and disbelief, he collapsed to the ground. The last thing he saw was an armored dragon standing over him, holding a spear, laughing.

In the dim torchlight, Peacefinder wasn't sure if her arrow had hit its target. The glowing orb was still quite far away, and she was being hunted by a giant, angry creature when she fired. The explosion she saw seconds later may not have been enough. But then, she heard the creature collapse, and a Jadeclaw's bellowing laughter, followed by Firesneezer's yelp of victory.

"We did it!," yelled Firesneezer. "That's two for two monsters defeated, for those of you at home keeping score!"

The cavern was now filled with the sounds of celebration. Firesneezer and Jadeclaw joined up with Lavender and Bubbletail and they all jumped up and down and hugged each other. They then came over to Daybringer and Peacefinder, who were on the far side of the cavern. They all celebrated once again. Daybringer sat down on the stone ground, sweating and shaking. Peacefinder noticed this. He was very different from the dragon she remembered. That cool, confident dragon that always knew what to do was now looking very uncertain of the future. When they settled down, Bubbletail turned to Daybringer.

"So, did your vision of the future show how we would completely out-wit that beast?"

Daybringer smiled slightly. "Yes well, the outcome is never certain, but you and the others have proven extraordinarily brave," he replied.

Peacefinder was surprised by his answer.

"Why is the outcome never certain for a Future Seer?" she asked Daybringer.

He was flustered by the question, and tried to dodge it. "At any rate, the hard part is done, but I still have to locate the orb I came here for, and I'll need all of you to help," he continued.

"Wait a minute," said Lavender. "You've been trying to stop us from following you at every step," she said, with anger in her narrowing eyes. "You scared me out of my visions, when all we were doing was trying to save you. But now you want us to help you? Why?"

The rest of the group grew silent, all of them agreeing with Lavender and awaiting an answer. Daybringer smiled the nervous smile again.

"You're right, I did try to throw you off of my path, and I did try to scare you. For that, I am sorry," he said. "I wasn't sure who you were," he continued, but then you came down to this cavern and I finally saw Peacefinder, and I knew you weren't bandits or thieves, so that's when I realized you were here to help," he concluded.

And he immediately saw that he had said too much.

"You mean, you only saw me in your future when that future was moments away?" asked Peacefinder, still in disbelief that this was the same dragon she knew so many years ago.

Daybringer once again shifted uneasily.

"Yes well, I knew you would find me, sure, but I just didn't know when, or who you'd be with…." he said, but Peacefinder interrupted him.

"You used to be able to predict which side a coin would land on with perfect accuracy. You used to be able to tell if it would rain the next day, even tell at which hour the rain would begin, and you were never wrong. You could see in great detail what the king would be serving for dinner at a feast scheduled three months in advance…and you were always right. But now, you could not even see that I, your old friend and student, would find you here in this cave…how can that be?" she asked.

Daybringer now looked like a child who had just been caught in a lie. He sighed deeply, and said,

"I'm not the dragon I was all of those years ago. Even before I left Sagestone, my Seer ability was fading. I can still catch a glimpse of something here or there, some random moment in an unknown time, but as far as a Future Seer goes…I cannot call myself that anymore."

Everyone sat in stunned silence.

Then Firesneezer said, "So, that whole plan you made, the plan to kill that monster, the plan where I was the bait and you said it'll be fine because you can see the future...was all of that…"

"Made up?" finished Daybringer. "For the most part, yes," he said.

Firesneezer's jaw dropped.

"I need a moment to consider my life choices," said Bubbletail.

"I think we all need a moment," said Jadeclaw, sensing the disappointment and outrage in the room. "I suggest we get back to the surface and leave this cave behind," she continued.

"No!" yelled Daybringer. "We have to find the orb- the Orb of Understanding," he continued. "It's here, I know it! It's the only thing that can stop the great calamity that's coming," he said. But after revealing that his ability to see into the future wasn't there anymore, his words had little meaning to them.

"We risked our lives to find you," said Jadeclaw, "now you're found and we're leaving," she concluded.

But Peacefinder hesitated. Even if Daybringer wasn't the dragon of the past, and even if he had deceived them into thinking he was, he was also still her friend and someone who helped her become who she is today.

"Wait," she said to Jadeclaw. "We're down here already, we can look around a little while for this orb," she said.

Jadeclaw frowned. "Fine," she finally said.

"What does it look like?" asked Bubbletail.

They each held a torch and looked around the large cavern.

"The treasure that monster was guarding must be through here," said Daybringer, pointing at another entrance at the far end of the cavern.

This entrance was carved into the cavern walls, and it looked like someone had simply blasted a hole through the wall into another chamber behind it. The wall was thick, and Lavender wondered at what kind of magic it would take to blast a hole in such thick stone. The torchlight threw shadows on the wall, and made the cave look scary. Lavender wondered if there could be another monster hiding inside. What they found inside wasn't another monster, but something just as unbelievable. The room they stepped into wasn't as large as the creature's cavern, but it was still quite spacious. There were no pillars or structures inside, just a large, round, open room. What made it unbelievable was all of the gold, jewels, diamonds, and other treasures just laying around all over the room. Everyone was stunned into silence at the sight. Everyone- except Firesneezer.

"Jumping bananas, this must be the biggest treasure in the entire world!" he screamed, and ran into the center of the room where a huge pile of gold coins awaited.

He tried to climb to the top, but kept sliding down and sending gold coins flying all over the floor. It didn't matter- there were so many that they could never even count them all. Bubbletail joined Firesneezer, lifting up as much gold as he could hold and throwing it in the air over his head.

"I always imagined this would be fun," he said, "but I never thought about how throwing gold into the air meant that it would just come back down and bonk you on the head later," he said, laughing.

Lavender also laughed, and joined in on the fun. This room had torches placed all around, and Peacefinder circled the room and lit them all. The treasure looked even bigger and more grand when the room was all lit up. Even Jadeclaw had to drop her stoic look and admired the shiny jewels with amazement.

229

"Quick, someone, find some sacks," yelled Bubbletail.

"Yeah, big ones!" added Firesneezer.

While Lavender and the other two small dragons went to find some sacks, Peacefinder and Daybringer searched for the orb.

"I'm not sure what it'll look like," said Daybringer. "The dragons who escaped Frosthall's doom brought this treasure here, along with several orbs of power," he added.

Towards the back of the room and along the wall, they found a bronze pillar with fancy decorations. On top of the pillar was a beautiful green and blue orb, placed on a pillow. The orb looked flawless, without a single scratch on it. Peacefinder's eyes lit up.

"There it is," she said. But Daybringer didn't look excited.

"Yes," he said, "just that easy."

"Easy?" questioned Peacefinder. "You call all of what we went through to get here *easy*?"

"No, no, but after all of that, why would they make the last step so obvious?" he asked.

Peacefinder gave it some thought.

"Maybe they were sick of puzzles, traps, and monsters by the time they got here," she said, though she knew it wasn't a good reason.

Daybringer took the orb into his hands and closed his eyes. Nothing happened.

"How will you know if the orb is the one you're looking for?" asked Peacefinder.

"I'll know, because I'll be able to speak to the king," said Daybringer.

"What?" asked Peacefinder.

"The Orb of Understanding allows the user to communicate with anyone, anywhere, and immediately" said Daybringer. "It would be as if the king was right here in the room with me, but in fact he is thousands of leagues away," explained Daybringer.

Peacefinder was amazed. "But how could the king hear you?," she asked.

"He wouldn't hear me; my voice would come into his mind," he explained.

At that moment, Lavender, Bubbletail and Firesneezer dragged three large sacks into the room.

"Where did you get those?" asked Jadeclaw.

"These are our sleeping bags," replied Bubbletail, as he began to shovel heaps of gold coins into his sack.

"But, we still have a long journey ahead," said Peacefinder.

"Where will you sleep?" asked Jadeclaw.

"In your sacks," said Firesneezer, as if that detail had already been agreed to a long time ago.

Peacefinder and Jadeclaw just shook their heads. As Daybringer continued to search for the orb, Peacefinder found some scrolls in a chest. She unraveled one and tried to read it. It was written in an ancient text, most of which she didn't understand. Since the scrolls were small and light, she figured she could take them back to Sagestone and ask the scholars to translate them.

"Look here," she heard Daybringer say from a far corner of the room.

He was standing next to what looked like broken and unused wooden furniture. There was no torchlight in this corner of the room, and it looked like the builders used it as a dumping area for unwanted items. Daybringer had been searching through the rubbish, and had found a dark, dust-covered orb. The orb was the same size as the one they found earlier. It was green and gold, but it didn't shine at all and there appeared to be cracks all over it. It looked more like a ball of shattered glass than a magical orb.

"It looks like this one was broken, so they threw it away," said Peacefinder.

"Maybe," said Daybringer, "or maybe this is how they hide it," he said.

"By making it look like junk?" questioned Peacefinder.

"Let's find out," replied Daybringer.

He carefully lifted the orb and held it between his talons. Suddenly, the orb began to shine in many different colors. Greens, reds, blues, purples…every shade blinking in and out. Everyone stopped what they were doing and looked over. Daybringer was in a trance. He felt like he had jumped out of his body and was being transported high into the air. Then, he focused his thoughts on a specific place and a specific dragon. Moments later, he was face to face with the dragon King Everwise, though the king could not see him. Then, Daybringer pushed a thought into the king's mind.

"Your Majesty, this is Daybringer. It's been many years, but I have finally found what I was looking for. With this new power, we will do everything we can to save our world from the great calamity."

Far away, a look of total astonishment on the king's face. The king tried to speak, but Daybringer couldn't hear his words and then the connection faded. Daybringer opened his eyes.

"This is it," he said. "This is what I've been searching for all of these years," he said quietly, with a smile of relief on his face.

They spent another hour in the treasure room. Daybringer sent another message to the king, informing him of where they were and that they would depart the Icelava fields as quickly as possible. Bubbletail and Firesneezer realized that their sleeping bags full of treasure became too heavy to carry, so with great sadness, they emptied out about half of their treasure.

"I guess we'll only be half the richest dragons in the kingdom now," said Bubbletail.

Lavender didn't take much, but she did fill her carry bag with precious gems.

"I want to donate these to the orphanage at Talonwing," she said. "They are always short on supplies," she added. "And those lunches…don't get me started on those lunches." Peacefinder smiled at this.

"With this donation, they will never be short on anything again, and can eat like kings," she told Lavender.

On their way out of the treasure room, Jadeclaw saw a beautiful silver necklace with several green jade stones. She couldn't help but take it for herself.

*Jade, like me. I did help slay a monster after all*, she said to herself. They put out the torches and the remaining treasure was once again shrouded in darkness.

"Should we tell people where it is?" asked Bubbletail.

"We'll notify the history department at Sagestone University about it," said Peacefinder.

"Not if the Firesneezer tribe gets to it first," mumbled Firesneezer under his snout.

Suddenly, they heard a rumbling sound and the earth began to shake.

"Earthquake!" screamed Daybringer, "we need to move!"

They all began to run. The tremor continued, and rocks began to fall into the corridor. Just as they arrived at the shaft leading up, a massive rock broke away from the wall and fell towards them.

"Get down everyone!" screamed Peacefinder over the sound of rumbling and falling rock.

They all jumped out of the way as the huge rock came crashing down. It made a terrible noise, and dust filled the air. Then the tremor stopped. They were all coughing and wheezing, and trying to see through the dust. Once it settled, they could see the damage done.

"Oh no," said Lavender, seeing the mass of broken rocks ahead of them.

Jadeclaw tried to climb over and throw the rocks out of the way, but it was no use. The amount of rock debris now blocking the shaft was too much to move.

"It's no use," she said. "We're not going out that way," she said with a sigh.

"You mean we're trapped down here?" said Bubbletail with a panic in his voice.

"We're all going to DIE!" added Firesneezer, his panic growing.

It was in moments like this that Lavender found herself surprised by her own calm. She knew the situation looked very bad, but she didn't feel panicked or scared. She just felt that she needed to do everything she could to help.

"There's another shaft we haven't explored yet," said Jadeclaw.

"Yeah but that goes straight down, and we're trying to go up," said Bubbletail.

"Sometimes, you need to go down before you can go up," said Daybringer.

"Oh thanks, wise one," said Firesneezer. "Can't even see the future…" he mumbled under his breath.

They walked to the edge of the dark shaft and peered down. Jadeclaw once again took a rock and threw it down. To her surprise, it didn't fall very far before a splash could be heard.

"There's definitely water down there," she said. "If the shaft is flooded, we won't be able to use it," she added.

One of the torches went out. Daybringer managed to re-light it with a spark from his staff. Bubbletail was right back in panic mode.

"No food, no water, no light…it's only a matter of time," he said to himself.

"Come on you two," said Jadeclaw with a thunder in her voice. "Pull yourselves together," she continued. "Kingsguard never give up, never quit," she said.

"Look at us," said Firesneezer with tears in his eyes. "We're not Kingsguards, we're nothing, and soon we'll be dead!" he screamed back at her.

"Wrong," said Jadeclaw. "As a Kingsguard myself, I have the power to make anyone a deputy Kingsguard if they show bravery and strength in difficult situations," she said. "You two have shown great bravery throughout this journey, and you've faced challenges that most Kingsguards have only read about in books," she continued. "Therefore, I now name both of you deputy Kingsguards," she said, raising her spear.

Bubbletail and Firesneezer forgot about their panic.

"Really?" asked Bubbletail.

"Yes," replied Jadeclaw, "but you can only keep your title if you stop panicking now and continue to show the qualities of a Kingsguard," she told them.

The two dragons looked at each other, and then back at Jadeclaw.

"We won't let you down," they both said. Jadeclaw smiled.

"Good, now I want both of you to take stock of what rations we have," she said.

They got up and got to work.

"Well done," said Peacefinder.

"It'll keep them calm for awhile, but we still don't have a solution to our problem," replied Jadeclaw.

"We might," said Lavender.

She had been sitting on the edge of the shaft, deep in thought. In fact, she was peering into the past.

"I saw a small rodent pass through this cavern a few days ago," she told the group. "Well, it wasn't being careful and it fell into this shaft," she continued. "It fell into the water and was swimming inside the shaft, but couldn't climb out. But then after a few hours, the water level started to fall and a tunnel was revealed. The rodent, super tired from swimming, was able to get into the tunnel where it was dry. The rodent then ran through the tunnel," she said.

"Then what happened?" asked Firesneezer.

"I don't know," replied Lavender. "I couldn't see where that rodent went after that," she concluded.

"I don't think we have any other options," said Jadeclaw.

"Peacefinder, will you be able to see when the tunnel is above the waterline?" asked Jadeclaw.

"Yes, I think so," replied Peacefinder.

"In that case, we get ready to go down and wait for the moment to come," said Jadeclaw.

Peacefinder then used her ability to concentrate on the water level below. Although it was totally dark, she could tell by the sound the water made when it cleared the hidden tunnel. After what felt like a few moments, she could hear that the tunnel had drained and was clear to go through. She returned to reality.

"Woah," said Bubbletail, nice to have you back.

"How long was I gone?" she asked.

"It's been nearly three hours," said Daybringer.

"Well done everyone, we have a way out. Now let's move," said Jadeclaw. "Who knows when another earthquake will hit," she added, as she made her way down the shaft using her rope. "I'll check it out first, then give the signal for you to come down," she said.

She lit a torch as she proceeded down the dark shaft. While they waited, Peacefinder looked at the dark figure sitting across from her. The old dragon had gotten even older, and now, without his Future Seer ability, looked very frail.

"Why did it take you ten years to find this place?" asked Peacefinder.

Daybringer looked at her with weary eyes.

"Most of that time was spent trying to find out what I was searching for in the first place," he said. "I knew that the ancient dragons of Frosthall were the most advanced dragons of all when it came to magic. Rumors of the orbs they used to store magical power have been around for generations," he continued. "But

238

separating the truth from these rumors- that is what took so long. Once I knew what I was looking for, it was only a matter of finding the various locations where the dragons of Frosthall escaped after the city fell from the sky. That was also no easy task, as there are dozens of possible locations and hundreds of so-called treasure maps that promise to lead you there. I had to sort through all of it and explore many caves, ruins, and outposts before I came to this place. You only arrived to see the end of my journey," he said.

Peacefinder thought for a moment, then said, "we're not at the end of the journey yet; we still need to get out of here and make it back to Sagestone."

Just then, they heard a sound from inside the shaft. They looked down and saw the dim light of a torch moving back and forth.

"That's the signal," said Peacefinder. "Let's go."

They each made their way down the rope the same way they had done before. Jadeclaw greeted them at the bottom and untied the ropes once everyone was done. The tunnel was damp but dry enough to walk through. Their torch lights lit the way, though they couldn't see very far ahead. The tunnel continued on for a while before opening up to a much larger cave. Jadeclaw gave the signal for everyone to stop. She listened intently. The only sound was the slow dripping of water off the distant walls.

"What's wrong?" asked Lavender in a hushed voice. "I don't like it," whispered Jadeclaw. "This cave is a perfect den for all kinds of beasts," she continued, stepping forward carefully.

She then unraveled her rope and urged each dragon to tie themselves around the waist to it. "We need to be silent, but also invisible," she whispered. "Put out your torches, I'll lead you by the rope," she said. They each put out their torch, until only the only light in the huge cave came from Jadeclaw's tiny torch. "Now, we move, as quietly as possible," she told them.

With small, quiet steps, she led the group through the cave. Lavender could barely see the torch light. She just focused on not tripping over anything or falling down. Fortunately, the water that passed through this cave made the floor smooth and free from rocks or other objects. They walked in darkness like this for what felt like an hour, when they began to hear noises from both sides of the cave. At first it sounded like talons scratching on rocks, and later they could hear rapid tapping.

"Is anyone hearing that?" asked Bubbletail, as quietly as he could.

He then felt a tug on his rope which urged him to walk faster. As they continued to be pulled along, the noises gradually began to move away. Then, they saw faint daylight ahead.

"A light at the end of the tunnel!" shouted Firesneezer. The sound of his shout echoed through the entire cave.

Everyone froze. Firesneezer realized his mistake.

"Oops," he said under his breath.

Just then, the sounds of roaring beasts could be heard from deep inside the cave. They all looked back and saw hundreds of small, red dots moving towards them. Those dots were eyes.

"Ash-claws!" yelled Daybringer.

"Run!" yelled Peacefinder.

They all began to run towards the light. The sound of the ash-claws running after them was like an avalanche of falling rocks. Their long, sharp talons could be heard scraping along the ground as they chased. Bubbletail and Firesneezer fell behind, so Peacefinder lifted them up, but they were too heavy for her to carry on her own.

"Help!" she called out.

Jadeclaw came to the back to protect them, but it was Lavender who grabbed Firesneezer and heaved him onto her back. They were running through the cave exit now at full speed. As the daylight hit their eyes, they were momentarily blinded. The sound of the rushing ash-claws was now replaced but the sound of rushing water. Daybringer was the first to open his eyes and see that he was speeding towards the edge of a cliff! He slammed his talons into the ground and came to a screeching halt. The rest of the dragons nearly ran into him. Lavender quickly looked around. Above them, a waterfall roared down past the cave entrance. Below them, a crystal-clear lake formed from the waterfall. Lavender peered out over the edge of the cliff.

"It's too high to jump!" she said, grabbing her pack and reaching for her Gliderwing. Then, a dozen of the blood-red eyed beasts emerged from the cave, running at full speed. Jadeclaw raised her shield and buried her talons into the dirt. The ash-wings crashed into her shield, their long talons swiping at Jadeclaw. The beasts roared and raged, and rapidly more and more of them closed in. They piled on top of each other, all of them swiping at Jadeclaw. She pushed them back and lodged her shield in the narrow cave opening. Peacefinder grabbed her bow and rapidly started firing arrows at the ash-claws. The arrows bounced off their thick, midnight-black armor.

"Quickly, grab your Gliderwings," shouted Lavender.

Daybringer unfurled what looked like an ancient kite from his pack, and instructed Bubbletail and Firesneezer to help. Peacefinder also began to unfurl her Gliderwing. They heard Jadeclaw scream. One of the ash-claws managed to slash her shoulder underneath her armor. Lavender could see blood on her arm, but Jadeclaw fought even more fiercely, slamming her spear into the mass of furious ash-claws over and over again. Daybringer was the first to unravel and harness his Gliderwing, which was larger than any glider Lavender had seen before.

"I can take Bubbletail, you take Firesneezer," he yelled over the roar of the waterfall.

Lavender strapped into her harness and Firesneezer jumped on. Daybringer jumped over the edge, followed shortly by Lavender. As she jumped, she felt the rushing air and sting of the water droplets against her snout. She spiraled down and down, waiting to get as much speed as possible. Then, she unfurled the Gliderwing. A rush of air lifted them up and out of the mist of the waterfall, but the Gliderwing started stalling. Lavender tried to maneuver to gain speed, but she couldn't.

"We're too heavy," she shouted to Firesneezer. "You have to drop that sack," she screamed.

Firesneezer looked down on the sack of treasure hanging from his side. "Are you sure?" he asked in a pleading voice. The Gliderwing began to buckle under the weight.

Lavender looked at Firesneezer and said, "it's just gold, it's not worth risking our lives over."

Firesneezer knew she was right, and unhooked the bag. The Gliderwing immediately rebounded towards the sky. Firesneezer watched his treasure disappear into the mist.

"Oh well, back to being poor," he said to himself with a sigh.

They lifted higher and banked around to see what was happening on the ledge where Jadeclaw and Peacefinder were still fighting for their lives.

"Jadeclaw, get ready to go," yelled Peacefinder.

Jadeclaw then un-latched her shield and kicked at it hard to jam it between the rocks, leaving it there. She then ran at the Gliderwing which Peacefinder had unfurled for her. The ash-claws bashed at the shield and it collapsed. Peacefinder then loaded her explosive arrow and fired at the ash-claws. The explosion blew many of them back and scattered the others. It was the moment Jadeclaw needed to escape.

"Let's GO!" screamed Jadeclaw as she sprinted to the edge and jumped off without a moment of hesitation.

Peacefinder followed. They both jumped clear of the ledge, just as another swarm of ash-claws emerged from the cave. They made it. The four Gliderwings climbed into the air and re-grouped high above the ravine. The Icelava fields once again stretched to every horizon. The sky was covered in white, wispy clouds, and the air was fresh and cold. Lavender was so happy to be out of those dark caves. They flew along the wind heading south for a few hours, until they could see the pine forests underneath. They had left the Icelava fields behind, and with the sun already setting, found a cliff to land on and camp for the night. Once they had set up camp, Daybringer removed some dried meat and cheeses from his pack.

"Yuck, cheese," said Lavender.

"You don't like goat cheese?" asked Daybringer.

"I don't like any cheese," replied Lavender.

Peacefinder and Jadeclaw were busy setting up tents, while Firesneezer and Bubbletail were gathering firewood.

"Hey where did you get that Gliderwing?" asked Lavender. "I've never seen that design before," she added.

"That's because this Gliderwing is older than you are," replied Daybringer. "It was built by a master wing builder on the far edge of the dragon realm. He used 50 layers of spider silk for the wings and a rare metal made from moon rocks for the frame. It's incredibly light, yet very strong."

He let Lavender lift the furled Gliderwing. Despite it being nearly twice as big as hers, it was lighter.

"Amazing!" she exclaimed.

"Yes, and best of all, it can carry a good amount of weight because the wingspan is so much larger. The one downside is that it's less nimble in the air," he said, as he cut the meat and cheese into portions.

The fire had been lit and the tents were ready, so the group gathered around the fire to have dinner.

"So are you happy that you found the orb that will save the future?" asked Jadeclaw.

Daybringer smiled and said, "although my visions of the future faded, one thing was clear- no matter what we did, we could not prevent the great calamity from happening. That was what I was trying to do, and that was my mistake. Realizing this, I no longer focused on trying to prevent it from happening, but stopping it once it began. And this orb has the power to do that. Only a united world can stop the great calamity. That means both of the great kingdoms- the dragons, and the humans, must work together."

"Humans?" commented Firesneezer. "I thought those were a myth!"

"Oh no, humans are real, and their kingdom is nearly as old as our own," explained Daybringer.

He brought the orb out of his sack and unraveled it from the cloth. The glass sparkled in the firelight, and seemed to give off a slight greenish glow.

"How can this orb unite dragons and humans?" asked Bubbletail.

"A very long time ago, humans and dragons worked together. At that time, we could even speak each other's languages. But that was so long ago. Then a great divide came between us. We haven't spoken to each other in over a thousand years. Nobody knows how to anymore. But this orb allows us to speak to the humans and to tell them that we need to work together again to save the world," replied Daybringer.

"Wow, that's amazing. But how do you know it'll work?" asked Firesneezer in between chews.

"I don't know for sure," replied Daybringer. "But this is our best hope. Once we get to the human kingdom, we'll try it."

"Why can't we try it now? You were able to communicate with King Everwise earlier today right? Why not with the humans?" asked Lavender.

"I want to understand the situation on their side of the world first," he replied. "They don't know us, and we don't know them, and contacting them at the wrong moment could do more harm than good. So we'll need to go there to see what's happening," he concluded.

"We're going to the human kingdom? Now?" asked Jadeclaw.

"I'm afraid so," replied Daybringer. "Our time has run out. We must act now."

"You keep talking about this great calamity, but you never mentioned what that actually means," she continued.

Daybringer put down his meal and looked out at the moon. "I first had this vision of the future over ten years ago. Since then, I've had it countless more times, and it's always the same. A young human boy defies death, then becomes a young man and defies death again, and again. Each time, he becomes stronger, but also more angry and terrifying. I could see him as clearly as I see you now" he said. "His name is Malon. This boy was able to unleash a terrible monster; one that dragons locked away a hundred years ago. A monster that answers to Malon, and one that cannot be stopped by the humans, or the dragons alone. If we leave the humans to fight on their own, they will fall, and we will be next."

They all stared at him in silence. Then Jadeclaw spoke up.

"Wait, you mean to tell me that all of this fuss is over stopping one human boy?" she asked. "Do you know where this human is now; because I figure I could have saved you about ten years with this spear," she said, holding up her shiny spear.

Daybringer smiled. "At first, I thought the same thing," he said. "That is why I asked Honeywing to go to the human-settled part of the world to find Malon and destroy him," he said.

Lavender sat bolt upright at these words.

"But I was wrong," he continued. "Very, very wrong. Because this evil faces death again and again, and always comes out on top," he continued.

Peacefinder looked to Lavender with concern. Lavender's face was red.

"You sent Honeywing on that mission?" asked Lavender in a cold, dark voice.

Daybringer looked at her, concern in his eyes. "She was the only one who believed me," he said. "She was my best student and dearest friend," he said. "When I told her how the entire world would suffer if we didn't stop this, she volunteered to go, even though she had an egg to care for. I told her she shouldn't, that I should be the one to go, but she insisted that I was too old and that the king needed me. And so she went," he said, his face pained. "When she didn't return, I knew that she had failed, and that my mission to stop Malon had to continue without her."

His words were quiet and full of regret. Lavender wanted to pounce on the old dragon, but as he continued the story, her anger cooled.

"Have you heard from her, or have any idea where she might be?" was Lavender's next question.

"I never heard from her again," admitted Daybringer.

"Then use your future sight!" yelled Lavender. "She might have survived, she might be out there even now" cried Lavender. Daybringer sighed.

"I'm sorry child, but I tried. And I never saw her in the future," he said.

"But it's not impossible. I survived," said Lavender.

Daybringer looked up at her, finally noticing the resemblance. "It cannot be," he said in awe.

"It is," said Peacefinder.

Daybringer still couldn't believe the words he was hearing. "You, you're…"

"Honeywing's daughter? "Yes, I am," said Lavender, calming herself.

"But how?" exclaimed Daybringer.

"I know that the king sent a huge team who searched for months for Honeywing and found nothing," he said.

"I don't know how, but I survived. And if I survived, my mother may have as well," said Lavender.

Bubbletail and Firesneezer were both fascinated by the story.

"Does that mean Lavender is something like royalty?" blurted out Firesneezer.

248

Lavender gave him a look that told him to shush.

"It means that she inherited her mother's ability, and that she is an incredibly lucky dragon," said Daybringer.

"I never even met my mom, I don't feel lucky" replied Lavender.

Daybringer realized that he had mis-spoken.

Firesneezer whispered to Lavender, "don't take that too seriously, he said himself he can't see the future anymore."

Lavender felt a little better. She could still keep hope alive in her heart.

After an uncomfortable silence, Peacefinder said, "It's been a very long and difficult day, and we have a long flight tomorrow. We should get to bed."

They all went to their tents, but Lavender's sleep was restless. She couldn't stop thinking about her mom.

## CHAPTER EIGHTEEN: THE GREAT CALAMITY

Malon watched from a high cliff as a town burned. Cloud Hill was the name. *Now it was a cloud of ash*, he thought to himself.

"It seems you've lost your appetite for becoming king," said the voice of Doomswing in his head.

"What do you mean?" he asked the dragon.

"You've gone from scaring the humans to simply killing them. It's hard to rule over a kingdom if you have no people to rule over," said the dragon in an annoying, humorous tone, as if he was laughing at Malon on the inside.

Malon didn't trust Doomswing. He was sly, crafty, and mean. But he was the only thing that gave Malon power. Or rather, the only thing that kept Doomswing from killing Malon was the jewel he wore around his neck. Without that, Doomswing would fade back to being an old, weak dragon; just a shadow of his former self.

"There are plenty of towns left, I am just sending a message to the king," replied Malon.

"But the king doesn't reply," said Doomswing. "It seems we will come to a battle after all," he continued.

A battle with the king's army wasn't what Malon had wanted. He hoped that burning a few towns to the ground would scare the king enough to make him give up and make Malon the new king. But no messengers arrived from the capital. Malon knew that Doomswing was nearly invincible against anything the human army could throw at him, but Malon himself wasn't, and this was the problem. After he lost his leg in the first battle, he began to wear steel battle armor from head to toe and built a much sturdier saddle for himself while he rode Doomswing. He was more confident that he would not be so easy to kill now, but he also knew that no amount of armor made a human invincible. And with only one dragon to attack, the king could focus all of his soldiers on Doomswing and Malon. All they needed was one lucky shot, and Malon would be done for. Since the king didn't seem interested in giving up without a fight, Malon had to change his strategy. But re-building an army of bandits and misfits wasn't what he wanted either. That didn't work out too well in the first battle. As he thought about what he should do, Doomswing turned his gaze towards the road heading north.

"It seems we have a visitor," said the dragon in Malon's mind.

Far in the distance, a single rider was coming towards them. It was a messenger.

*Finally*! thought Malon. *The king had given up.*

They met the messenger on the road. Malon came down from Doomswing. As the messenger approached, Malon noticed that he wasn't wearing the usual clothing that a royal messenger would wear. In fact, he looked more like a soldier. Sensing danger, Doomswing raised his head and prepared to send a bolt of fire at the stranger. But the messenger held up his hands and got off his horse.

"I am unarmed, and this isn't a trick," he said, with obvious fear in his voice.

"I'm going to place this message on the ground here, and then back away. I'll wait over there for your reply."

The messenger did exactly that, and Malon went to pick up the message. It was sealed with a stamp he didn't recognize.

Malon read:

*To the future king,*

*My name is Veralus. I am the loser King Steadfast's strongest general. I fought and defeated your Blood-Red Army at the battle for Grapefine. Although you lost that battle, I know you will win this war. We have no chance of defeating you. This is why I have sent this message; I want to join forces with you. I have the army on my side. Nobody likes the current king. He is weak and he doesn't care about his people. With you as king, we will be stronger than ever. We could even conquer the dragon realm.*

As Malon read this, one thought came to his mind- it's a trap. But there was more:

*I know what you're thinking- it's a trap. But I promise you this is real, and you don't have to take my word for it. I will prove that we are ready to join you. Stay in Cloud Hill for one more week. I will be able to march my army out to you by then. I will meet you in person, along with all the soldiers. Then we will march on Ravensthorn together and take the city. When the king sees that his army has turned against him, he will have no choice but to surrender. Your victory will be complete without a fight.*

Malon considered this carefully. It made sense, and it was what he wanted from the beginning. But this was the commander that nearly killed him. Malon hated what happened to him at that battle, and Veralus was the perfect target for his hate. He decided he would play along with this plan, and once he was crowned the new king, he would get rid of Veralus. Malon turned to the messenger.

"Tell Veralus that I agree, and will be waiting for him here. He has one week."

The messenger bowed and immediately rushed off. A few days later, when Veralus received the reply, he smiled a wicked smile. Soon he would be rid of the pesky king, and then once he was close to Malon, he'd figure out how he controls the dragon. Once Veralus seized that power, he'd get rid of Malon, and have the power of the dragon for himself. But first, he'd have to convince the army to follow him against the king's orders. He gathered them at the army headquarters and stood on one of the tower balconies overlooking the central square where the soldiers were gathered.

"You all know of the dragon threat," he said in a loud voice.

"But rather than fight, the king asks us to hide!" he continued.

The soldiers started nodding in agreement.

"Rather than defend our home, we are told to wait here for death to come to us!" he continued.

Now some soldiers were yelling and stomping their spears on the ground.

"I say, we fight! I say we meet the dragon when it leasts expects us. I say we forget about the cowardly king!"

At this statement, many soldiers screamed "yeah", but several others got silent.

"Those of you who are not cowards, follow me!" said Veralus.

He started marching out towards the city gate. A messenger who saw the whole thing ran up to the king's chamber to let him know what was happening. But by the time King Steadfast the 25th realized what was happening and went to stop Veralus, roughly half of his army had made their way out of the city.

"The last thing we need now is our own army fighting each other," said the king. "If they want to march out and fight the dragon, let them. We will defend our home here," he told the council.

After a day of marching south, Veralus stopped and made camp. Now came the hardest part of his plan. He had to convince the soldiers to turn on the king.

"Soldiers, we have a decision to make," said Veralus. "Many of you were at the battle of Grapefine. You saw the power of the black dragon. You know what I know- we cannot beat it."

Many soldiers gasped as Veralus said this.

"If you believe that, then why are we out here?" asked one of the soldiers.

"Because there is another way to save our families and our kingdom, and it won't even require us to fight," replied Veralus. "Imagine, if we didn't have to fight the dragon, but instead, had the dragon on our side," he continued. "Imagine how unstoppable we would be. The kingdom would be safe from any threat. Would you like this to come true?" he asked.

Some soldiers nodded, but most just looked at him in confusion.

"Well, I can make this come true. All you have to do is trust me," he continued.

"But Malon controls the dragon, and he wants to be king!" yelled out one of the soldiers.

"Exactly," replied Veralus. The soldiers thought about this for a moment.

"Wait, so you mean…" the soldier trailed off.

"I mean it's time for us to pick the winning side. A king that can give us peace and an unstoppable army, or one that hides in his castle, waiting for defeat," continued Veralus. The soldiers just stood there, shocked by what he was saying.

"But that's…that's treason!" yelled out one of the soldiers.

Veralus looked at him. "I say King Steadfast is no longer capable of being king, and we should now look to our new king to save us from this disaster," said Veralus. "When that dragon arrives at Ravensthorn, nothing we do can stop it. Everyone will perish. Or, everyone will survive and live peacefully in a new era."

As Veralus looked around the field of gathered soldiers, he could tell some of them were convinced, while others were clearly about ready to abandon him. He expected that would happen, and he didn't want a battle on his hands between the two groups.

"You know where I stand," he said. "Those of you who want to join the winning side, stand by me now. Those of you who want to perish in the coming battle, you're free to return to Ravensthorn."

Now came the moment he was waiting for. How many would stay, and how many would leave? The soldiers realized that this could be the most important decision of their lives. It could literally mean the difference between life and death. For some of them, it was an easy choice. A group of soldiers screamed out "Traitors!" and made their way out of the camp and back to Ravensthorn. But most of them didn't know what to do. They were looking around, not really sure. Eventually, most of them stayed, as they believed they would already be considered traitors anyway and didn't want to return to Ravensthorn in shame. Even so, Veralus lost about half of the army that marched out from Ravensthorn. It was more than he'd expected. He was enraged, and continued yelling abuse at the soldiers leaving long after they were gone, but there wasn't anything he could do. This was the army he had now. He hoped it would be enough.

## CHAPTER NINETEEN: REUNION

Lavender woke up with the sunrise. The clouds had passed and it was going to be a beautiful day. She felt better, but still had some thoughts of her mom that wouldn't go away. She really wanted to question Daybringer and find out where she was so that she could go look for her. But she knew the time wasn't right for that yet. As they sat around the crackling fire to warm up and have some porridge, Peacefinder looked to the west and said,

"I'll scout ahead to see what the road looks like," and then she went into a deep concentration. She gazed beyond the pine forests and the rolling hills, and then, at the very edge of her vision, beyond the borders of the dragon realm, she noticed black smoke.

She turned her gaze in that direction, but it was very far away, and her sight would only blur. She returned to the campsite in a flash.

"What did you see?" asked Jadeclaw.

"I saw...something. It was very far away so I couldn't see clearly, but something is definitely not well in that part of the world." said Peacefinder.

Daybringer frowned and his claws dug into martian soil. He was clearly upset by this vision.

"It's just as my earlier visions predicted. It would start far away- in the part of the world where humans live. But eventually, it would spread to the entire world. And I believe it has begun," he said.

"We must inform the king," said Daybringer, as he took out the Orb of Understanding. He then closed his eyes and focused on the dragon he wanted to communicate with. He pushed a thought to the king.

"We believe the great calamity has started in the human realm, and we are going there to learn more and to try to stop it. Please, order our army to meet us at Ravensthorn. The fate of the world is at stake."

Next, Peacefinder also spoke to the dragon king through the orb- something she had never done before. It was a strange feeling, as if she had left her body and was somewhere else. She could see King Everwise, but he couldn't see her or respond to her. She told him what had happened, and confirmed their plan to proceed to the human kingdom. She noticed that the king seemed very eager to share some news with her, and she really wished that she could hear what the king had to say, but the orb couldn't help her.

Back in Sagestone, King Everwise did indeed have important news to share, but he knew there was only one way to share it. He acted quickly, ordering the entire dragon army to prepare to fly to the human kingdom and face a threat they still knew very little about. But in addition to this, he ordered five of his best royal guards to fly immediately out to meet Daybringer, Peacefinder, Lavender and the others. With so much danger in the vast world, and now that they had a powerful orb, the king felt they needed more protection. But there was one other reason why he wanted to send out this group immediately. In addition to the five royal guards, the king sent one other dragon to meet with the group.

Lavender flew behind Peacefinder, with Jadeclaw and Daybringer on her left and right sides. They had been flying in this "V" formation for the past three hours. It was their third day of long-distance flying. Lavender's shoulders ached and her muscles were sore, but she knew they had to reach the human kingdom as soon as possible. Suddenly, she heard a tearing noise from Jadeclaw's side. She looked, and saw Jadeclaw spiraling out of control! Lavender yelled out, and Peacefinder quickly banked and dove towards Jadeclaw. Daybringer was carrying Firesneezer, but Bubbletail was with Peacefinder. That meant she couldn't dive as fast as she normally could, nor could she maneuver as well.

"She needs my help," decided Lavender, and banked into a dive.

She focused in on Jadeclaw's spiraling Gliderwing as she felt the rush of wind and the sense of gravity disappearing beneath her. Peacefinder was further ahead, but Lavender was faster. She estimated that Jadeclaw had about ten seconds before she hit the ground. Lavender rushed past Peacefinder and slowed as she approached Jadeclaw. She then got right under Jadeclaw and unfurled her Gliderwing. As soon as she did, she felt a powerful jolt on her back. Her Gliderwing buckled under the additional weight, but the wings held. She was now being pulled hard towards the ground, but she managed to stabilize just enough to level out. She then made a smooth arc in the air and skidded to a stop in a wheat field. The wheat smacked against her face and arms as she crash-landed. The landing left some bruises, but other than that, Lavender was fine. Jadeclaw had rode with her all the way down, and now she untangled herself from the two Gliderwings.

Lavender spat out grains of dirt and shook her tail vigorously. Jadeclaw touched her shoulder gingerly and faced Lavender with pure shock etched onto her bruised snout. She opened her mouth to speak but it was dry and she just stared at her with wide eyes.

"That was close," Lavender said, finally breaking the shocked stillness.

"Yeah, it was close. Thank you, by the way," Jadeclaw muttered awkwardly.

Soon, Daybringer and Peacefinder landed nearby.

"Is everyone ok?" shouted Peacefinder.

"We're fine," replied Lavender.

Peacefinder freed herself from her Gliderwing and ran over to them.

"That was very brave of you, and very smart," said Peacefinder to Lavender. "I can't believe that just a few months ago, you didn't even know what a Gliderwing was. Now you're flying like a professional!"

Lavender beamed. But they did have a problem- Jadeclaw's Gliderwing had a huge tear in it.

"It must have happened during our escape from the cave. Maybe a rock hit it, or maybe I just pushed it too hard," said Jadeclaw.

"I can fix it, but you'll have to take it easy from now on," said Peacefinder.

They spent the rest of the day camping out near the wheat field while Peacefinder and Jadeclaw worked on fixing the Gliderwing.

"Do you think we are already in the human kingdom?" asked Bubbletail, bounding through the neat lanes of wheat. "I didn't see any signs or flags," said Firesneezer.

"Don't be ridiculous," replied Bubbletail. "Do you think we'll be seeing a 'welcome to humanity' sign with flags and a gift shop at the border?" said Bubbletail.

"A gift shop would be nice," Firesneezer retorted.

"Well, someone planted this wheat field," said Lavender. "And I think that someone might be approaching now," she continued, pointing to the dirt road that ran along the field.

There in the distance, they saw a horse pulling a cart, and a small, skinny creature sitting on top.

"Woah," said Firesneezer. "Aliens are real."

"Quickly, hide," said Lavender.

Peacefinder looked up and kicked herself when she saw the farmer approaching. She was so busy trying to fix the Gliderwing that she didn't bother using her ability to check their surroundings. Fortunately, this farmer didn't look dangerous at all. As the farmer rode past the what field, he noticed the massive chunk missing in the center. *What happened there*, he thought to himself. He got off his cart to investigate.

"Well, I guess it's time to meet the aliens," said Firesneezer.

As the farmer walked into the field, he came within arms-length of touching Bubbletail. But the farmer was focused on the area of destroyed wheat in front of him. Then, he suddenly stopped. His face filled with terror, and he ran off. He jumped onto his horse and bolted back the way he came.

"What was that all about?" asked Firesneezer.

"That was me," said Daybringer. "I used the orb to make the farmer think that a ghost was talking to him and haunting the field. I think it had the right effect."

They all laughed.

"That was clever," said Jadeclaw.

"Well, it really didn't matter," said Daybringer. "If he said he saw dragons or heard ghosts, either way nobody would believe him."

"Yes, but he might have encouraged others to come if he saw a bunch of dragons," said Peacefinder. "This way, I don't think he'll be bringing anyone anytime soon."

"But I'm afraid I have bad news," continued Peacefinder. "The tear in this Gliderwing isn't the only problem. One of the support beams is cracked," she said, holding up a long piece of wood that looked like it was about to break in half. "We can't repair this, we need to replace it."

"How do we do that?" asked Jadeclaw.

"That farmer must live nearby, which means there's a human village around here. They build things out of wood. All we need is to find a long, slender pole, grab it, and bring it back here," said Peacefinder.

"Oh, that's all we need to do?" asked Firesneezer. "Break into some alien's house and steal a piece of his furniture? Sounds super easy," he said sarcastically.

"I'm glad you think so," replied Peacefinder. "Because I'm assigning you two to this mission." Firesneezer looked at Bubbletail.

"What?" they both said at the same time.

"You two are the smallest, and you're most likely to get in and out without being seen. I'll fly you out there and then wait just outside of the village. If you run into any trouble, just get back to me."

Neither Firesneezer nor Bubbletail were willing to go through with it.

But then Lavender said, "Without that wooden pole, we cannot warn the humans, which means they will all perish, which means we will too. You two are literally saving the world by doing this."

Bubbletail's eyes lit up. Firesneezer puffed out his chest. "Well, we are deputy Kingsguards anyway. Ok, we'll do it," they said. Lavender grinned.

After being dropped off near the village, they made their way quietly through more wheat fields until they reached the first houses. As they scampered through the narrow alleyways, Bubbletail and Firesneezer kept close to the rotten wood of the abandoned houses that lined the outskirts of the village.

"Where do you think all the new wood is?" Bubbletail whispered as he prodded the molded wood. It fell beneath the weight and crumbled onto the ground. He glared at the pile of wood frustratedly.

"This is just the outskirts, remember? The good stuff is on the inside. Just keep looking for it," Firesneezer hissed urgently as he backed into the safety of the shadows.

"But this alley is so narrow I can hardly breathe!"

"Then don't breathe!" Firesneezer retorted.

They pressed onward and slithered further into the alleys without another word. Once they were at the back of a larger building which had cold, stone pillars, Firesneezer blurted out, "do you think the aliens have an actual wooden pole here?"

"Keep your voice down. They'll hear you and by the way, they're called humans," Bubbletail said.

Firesneezer rolled his eyes and casually said, "relax, the alien-I mean humans hearing range can't be that far. I mean, have you seen the size of those ears? Miniature!"

Bubbletail stopped listening when he glanced around a corner and saw what looked like a perfectly good wooden pole standing in the middle of the square. It had a funny piece of fabric hanging from the top with some markings stitched onto it. He craned his neck to see the short, slim humans bustling around the stalls and various markets. There must have been a hundred of them, all dressed in various colors and carrying packages and pushing carts.

"The pole we need is right there. We have to get it!" he whispered.

Firesneezer looked over. "Yeah, too bad it's right in the center of the town! How can we possibly get it without being spotted?

"We'll go after the humans fall asleep," muttered Bubbletail.

Firesneezer looked at the sun, which was casting long shadows onto the town square. "It'll take several hours," he said, but I guess it would be safer. But what if we get spotted while waiting in this alley?" he continued.

"We'd better hide," replied Bubbletail. They cautiously scanned the narrow alleys for any hiding spot they could cower in or behind but there was none in sight.

"Humans might not have as good eyesight as ours but they will definitely spot two dragons just chilling in an alley," said Firesneezer.

Bubbletail inspected a pile of compost carefully.

"Hey, this could work."

He motioned to Firesneezer. Firesneezer took one glance at the pungent pile and immediately said, "no way am I sitting in that pile all day. I'd rather be seen by the aliens!"

Bubbletail gritted his teeth in frustration. "We're doing this," he said, snatched Firesneezer's talon, and hauled him to the rotting pile of fruits and vegetables.

They sat there for what seemed like hours. The sun had already gone down, and the noises from the town square were gone.

"Is it time now?" asked Firesneezer.

But before Bubbletail could answer, a small human rounded the corner and walked towards them. She was carrying a large bucket.

"That better not be garbage," whispered Firesneezer.

Bubbletail held his breath in worry as they sunk into the compost and out of view. The human took one look at the pile of compost and dumped her bucket full of old potatoes onto the pile. Just then, she saw a flaming red, scaly tail jutting out of the pile. She screamed and ran toward the town square, dropping her bucket along the way. She hurried to the main street and Bubbletail could hear her terrified howls across the village. Firesneezer immediately leapt up from the pile and beat his tiny wings vigorously until he was up in the air.

"Come on! They already know we are here! We should make the most of it!" he yelled.

Bubbletail groaned and muttered "I guess you're right," before taking off.

They clumsily flew out of the alley and around the corner until they reached the town square. They dipped down and landed onto the grainy ground, dust bellowing up below their talons. Bubbletail dashed forward and yanked hard on the wooden pole, hoping that it would easily slide out of the ground. It didn't. Firesneezer ran over.

"Pull harder! It's just a pole, not an elephant!"

"I'm trying! It seriously won't budge!" bellowed Bubbletail, tugging at the wood with all his might.

"I know, maybe I could sneeze on it to burn a hole through," said Firesneezer, taking out the little feather he used whenever he wanted to activate his superpower.

Bubbletail stopped pulling on the flagpole and stared at Firesneezer.

"What now? Are you trying to burn this whole village to the ground?" he questioned.

Firesneezer's cheeks flushed red. "So you're saying it won't work," he murmured.

Bubbletail then had an idea.

"I know what to do! Just like my ancestors did, I can use my tail to chop the pole down!" he exclaimed.

Without waiting for a reply from Firesneezer, Bubbletail swung his massive tail back and let out a solid blow at the base of the pole, but it bounced back into its place, unphased.

"Hmm... I was sure that that was going to work," he muttered.

"Just try again!" Firesneezer urged.

Bubbletail reluctantly swung his tail back again and whacked the wooden pole. This time, it sliced through the wood and it came crashing down. They cheered victoriously. Just then, the ringing of a bell could be heard across the village. To their horror, a group of humans appeared from behind some hut, armed with bows.

"Quick, grab the pole! Firesneezer screamed.

They snatched up the pole and sprinted out of the village. The humans saw them, and had no idea what they were seeing.

"Were those...goblins?" asked one of the humans.

"No no, those were grumpkins," replied another.

"But why did they take our flag pole?" wondered another.

They just stood in stunned silence as the two dragons disappeared around the corner and out of the village. Bubbletail and Firesneezer returned to the wheat field in triumph.

Peacefinder took one look at the pole and said, "Wow, this is a really good piece of wood. You two did great."

Bubbletail and Firesneezer were now doing their victory dance.

"Were you seen?" asked Jadeclaw.

At this, they stopped dancing.

"Well, we weren't exactly invisible, but we definitely weren't super visible either," replied Bubbletail.

"And what's that smell?" asked Peacefinder. "We're not talking about that," replied Firesneezer.

268

It took them all of the next morning to shape the wooden pole and tie it into place. The Gliderwing failure cost them a lot of time, but the most important thing was that nobody got hurt in the incident.

"You'll have to fly more carefully," said Peacefinder to Jadeclaw.

"This wooden beam isn't a perfect fit, and too many sharp turns or dives could make it shake loose."

Jadeclaw eyed the beam with a distrusting look.

"Better not shake loose," she said to the beam.

After packing up their gear, they finally took off again and left the farmer's wheat field behind. Even taking off from there was hard work, as they were all loaded with gear and without a good slope to start from. By the end of that day, they were only able to fly a short distance before they had to camp for the night. They were flying along the coast now, with the sea on their left side and the rolling hills and forest on their right. The coastline was rough, with rock formations and cliffs jutting in and out. They saw a large boulder with a flat top that was sticking right up from the water. It made a very nice landing spot. After landing, they set up camp and started a fire. The wind was calm and the sun had just set, leaving the sky in deep hues of pink, violet and purple. Lavender was enjoying the view, when she noticed something in the sky. Far off in the distance, she saw what looked like a bunch of geese, but they were flying in an odd formation. She continued watching them, and they were getting closer.

"Don't tell me- the aliens learned how to fly," said Firesneezer when he saw what Lavender was looking at.

269

"Hey, have either of you seen something like that before?" she asked, turning to Peacefinder and Jadeclaw while pointing at the sky.

They both came over. Jadeclaw gasped with excitement.

"Gliderwings….it's the Royal Guard! I would know that flying formation from anywhere. Quickly, Peacefinder, fire the beacon arrow!"

Peacefinder took a moment to fumble through her pack, then took out a long, thin arrow with an odd bubble on the tip. She then placed the bubble tip in the campfire, and it sparked and lit up. She loaded it into her bow and fired directly up into the air. The arrow seemed to disappear as it flew higher and higher.

"Well that was disappointing," commented Firesneezer.

Then an explosion of light and sound came from above, leaving lines of blue, red and green across the sky, pointing in various directions, as if a colorful ball of paint had exploded onto the sky. Everyone gazed up in amazement.

"I take it back," said Firesneezer.

"I want that for my next birthday party," commented Bubbletail, still looking up.

Jadeclaw watched the formation of Gliderwings in the distance. They started to turn towards them.

"It worked!" she bellowed in excitement.

The formation of Gliderwings was swooping in , getting lower and lower and coming closer and closer. Lavender was excited to soon hear news from the capital. But as she looked over to

Peacefinder, she noticed that she had a look of utter disbelief on her face.

Then, Peacefinder walked over to Jadeclaw and said in a low voice, "I just took a look at who is coming to visit us…and…and I…I don't have the words."

Jadeclaw looked to Peacefinder with a look of shocked concern. "Are we in danger?" she asked.

"No, it's nothing like that, these are the Kingsguard, it's just that, they have someone else with them," said Peacefinder.

Before Jadeclaw could reply, the Kingsguards swooped down and pulled their Gliderwings forward hard, creating a loud, cracking noise as they landed on the rocky surface, not far from where the group was standing. Jadeclaw looked them over. Five of the dragons were wearing the same crimson and gold armor that Jadeclaw had, and carried spears and shields in their packs. She recognized them all. The sixth dragon was unknown to her and looked like a schoolteacher. *This was the one that got Peacefinder so bent out of shape*, she thought to herself. This last dragon was also clearly the least experienced with a Gliderwing, as instead of making a graceful landing, she came in snout-first, and was now lying belly-down on the ground, trying to get herself un-tangled. Peacefinder remained frozen, so Jadeclaw stepped forward to speak.

She approached them saying, "Tailwind, Skyrider, Goldenwing, welcome! I'm so glad you saw our flare."

The Kingsguards at the front of the formation saluted Jadeclaw and said, "Jadeclaw, it's good to see you. The king sent us out to find you as soon as he learned which way you were headed. I'm

271

still not sure how you managed to tell him that, but no matter. We're glad we finally found you."

Daybringer also came forward and began to speak to the Kingsguards, none of whom knew who he was. Lavender moved to the dragon on the ground who was just now getting untangled from her Gliderwing.

"Here, let me help you," said Lavender, and un-did the latches on the Gliderwing to help it fold.

She looked at the dragon now, who was staring at her. She was older, with a deep purple color and shiny, bronze outlines on her scales. Lavender couldn't help but feel that she'd seen this dragon before.

"Thank you, my dear," she said to Lavender, and once again her voice brought Lavender a sense of familiarity.

"Have we…" she started to say, and then noticed that Peacefinder was staring at her.

"Peacefinder," said the mysterious dragon, "it's so good to see you again." She then noticed Daybringer, who also stopped mid-sentence to look at her.

"Can this be real?" he said, his voice quivering. He walked over and touched the dragon's snout. Tears welled up in his eyes.

"So long I looked for you, and every vision showed me nothing but emptiness. You eluded me for so long."

Peacefinder's jaw had dropped by now. Lavender was completely confused.

"It...how...when..." Peacefinder seemed to struggle to say a full sentence.

The mysterious dragon smiled.

"It's not every day that you get to surprise a Future Seer, and get one the finest diplomatic speakers tongue tied." she said.

Bubbletail chose this moment to break into the conversation.

"Hi, my name is Bubbletail," he said to the mysterious dragon, while holding out one talon."

She took his talon gently and said, "greetings, Bubbletail, it's nice to meet you. My name is Honeywing." She looked at Lavender as she said this, her eyes welling up with tears. "Lavender, I'm your mother."

Lavender dropped to the ground, her knees giving out from the raw emotion of the moment.

"But... you..." she tried to make sense of all of it, but instead gave up and just dashed forward, wrapping her arms around her. "Lavender," she whispered. "Oh how I've missed you!"

All the dragons looked on at the reunion, ten years overdue. Firesneezer jumped up and down.

"I love family reunions," he remarked.

They trotted over to Lavender and beamed at her.

"Hi Miss Lavender's mom! I'm Firesneezer!" Firesneezer said cheerfully.

"Well, it's nice to meet you, Firesneezer. Please, call me Honeywing," she replied.

Once they were all settled around the campsite, Peacefinder finally had a chance to have her own reunion with Honeywing.

"We searched for nearly a year, you know," said Peacefinder. "You have to tell me what happened."

"Why don't we ask Lavender?" Honeywing suggested encouragingly. Lavender had a look of uncertainty written across her snout. "I-I don't know if I can go back that far..." she whispered.

"Take my hands, child. I will help you. Just focus your mind, and see what my eyes have seen," Honeywing murmured softly.

Lavender did so, and tried very hard to clear her mind and settle her emotions. Suddenly, she was flying...no, falling. She was in a terrible storm, being thrown in every direction. Water, cold, then dark. She was on a beach, her head hurt. Her arm couldn't move. Who was she? Where? She had lost something...something terribly important. But what...Then some dragons come to help her and take her to their fishing village. They ask her name....she can't remember. She stays there, her body heals. She still can't remember. She helps some local dragon kids with their lessons. She knows a lot, but she doesn't know why. She walks along the beach every evening, searching for...something. Years go by. She still doesn't remember.

Then one day, one of the mother dragons gives birth to an egg. She touches it...and suddenly her mind is in another place, another time. She has a vision. She remembers...everything. She is a Seer in the Royal Court. She is special, important. She was on a mission to save the world. She drops to the ground, sobbing. She lost her egg. Then she remembered her own name-Honeywing. For ten years she's been someone else...she's been

274

no one. But now, she had to return to the world in hopes that somehow, some way, her baby survived. She treks across the continent and gets to Sagestone. She meets with the king, who tells her that a dragon girl called Lavender came to Sagestone and went on a mission with Peacefinder. Honeywing couldn't believe it. Could it really be her? She begs him to give her a Gliderwing and let her go after Lavender, but the king tells her to be patient. They need to wait until Peacefinder sends them a message. They could be anywhere by now. She waits, and waits, until finally, the king tells her that he knows where they are. She wastes no time and flies, flies day and night to find her child. Lavender opens her eyes, tears streaming down her face.

"Mom," she says again, as Honeywing hugs her tightly.

"I'm so sorry I missed so much of your life," said Honeywing. "But I'm here now, and I'll never miss another moment."

Lavender had been dreaming about this day for most of her life. She imagined every detail of what it could be like. But she could never have imagined that it would be like this. Sitting on top of a cliff overlooking the ocean, seeing the sunset, surrounded by friends, hugging her mom. It was the best moment of her life.

## CHAPTER TWENTY: THE TRAITORS

Malon watched from high overhead as an army marched towards him. He flew on Doomswing, who was circling lazily over the fields below.

"Well, either Veralus made good on his promise, or they're here to kill you," said the dragon, with his usual amused tone, as if he was just there to watch the drama play out.

"We're about to find out, let's go meet them," said Malon.

With that, Doomswing dove and picked up speed- so much speed that Malon's eyes watered and his stomach turned. Malon felt a wave of terror come over him as Doomswing continued to dive, even though they were now just seconds from hitting the ground. Then, at the last moment, he unfurled his massive wings and caught the wind, propelling him upward and crushing Malon into his saddle. The quick reversal of gravity's pull made Malon nearly pass out. Doomswing swooped directly over the marching army, spooking horses and knocking several soldiers onto the ground from the rush of air alone. He looked back at Malon, who's face had turned blue. The dragon let out a terrible laugh.

"Come now Malon, we must make the right kind of entrance," he said. Malon wanted off this roller coaster, but he couldn't show Doomswing that he was at his mercy.

"You had your fun, now land," he said, in the most commanding tone he could put on. Doomswing did so, and Malon fell off the dragon, his knees giving up at soon as he touched the ground. Doomswing was wearing his usual smirk of satisfaction. It took Malon a moment to pull himself together, but once he did, he stood tall and waited for the army to approach. A few minutes later, a smartly-dressed soldier came riding up on a white horse, with the messenger that Malon met before riding next to him. Doomswing was curled up on the ground behind Malon, grinning his razor-sharp teeth. Veralus came down from his horse, and knelt before Malon.

"Your majesty," he said.

"I'm not king yet," said Malon. Veralus looked at him and smiled.

"With the dragon you command and the army I have brought you, there is nothing that can stand in your way," he said. Malon looked at the soldiers who were now filing in behind Veralus. They were all dressed in the gleaming silver armor that Malon remembered seeing at the battle. It was an impressive sight. Veralus turned to the soldiers.

"I, commander Veralus, present to you, our new king!" he roared. The soldiers replied with powerful shouts and cheers.

"King Malon, King Malon," they chanted. Malon felt the doubt disappear from his mind and felt the feeling of victory take over. It was really true, he really did have the most powerful army in the world. But now Doomswing stirred, and he sent a thought to Malon.

"Is this all they have?" he questioned.

"What do you mean?" Malon asked.

"The king's army should be much bigger than this," commented Doomswing. Malon considered this. The army was impressive, but Veralus said he would bring the entire army. Doomswing had a point; this was definitely not it. Malon turned to Veralus.

"This is an impressive sight, but where are the rest of them?" asked Malon. Veralus grew uncomfortable.

"The king still has a group of weak, cowardly soldiers defending the city. All it will take is one look at the dragon, and they will all run away," said Veralus, trying to sound as confident as he could. Malon wasn't happy about this. Even a small group of soldiers could put up a good fight, and it would mean Malon would have to risk his life flying on Doomswing again to fight them. It was the exact opposite of what he was hoping for, but he had no other options now.

"If this doesn't work, you'll be the first to feel the heat of dragonfire," said Malon to Veralus in a low, angry voice. Veralus glanced over at the dragon and felt a shiver run down his spine. *If this doesn't work, we're all dead anyway*, he thought to himself.

Several days later, a group of weary soldiers returned to Ravensthorn. They told the king how Veralus had deceived them, and how he had turned against the king. When the king heard this, he knew that the battle for the capital was coming, and there was nothing they could do to stop Malon and his dragon from attacking. He felt oddly calm, like he was reading a book about his life, rather than actually living it. He accepted that this could be the end of his story, but wanted the ending to be remembered. It was the first time ever that he truly acted worthy of his name- King Steadfast.

"We need every soldier we can get," he said to the soldiers who returned from Veralus. He didn't punish them, and set them to work right away in preparing the city for the attack. "We also need to evacuate the city," he said to his council. "Everyone who is not here to defend the capital must leave immediately. Go to towns further west. Anywhere is safer than Ravensthorn right now. Everyone else needs to find shelter inside the caverns. This castle was built to survive a dragon attack, and now we will need to use every bit of that protection."

The council quickly got to work organizing horse carts, getting people packed and ready to move, and clearing out the caverns and tunnels that had long been abandoned and where the remaining soldiers would hide during the attack. They didn't have much time; Malon and Veralus were only days away. After the meeting with his council, the king went out onto his balcony. He could see the entire city from there. The air was chilly and autumn leaves were already turning brilliant hues of red, yellow and orange. For a moment, he forgot about the desperate situation they were in and felt at peace. But only for a moment.

## CHAPTER TWENTY-ONE: THE TRICK

Honeywing was dismayed about Lavender wanting to continue the mission to stop Malon, but Lavender insisted on seeing it through to the end.

"Why can't we just go home, the two of us. We have both done more than enough for the kingdom, and already sacrificed so much," said Honeywing, pleading with Lavender. "Besides, this is a very dangerous mission, and…I can't bear the thought of losing you," she continued.

Lavender hugged her mom. "This is my purpose, and I feel my friends will need me," she insisted. "And now that we are together, nothing can stop us," she added.

Honeywing looked at Lavender with pride-filled eyes. "We are too much alike after all," she said.

Daybringer was speaking to Peacefinder, who was trying to use her ability to figure out where Malon was now.

"We're already in the human part of the world, but it's a vast area," said Daybringer. "It's unlikely that Malon is nearby, but we can guess where he's going," he continued. Now everyone was listening. "In my visions of the future, Malon attacks the human capital city of Ravensthorn. That's where he's going, and that's the direction we need to fly now," he told the group.

"How far from here?" asked Jadeclaw.

Daybringer brought out an ancient-looking map that had yellowed and flaked with age. "If we fly hard for most of the day and night, we'll get there in two days," said Daybringer. Lavender frowned.

"What about the dragon army, how far away are they?" asked Jadeclaw. "We left before they did," said Skyrider, who was one of the guards accompanying them. "They'll be slower, but they were flying directly towards the human capital city while we spent many days searching for you," he continued. "I believe they will arrive at around the same time we will."

"Then we don't have a moment to lose," said Daybringer.

They all got started packing up their gear and preparing their Gliderwings. Soon, ten Gliderwings took flight, with the Kingsguard leading the way and the others following closely behind. Honeywing watched how easily Lavender handled the Gliderwing.

"I still haven't gotten the hang of this," she said to Lavender in a loud voice so that she could be heard over the whistling wind.

"It took me a while to learn, and at first I thought I was going to crash," replied Lavender.

They were flying over green farmland now. They could see humans running around, staring and pointing up at them. Bubbletail giggled.

"To them, we're the aliens," he told Firesneezer.

The two of them had gotten comfortable sitting on top of the Gliderwings, and Daybringer even taught them how to control the big one he was using.

"This big Gliderwing would be suitable to take the weight of two pilots," he had told them.

They dreamt of the day when they could soar in the skies on their own. But first, they would have to survive the upcoming battle. They flew all day without a single break, and finally landed late at night on a dusty ridge overlooking a river valley. The entire group was super tired, and they didn't even bother making a fire. They just swallowed down some dried fruit and went to sleep. The Kingsguard took shifts patrolling during the night. The next morning, rain had rolled in and soaked their camp. Having skipped putting up tents, their gear was now soaked and would have to dry off before they could fly again. Lavender shook herself vigorously in attempts to dry herself but the rain was relentless and left her as wet and dripping as before.

"We need to dry ourselves somehow!" she said.

"This will pass," Peacefinder said calmly, "We've been through harder things than a rain storm," she added.

"What we need here is a fire!" Firesneezer exclaimed excitedly.

Making a fire now was difficult, but when Firesneezer made one giant sneeze, the wet logs lit up and started bellowing smoke into the air. Meanwhile, the others were heaving fallen logs and thrusting them into a pile, making a bonfire.

"It's amazing how fire can exist even when it's raining," Lavender stated, admiring their work and listening to the raindrops hiss as they hit the hot wood.

"You must be descended from the ancient dragons of great power," said Goldenwing to Firesneezer. He just smiled back.

They all started gratefully warming themselves by the fire. "We're just lucky he's not allergic to anything," commented Bubbletail.

"I'm allergic to your jokes," Firesneezer snorted, while standing over the fire, bundled up in a blanket and looking miserable. Lavender was standing by the fire as well, with Daybringer on one side and Honeywing on the other.

"I'm sorry," said Daybringer suddenly. Honeywing looked up at him.

"You have nothing to be sorry for," she reassured, "It was my choice. And in the end, us being here together now is all that matters." He smiled at her.

"But there is one thing I'd like to know," continued Honeywing. "How are you planning to defeat Malon? As long as he has Doomswing, he is nearly unstoppable."

It was clear that this was a question that many of them wanted to ask, because the entire group now huddled around the fire to listen.

Daybringer said, "I thought long and hard about how Malon was able to control Doomswing, and I believe that there's only one way- he must have found an artifact of power. Somehow, something must have survived from the last dragon-human war, and this artifact is now in Malon's hands. If we steal it from him, we will end his control over the dragon."

"Then will we have control of Doomswing?" asked Lavender.

"Isn't that kind of…mean?" Bubbletail questioned.

"It is, Bubbletail, but I'm not sure it will be that way," Daybringer remarked. "If that artifact has kept Doomswing from making a snack out of Malon, then clearly it has power over him. And if we take away that power, that could be all we need to stop Doomswing."

"What if we accidentally smash that artifact while trying to steal it?" asked Jadeclaw.

"I'm not sure what would happen," Daybringer contemplated.

"What does this artifact look like?" Bubbletail pressed on.

"It'll be something that Malon is never away from. So it's probably something he is wearing. It might be a ring, or a necklace, or maybe even an orb he keeps in his pocket. Don't worry, once we get closer, I have a plan to learn more about it," said Daybringer.

"What plan is that?" asked Peacefinder.

"I plan on using your ability plus the Orb of Understanding to talk to Malon and trick him into showing me the artifact," replied Daybringer.

Everyone looked at him like he was speaking some sort of foreign language.

"I have a feeling that's not going to work," Goldenwing admitted.

"Don't worry, it will, Goldenwing," Honeywing assured, "If anyone can figure it out, it's Daybringer," she explained whilst casting him a small grin. He smiled gratefully.

The sun was now starting to peek out from behind the clouds, and the air quickly got warmer. They managed to dry out their packs and got ready to fly. They spent the next day flying over the countryside. Lavender saw lakes, rivers, and far-off mountains. She also saw human towns, which in many ways looked like smaller versions of dragon towns, except that many of the buildings were made from wood, while most dragon buildings were made from stone. Daybringer told her that humans had many of the same things dragons had- books, schools, markets, castles, and they like to make things like paintings, jewelry, and crafts. One thing that shocked her was that humans had pets.

"Dogs and cats," Daybringer explained. "They are small, furry lumps that run around making noise. Well, the dogs do. The cats just sort of sit there."

"And the humans feed them?" asked Lavender.

"Yes, and walk them and keep them clean. It's all very strange," said Daybringer. "The dogs at least use their noises and

285

even their bite to protect the humans from danger. But the cats…no dragon has understood cats," he concluded.

"Now that we have the Orb of Understanding, maybe we can ask the humans about that," said Lavender.

Daybringer smiled. "With this orb, there is so much we can learn. It will truly be a new age of understanding. But…" he trailed off.

"But first we need to survive the great calamity," finished Lavender. Daybringer smiled at her as best as he could and nodded.

After another long day of flying, they finally landed for the night on top of a grass-covered hill. There wasn't much room to land, as the hill was covered in trees and bushes. They set up camp and cooked a proper meal this time because they were all starving. After filling their bellies, they settled in around the fire and got ready for bed. Then they heard a scream coming from Peacefinder. They looked over with concern.

"What happened?" asked Jadeclaw.

Peacefinder was sweating and panting. "I saw him," she replied. "I saw Malon in my vision. He's about thirty leagues to the west, and he's got an entire army with him," she continued. "I also saw Doomswing." She shuddered as she said this. "That's the biggest dragon I've ever seen." Honeywing rushed to her side and patted her shoulder gently.

"We will be fine," she assured, "Daybringer knows what he's doing."

Peacefinder let out a shaky breath and muttered "You're right."

"This is very good news," said Daybringer.

"How is Peacefinder breaking into a cold sweat at seeing an enormous evil dragon that's planning on eating us good news?" commented Firesneezer.

"It's good news because we know where they are, and that we are not too late," replied Daybringer.

He reached into his pack and brought out the Orb of Understanding.

"And now that we know these things, it's time for me to have a little chat with Malon. Peacefinder, I'm sorry but I have to ask you to look again, but this time only focus on Malon."

Peacefinder composed herself and got ready. Daybringer focused on the orb, and it began to glow. They all stared into it, expecting to see something magical happen. Instead, Daybringer entered into what looked like a deep trance.

A long distance away, Malon was trying to sleep in his tent. They had set up camp for the night, and although his tent and his bed were comfortable, he could barely sleep these days. He was constantly worried that someone would break into his tent and steal the Jewel of Dragonsmight. Just as he closed his eyes again, he was awoken by a voice in his head.

"You are the one who seeks the power of dragons," said the voice.

Malon sprang up in his bed, looking around but seeing nobody. He grabbed a sword and thought about calling to Doomswing, but decided not to.

"I am the one that gives you the power. I am the one that you keep safe and away from all the others," continued the voice.

Malon stopped looking around. *What magic is this?* he thought to himself. He reached for the jewel hanging around his neck. Far away, Peacefinder could see Malon, and the jewel. "So that's where you keep it," muttered Peacefinder with a smile.

"How can you speak to me?" Malon asked the jewel.

But the jewel had no reply.

"Why do you only now speak to me? Why not before?" asked Malon.

With Peacefinder's help, Daybringer was able to figure out what Malon was trying to say. He replied, still impersonating the jewel, "I have seen that you are an evil person, and you intend on using this power to hurt a great many people. That's why I've decided to leave you."

Malon turned pale at these words. "How can you leave me, I stole you fair and square."

"The power will soon leave you, and as soon as he knows that, Doomswing will turn against you. It will be your end."

Malon's hands were shaking as he held the jewel. "NO!" he yelled out. "It can't be! I don't believe it!"

Daybringer opened his eyes, and the Orb of Understanding stopped glowing. He said all that he wanted to say.

"Did it work?" asked Honeywing.

"Oh, it worked," replied Daybringer. "We've got him spooked. More importantly, we know what the source of his power is. It's a jewel that he wears on a necklace."

"Then we have our target," said Goldenwing. "We'll steal that jewel from him and end this battle before it even begins," he continued. The other Kingsguards nodded in agreement. Jadeclaw wanted to believe that it would be that simple, but she knew that these "easy" plans usually fell apart. But this time, they had no room for mistakes. They had to succeed.

## CHAPTER TWENTY-TWO: THE MISSION

King Steadfast the 25th knew that Malon's army was nearby, but he wanted to know exactly where they were. So he sent scouts out to patrol the countryside around Ravensthorn. The king was in his council chamber, discussing plans to fight the dragon, when one of his scouts burst through the door.

"Your Majesty, we've spotted the army!" he stuttered, out of breath.

The king looked to his council.

"Then the time has come to make our stand," he said. Although the king intended on keeping most of his soldiers protected inside the city, he asked a group of volunteers to ride out at night and launch a surprise attack on Malon and his army while they slept. With Doomswing protecting Malon, it was a mission that was certain to fail, but maybe, just maybe, if they got super lucky, they could stop the battle before it even began. They had to try. So that evening, a group of brave soldiers rode out of the city, facing what most thought would be certain death.

Meanwhile, back at the dragon camp, the Kingsguards flew out to get close enough to where they could sneak into Malon's camp. Everyone else stayed behind. Jadeclaw pleaded to join them, but they insisted that she stay behind to protect the others.

"You've made the Guard proud," said Goldenwing to Jadeclaw, "but your job isn't finished yet. The king told you to protect them, and that's what you have to do."

Jadeclaw reluctantly agreed, and wished them all good luck before they flew off towards Malon's camp. The dark of night had come when they arrived at the clearing where Malon was camped. They landed far away and hiked closer to the camp, using the nearby forest as cover. The sky was clear and there was plenty of moonlight, which would make them easier to spot. The five of them had left their gleaming armor behind and put on dark robes instead to make themselves less visible. Malon's camp was large, with many small tents arranged in a circle. There was a large campfire in the center, and two larger tents along the outside of the camp. Behind those larger tents was a huge, black dragon who seemed to be resting. There were soldiers walking around on patrol, and a few were still gathered around the campfire, but other than that, the camp was quiet.

"Malon must be in one of those larger tents," said Goldenwing.

They all nodded, and started to crawl along the ground. They're movements were nearly silent, and they looked like shadows snaking along the ground. None of Malon's soldiers noticed anything. Moments later though, they were almost spotted as they crossed the path between two rows of tents, but the soldier walking by wasn't quick enough to realize what he had seen. By the time he went over to investigate, they were out of sight. They found a hiding spot underneath some carts. The large tent in the center was very close now. They heard Doomswing move and huff out air from his snout. His eyes remained closed. They slowly crept closer to the tent.

At that very moment, an explosion rocked the sleeping camp. The Kingsguards all looked in the direction, shocked by what was happening. Hundreds of flames streaked across the night sky, hitting the camp tents and setting them on fire. The peaceful night had erupted into chaos. Soldiers started running in all directions and an alarm bell began to ring. Doomswing lifted his giant head and felt the impact of fire arrows against his scales. He immediately stood up and started running, the ground rumbling beneath him. Within a few moments, his wings spread out and he took to the air. Back inside the tent, the first explosion threw Malon off his bed and onto the ground. Dazed, he quickly gathered himself up and emerged from his tent to look around. He thought it was a bad dream. The entire camp seemed to be on fire. He looked around the back of his tent; Doomswing was gone. He felt a moment of sheer panic, but then he saw the giant dragon making a wide arc in the night sky and flying towards the tree line on the far side of the camp. Soldiers were running around and screaming.

Malon turned to grab his armor from the tent, but just as he did, he felt a powerful impact on his back and was violently pushed forward. The force of the push threw him to the ground and back into his tent, where he rolled on the ground and finally stopped against a wooden table. Before he could get up, he could just make out two large shadows breaking into his tent. They almost looked like...but that couldn't be. Before his brain had time to process what he thought he saw, he was picked up and thrown into a large sack. The world became dark. He struggled to try to get out, but it was no use. Then he felt that he was being dragged on the ground. Moments later, he felt gravity shift; and the sack he was in was swinging around in the air. He was flying! But how- was it Doomswing? He reached down to grab the Jewel of Dragonsmight and called out to Doomswing, but when he reached for it, all he felt was empty space around his neck. His heart sank, and panic took hold; the jewel was gone.

The army of King Steadfast the 25th attacked Malon's sleeping camp with all fury. They lit arrows on fire and launched them at the camp. They even brought some explosives that they launched with a catapult, hoping to blast the dragon as well. But they all knew that the chances that they would stop Malon and the dragon were slim. Still, they had to try. At first, it was looking like they might just succeed. The attack was a complete surprise, and Malon's soldiers were running around in panic. It even looked like the giant dragon was flying away. But then, the dragon looped around in the sky and dove right for them. They retreated as a burst of flame lit up the forest. Now that the dragon knew where they were, it was only a matter of time before the dragonfire would get them. They did all they could, and now they ran to their horses and retreated back to Ravensthorn.

Doomswing flew after the retreating army for a short time, but as he got further and further away from the Jewel of Dragonsmight, he felt weaker and weaker, so he looped back around to return to the camp. As he landed near Malon's tent, he felt the strength of the jewel return. Veralus was busy organizing his soldiers and putting out fires. The fact that the king's army managed to surprise them like this was embarrassing, and Veralus was angry. Once the attack was over and the fires were put out, he had time to check in on Malon. That's when he noticed that Malon's tent was open, and there were signs of a struggle inside. Malon was nowhere to be found. Veralus felt a shiver go down his spine, but Doomswing looked totally calm, as if nothing had happened. *Could it be that he didn't know Malon was missing?* Veralus took a moment to look around Malon's tent. It didn't take him long to notice a beautiful necklace on the floor, with a shiny jewel glowing in the center. Veralus had never seen anything like it before. He picked it up carefully. The jewel glowed in his hand. He put the necklace on. He wasn't sure what to expect, but he didn't feel any different. Suddenly, he heard a voice inside his head.

"Did you sleep through the attack?" asked the rumbling voice, seeming to come from nowhere. "I've been trying to contact you," it continued.

The voice sounded ancient. A thought entered Veralus' mind; *can this be the voice of Doomswing? Is this how Malon did it?* He stepped outside of the tent and looked at Doomswing, who then turned to look at Veralus.

Veralus decided it was now or never. He formed a thought in his mind, "Malon is gone, but the Jewel is safe...with me."

Incredibly, the dragon seemed to understand. A look of amusement crossed Doomswing's face. "Should I bother to ask what happened to Malon?" he asked Veralus, the voice sounding in his head.

Veralus knew that the dragon could destroy him at any moment, but he felt that, with this jewel around his neck, he was in charge. "I don't know, and it doesn't matter. He doesn't have the jewel, and I do. So now I will fly on your back tomorrow when we take Ravensthorn, and I will be the new king!"

Doomswing continued looking at Veralus in amusement.

"Malon or you, or some other human....you're all just the same: greedy, power-hungry, selfish. I'll tell you the same thing I told Malon; I'll help you become the new king. And after that, you'll help me take revenge on the dragon kingdom."

Veralus smiled. His dream was coming true. This would work out just fine. He would inform his army and then fly to Ravensthorn to take his crown. He stepped into the camp courtyard and notified his soldiers that Malon was missing, and that Doomswing was now taking orders from him. The army cheered. He then ordered them to search the camp and surrounding area. He wanted to be certain Malon wouldn't come back to ruin his plans.

The Kingsguards arrived back at their camp very late at night. They were very excited and happy that the mission was a success. They pulled Malon out of the sack and tied him up. Malon looked around and was shocked to find that he was surrounded by dragons. Then he heard a voice in his head say, "We know who you are, and we know what you're planning to do." He looked around the circle of dragons. One of them was holding a glowing orb. "We also know how you managed to get Doomswing to go along with your plan," said the voice. Then one of the other dragons stepped forward and reached for Malon's neck with a sharp talon. But the dragon suddenly looked confused. Malon realized what they were looking for, but he didn't have it. He must have lost the jewel when the dragons grabbed him back at his tent. The dragon checked his pockets and looked inside the sack he was transported in. Then he watched as the dragons backed away and spoke amongst themselves in the language he couldn't understand.

"Where is it?" asked Peacefinder.

"I don't know, and I looked everywhere," answered Jadeclaw. "He doesn't have it."

"But that can't be!" cried Daybringer. "We saw it with the Orb of Understanding; it was on the necklace around his neck." Then Daybringer turned back to Malon and, using the orb, asked, "Where is the jewel?"

Malon looked at him and cringed. Daybringer brought the orb close to Malon, so that its power would allow him to understand Malon's words.

"I'm not sure. Maybe I lost it in the struggle back at my tent," Malon replied.

Daybringer shared what Malon told him with the others. Their hearts sank.

"It was all for nothing," said Goldenwing, as he sat with his head down. "How could we have failed so terribly," he continued, dejected.

"We can still go back and get it," said Skyrider.

"No, it's too risky now, the jewel is out of our reach," said Daybringer.

"Then, what can we do now?" asked Lavender.

Daybringer looked at all of them. He tried so hard to stop this, but no matter what he did, it always came down to the final battle.

"Now, there's only one thing left to do," he replied. "We fight."

## CHAPTER TWENTY-THREE: FINAL BATTLE

Veralus grinned as he soared atop Doomswing across the horizon. This was the first time he'd experienced flight, and it was better than anything he could have imagined. His ears popped as the dragon dipped and swerved, and the wind rushed across his face. He was scared, but at the same time bursting with excitement. The whole world looked so much smaller, and he could see so far away. He could see his entire army marching far below him, and they looked like tiny ants. Off in the distance, the towers of Ravensthorn were just barely visible against a velvet-colored sky. If not for the coming battle, Veralus would think the whole scene was beautiful. But he was the commander of the world's most fearsome force, and he felt mighty, as if he could destroy an entire mountain with just a thought. He glanced down at his army and signaled for his scouts to ride ahead. Reluctantly, a group of scouts pressed forward. He would not be caught off-guard like he was last night. Doomswing beat his wings repetitively and the rushing wind from under his wings threw Veralus off balance. He gripped Doomswing's spikes until his knuckles turned white and yelped in fear as his foot slipped over the side. Veralus quickly regained his balance and shot Doomswing a icy glare.

"I know you did that on purpose," he hissed. Doomswing snickered but masked it with a fit of coughing.

"Whatever do you mean?" he asked innocently. Veralus rolled his eyes. "If you want to ride a dragon, you'd better be ready to be afraid" Doomswing bellowed.

"Just make sure you don't drop me, otherwise your precious jewel would shatter into a million pieces" Veralus retorted.

They didn't speak for the rest of the flight. It was clear that they didn't like each other. Finally, Veralus broke the silence.

"We are here, land in that clearing over there," he instructed.

Doomswing dove down and landed in a wide open floodplain. Ahead of them, the mountainside that the city of Ravensthorn was carved into towered over the landscape like a sleeping giant. Veralus gazed upon it.

"Soon, it will all be mine," he said to himself. Then he met up with his army and declared, "this is the day I've been promising you! This is the day we take over the kingdom!" The soldiers cheered.

Jadeclaw was the first to see Doomswing with her own eyes, soaring high over the fields below. At first, they still held out hope that the jewel had been destroyed and that Doomswing was no longer interested in attacking the humans. But this hope was now lost. But who was controlling Doomswing now? Jadeclaw could barely make out a figure riding on Doomswing. When she reported back, Daybringer asked Malon about it. There was only one possible person- Veralus. The dragons couldn't believe it. They got rid of one evil human only to have him immediately be replaced by another. But at least they knew where the jewel was now; it must be with Veralus. They also learned from Malon that without the jewel, Doomswing would lose all of his strength. They had to find a way to destroy the jewel, and that meant attacking Veralus. They were preparing to depart for Ravensthorn and face the final battle. But first, they had to think of a plan. They had to think of a way to distract Doomswing for long enough to give them a shot at Veralus.

"What if we pretend to be a ghost and send scary thoughts to him?" asked Lavender.

"Doomswing doesn't seem to scare easily," replied Jadeclaw.

"What if we challenged him to another riddle?" asked Peacefinder.

"After spending a hundred years trapped in a cave, I think the last thing Doomswing would do is fall for that trick again," replied Honeywing.

They went through idea after idea, but nothing seemed very good. They hadn't slept at all last night. Peacefinder was tired, and she sat back, letting her mind rest for a moment. She watched Bubbletail and Firesneezer tease each other, as they often did.

"I think you could just use that tail to fly…it's the size of a blimp anyway," said Firesneezer to Bubbletail.

"Oh yeah, well at least I don't burn my house down every time I catch a cold," replied Bubbletail.

Then, Peacefinder had an idea. "What if we tease him?" she said to the group.

"What?" asked Daybringer.

"You know…make fun of him. You said yourself that Doomswing is so proud and thinks he's the greatest dragon alive. Well, what if we just tease him and make him so angry and annoyed that he loses his concentration and gives us a chance to strike at Veralus," continued Peacefinder.

"The battle will be chaos…if Doomswing isn't focused, he could make a mistake. All we need is one chance. As silly as it sounds, it just might work," said Daybringer.

"So, we're going to use the Orb of Understanding to get into Doomswing's head…and talk about how he's a big bully?" asked Jadeclaw in disbelief.

"Not *we*," replied Peacefinder. "*They*," she said, while flicking her tail at Bubbletail and Firesneezer.

"Oh this just went from funny to completely silly," said Jadeclaw.

"It's the best plan we have," Peacefinder argued.

It took quite some time to convince Bubbletail and Firesneezer that Doomswing couldn't see them or know where they were when they started to make fun of him. They were really scared that he would somehow find a way and come after them. But then Jadeclaw promised to make them full Kingsguards if they did this, and that was the push they needed. They agreed to help. While they distracted Doomswing, everyone else would be focused on attacking Veralus.

"Are you sure you want to do this?" said Jadeclaw to Lavender. "You're not trained to fight, this isn't really your place."

"We'll need every dragon we can get," replied Lavender. "And besides, I've got my mom to protect me."

Jadeclaw looked at Honeywing, who looked as determined as ever.

"Very well," she said, and gave them each a long spear and armor.

"Did you see any new visions?" Peacefinder asked Daybringer. He looked at her and sighed.

"Does it matter?" said Daybringer. "I was wrong about Honeywing. Nowhere in my years of looking into the future did I see her here, now. As far as I'm concerned, the future is what we make it."

Peacefinder smiled. "Then there's hope for a victory," she said, as she moved to put on her Gliderwing.

"Yes," said Daybringer, "and perhaps it's time we send word to our new friends," he added, as he pulled out his cherished orb.

King Steadfast looked out from his balcony at the gathered army outside of the city walls. The sheer size of the dragon sitting there was enough to make anyone run and hide. But he didn't have that choice. Although the surprise attack on Malon's camp had failed, most of his soldiers managed to make it back to the city alive, which was already better than anyone could have hoped for. But now, facing what looked like an invincible enemy, he seriously considered simply giving up. Then he heard a voice in his head. It felt like it was coming from far away. It was faint, but the words were clear.

The voice said, "King Steadfast, I represent the dragon kingdom. I am speaking to you through a magical orb. We know you're about to face a terrible battle. Don't lose hope; we will do everything we can to help you. The entire dragon army is coming. Just hold on."

The king couldn't tell where the voice was coming from, and he attempted to reply, but he heard nothing more. *Could this be true?* he wondered to himself. The message brought him hope, and he called for a meeting with his council. When he told them what he'd heard, they all looked at him with confusion and doubt. The king announced that the moment the dragon army began to attack Doomswing, his own army should gallop out of the city and attack Malon's army. At this point, the king didn't know that Malon had been captured and that Veralus was now his worst enemy. The order was passed on to the soldiers, though nobody took it seriously. On his way out of the council chamber, he heard someone mumble, "the king has finally lost it." But King Steadfast believed the message was real. He had to believe. Then he felt a shudder in the floor, and the walls shook. He looked out of a small window and saw the shadow of a giant dragon passing overhead. The battle had begun.

Veralus gripped the saddle with both hands until his knuckles turned white as Doomswing swooped down on Ravensthorn. The dragon was spraying the towers and city walls with fire. Even through his helmet, Veralus could feel the heat on his face as Doomswing attacked the city. The wooden parts of the towers burst into flames and some even exploded. Sprinters of burning wood flew in all directions. Billowing black smoke poured from all sides, making Veralus' eyes water. Veralus expected to see arrows flying at them as the city tried to defend itself. But he saw nothing. In fact, he didn't even see a single human in the city. *Had King Steadfast abandoned the city?* wondered Veralus. Regardless, he had to get inside the king's castle to make sure. He ordered Doomswing to blast through the city gates so that his army could come in and start searching. Dust flew up from the ground as Doomswing beat his wings hard as he came in for a landing. When the dust finally settled, Veralus gazed at a huge steel gate in front of them. He instructed Doomswing to break it down. Doomswing took a deep breath and sprayed the gate with white-hot dragonfire. The steel started to glow red hot, and the hinges that held the gate in place started to droop as the steel started to melt.

Suddenly, the sky was filled with arrows, all aimed at Veralus and Doomswing. Veralus was wearing thick steel armor, but the arrows struck him again and again and he could hear the metal clanging and felt the impact as the powerful arrows connected. Doomswing looked up to see a hundred archers suddenly emerge from the ruined towers. He had no idea where they came from, but they were all spread out and shooting from so many angles that he wouldn't be able to destroy them with one burst of flame. Veralus hunched down and cowered while the arrows pummeled the huge dragon's back. Then one of the arrows hit Doomswing in his right eye. He felt a sharp pain, and he shrieked in agony and surprise. His vision blurred for a moment, but he recovered. The pain had dulled somewhat, and now he was annoyed. He decided to put this gate down, and then deal with the archers. He started charging at the gate, his head pointing down. The ground shook violently, and then Veralus realized what Doomswing was about to do. In total disbelief, he tried to get the dragon to stop his insane charge, but it was too late. Veralus braced himself. The dragon rammed the gate with a power unlike anything the gate was built to handle. The sound was deafening. The gate, which was already weakened from the fire, collapsed into the courtyard inside. The collision threw Veralus out of his saddle and into the air. He hit the ground head-first, and rolled onto the ground. Veralus gasped, as the wind was knocked out of him. His head throbbed and he couldn't breathe inside of his helmet. He removed it, and his world was spinning. He struggled to move. His heavy armor didn't help. Doomswing seemed totally unphased by the collision and glanced at Veralus with indifference. But he eventually lifted the little man with his talon and threw him onto his back. Then he got a running start and took to the air again. Veralus managed to crawl into his saddle just as Doomswing blasted another tower with dragonfire. With the gate down, Veralus saw that his army now charged towards the city. Veralus pushed aside his injuries and snapped back into focus. *Nothing could go wrong now*, he thought.

Just then, Veralus felt the sky grow colder as if the sun went behind a cloud. But when he looked up, there were no clouds in the sky. What was blocking out the sun was the thousand Gliderwings of the dragon army. The sight made Veralus' jaw drop. He couldn't believe it, and now a shiver of fear ran down his spine. It was the first time Veralus felt doubt in his victory. Doomswing saw the dragon army as well and was equally shocked. He knew he would have to face a dragon army eventually if he wanted to get his revenge on the dragon kingdom, but not so soon ...and not this many. When the soldiers that had hunkered down inside Ravensthorn saw the dragon army flying in, their hearts flickered with hope once more and they let out a cheer. King Steadfast was sitting in his throne room, feeling dejected, when he heard the cheers emanating from all over the city. He ran out onto his balcony and gazed up at the sky. His eyes filled with tears of joy. The message was true; the dragons had come!

Doomswing ceased his attack on the city and focused now on this new threat. The size of the army was truly impressive. *This battle would indeed decide the fate of the world*, he thought to himself. Doomswing flapped his wings hard to try to gain altitude, but the army dragons were already far above him. Then he heard a loud battlehorn sound wailing from above. He watched as the first of the dragons started their dive at him. Within a few seconds, they gained massive speed and plunged towards Doomswing, some using their spears to attack, others trying to bite or claw into his scales, still others ramming him directly. But his mass was so great that these attacks just bounced off of him. He shook them off with ease and swung his huge tail at the tumbling dragons. They swiftly veered toward the sides, but just the wind from the passing tail was enough to throw them about and into each other. Doomswing grinned. "Is that the best you can do?" he teased the army.

Back on the ground, Veralus' army had reached the city gate, and were expecting to stroll right through. But they were in for a surprise. The king's army poured out of the gate, and archers popped out of their hiding places along the walls and once again rained arrows down. Veralus' soldiers were stunned, but quickly regained their composure. Their illusion of taking the city without a fight was shattered. The fighting on the ground was fierce. Spears smashed into shields, axes smashed into swords and the clanging, banging, and screaming made it all the more terrifying. But the king's army had more soldiers, and they were fighting with all of their might, while the soldiers who decided to support Veralus were starting to doubt that they made the right choice. All around them, dragons were crash-landing, or just plain crashing, into the ground.

High above, Doomswing was tearing through the dragon army. Their armor was useless against his flames, and their spears and arrows did nothing to damage his scales. As wave after wave of dragons attacked him without any success, it was starting to look hopeless.

"Attack the human sitting on his back!" cried Jadeclaw, but her voice could barely be heard over the wind, and even when they did try to attack Veralus, Doomswing would expertly knock them away. Back on the ground and far from the battle, hidden in the forest, Daybringer was watching.

"It's time," he said.

Bubbletail and Firesneezer were ready. They sat in front of the orb, and Daybringer activated it. He searched for the target, which didn't take him long to find as Doomswing was the largest thing in the air by far. Then he waved to the two small dragons, and the show was ready to begin.

"Hey! Hey you! You there, the big ugly one!" started Firesneezer.

Doomswing craned his long neck, swinging it back and forth, trying to find out who was speaking. But there was no one around him.

"Yeah you, I know you can hear me but those tiny eyes must be making you blind, I'm right over here!" said Bubbletail.

Doomswing dove and banked, trying to shake the voice out of his head. But it kept talking.

"I bet I can walk faster than you fly," teased Bubbletail into the orb.

"Yeah I bet it takes you ten minutes just to lift off with those ridiculous tents for wings," continued Firesneezer.

Doomswing left out a roar of anger and furled his wings back. He dove for the ground, thinking that the source of these voices might be below him. But he saw nothing.

"Hahaha, look at your silly flying, I've seen horses fly better," said Firesneezer.

"Horses, why, I had a pig that could fly circles around you!" continued Bubbletail.

Doomswing was circling in the air now, infuriated and searching for the source of the voices in his head.

"Open your eyes, I'm standing next to the river," said Bubbletail.

Doomswing dove again and flew low over the river, took a huge breath in, and let out a roaring flame of white-hot fire. Water in the river boiled, and sent up a jet of hot steam all around. All the while, Veralus was sitting on his back, holding on for dear life.

"Stop!" he screamed to Doomswing. But Doomswing was so enraged that he was beyond listening to Veralus now.

"Hahaha, wrong river! Actually I'm riding on a dragon high above you now, come get me, stupid!" said Firesneezer.

They were really having fun now, and Doomswing was getting angrier and angrier. He had fallen for their trick. He used all of his energy to fly all the way back up, all the while being attacked by the dragons.

"No you just missed me, I'm below you!" yelled Bubbletail.

At this moment, Doomswing did a loop in the air, going completely upside-down. He barely heard the panicked screams of the human riding on his back. As Doomswing dove to catch the imaginary voice in his head, Veralus flew off the dragon and started falling.

"There!" screamed Jadeclaw, as she saw Veralus tumble out of his saddle and began plummeting to the ground. Lavender was flying lower and saw Veralus fall as well, and dove right for him. Honeywing followed, but she wasn't as good at flying, and so she fell behind. Jadeclaw and Peacefinder saw them and dove to distract Doomswing. Lavender's eyes watered as she reached her top speed. Veralus was tumbling below her, and she could just hear his screams. She was now seconds from hitting the ground. She swooped under Veralus and opened her Gliderwing. She felt a rush of air and a powerful thud on her back. She was slowing down, but not quickly enough. Lavender was going to crash. She tried to level off as much as possible before hitting the ground.

She slammed down, skidded, then rolled to a stop. A cloud of dust covered her. She tasted dirt and blood, and felt pain all over her body. Her vision was blurry and her ears rang, but she was alive. She gingerly got up and tried to untangle herself from the ruined Gliderwing. Then she noticed a small, shiny object lying a short distance away. She realized what it was- the Jewel of Dragonsmight! This was it- all she had to do was pick it up and put it on, and this terrible battle would be over. But just as she realized this, Veralus emerged from behind the Gliderwing. He was limping and she could see blood dripping from between his lips. His armor was broken in several places, but his face showed furious determination, and he held a shiny sword in his hand. He roared and lunged at her, swiping with the sword. The blade made a whooshing sound past her ear, but he was too far away and missed. Now Lavender tried to lunge at the jewel, but one of her legs was still tangled in the Gliderwing. Veralus noticed what she was trying to get to. He sneered and casually walked over to the jewel, picked it up, and put it back around his neck. His face covered in mud and blood, he gave Lavender an evil grin. Lavender finally got her leg unstuck, but it was too late. Veralus had his sword up, about to slash at her. Lavender closed her eyes. Then she heard a powerful blast, and the sound of armor shattering. She felt a wind pass right over her head. She opened her eyes, and Veralus was gone. Behind him, she saw another Gliderwing that had just crash-landed. It must have collided with Veralus. The force of that impact was immense. Veralus was on the ground, not moving. Lavender walked over to him. His eyes were closed and he showed no signs of life. Lavender cautiously took the jewel off his neck. It glimmered in her hands, and felt warm. She looked up into the sky, where she saw Jadeclaw and Peacefinder battling with Doomswing. The two greatest warriors she had ever seen; the two best friends she had ever known, were

310

in danger. Doomswing flung his tail at Jadeclaw and struck her. The wooden pole they had used to repair her Gliderwing cracked in two and the wings collapsed. She started to fall. Lavender screamed, and she felt a rage unlike anything she'd felt before. She hated the senseless violence and destruction, and all because of this terrible jewel. *As long this cursed thing exists, this will continue*, she thought. She looked down and saw the sword that Veralus had just used to try to kill her with, lying on the ground next to him. She picked it up, threw the jewel on the ground and slammed the blade down with all the force she had. She put all of her hatred for Doomswing and Veralus and Malon and all the evil in the world into that blow. Her aim was perfect, and the jewel exploded into a thousand shards of broken crystal. A wave of bright light left the shattered jewel.

Far above, Jadeclaw fell towards the ground. Peacefinder quickly moved to grab her, but Doomswing was on her. He lined up a blast of dragonfire that would end both of the dragons at once. And then, nothing happened. Doomswing's eyes grew wide. He tried again, but his breath held no flame at all. What was happening to him? He suddenly felt tired and weak, the energy draining from him. His sore eye felt worse, and his talons felt heavy. Peacefinder had caught up to the tumbling Jadeclaw and managed to snatch her by the talons, stopping her fall. She then looked up at Doomswing, who was rapidly diving at them. With her one free talon, she flung out her bow and pulled the string with her teeth. She lined up an arrow on Doomswing. The arrow left the bow with a 'thwack' sound and arched gracefully through the sky. It connected in between his scales, right in the center of his neck. Doomswing choked. He suddenly had trouble breathing. He panicked, and broke off his attack. Seconds later, another spear from above pierced his back, and then another. Siering pain ran down his spine, and he clawed at the arrow in his neck. He couldn't believe it, but the pain he was feeling and the weakness, which was growing worse with every breath, told him one thing-escape. He banked sharply and flew as fast as he could away from the battle. The army dragons gazed at what they were seeing in stunned disbelief. They didn't dare to believe they had beaten the terrible dragon. Several dragons started after him, expecting him to turn right around and attack at any moment. But he didn't attack. In fact, he almost looked scared while the dragons gave chase and hurried his retreat. They all let out a cheer of triumph; Doomswing's role in this battle was over.

As the soldiers loyal to Veralus saw this, they instantly knew that they had lost. Some of them turned and ran, while others surrendered. The battle was over!

Bubbletail and Firesneezer jumped up and down, hugging each other. "It actually worked," they said at the same time.

"That dragon really is easy to trick," said Bubbletail through his giggling.

They looked at Daybringer, who had tears streaming down his face.

"All of these years, all I did was dread this moment," he said, with a shaky voice. "And now, all I feel is joy…and immense relief." They ran up to him and did a group hug.

Lavender watched Doomswing fly off and away from her friends. She was ecstatic. But then she remembered the Gliderwing that had crashed into Veralus. She knew exactly who had been flying it. She ran as best as she could over to the wrecked Gliderwing. It had crashed some distance away because it was going so fast. As she got closer and closer, Lavender grew more and more concerned. She reached the ruined Gliderwing, which was partly buried into the ground. She flipped it over, and saw Honeywing. She wasn't moving. Lavender came down close to her.

"Mom! Mom, wake up!" she cried.

Terrible thoughts ran through her head. *After all that they'd been through, after all this time, please don't let it end like this*, she thought to herself. Then Honeywing groaned.

"Mom, you're alive!" yelled Lavender.

She hugged her mom, which made her groan even more. Lavender quickly stopped and instead helped her get out of the wreckage. Honeywing was bruised and battered, but her injuries were not too serious.

"Mom, you saved me back there," said Lavender.

Her mom smiled at her. "I wish I could take credit for that my dear," she replied. But it all happened so fast, and I wasn't really in control of that thing. I'm just glad I managed to knock that little man over for you."

Lavender laughed, and together they limped away from the battlefield.

Peacefinder managed a relatively graceful landing, considering that she was carrying Jadeclaw with her. Jadeclaw was alive, but the impact with Doomswing's tail had crushed her armor and probably broken several bones. Peacefinder stayed with her until help arrived.

"Am I dead yet?" asked Jadeclaw jokingly.

"I'm afraid not," replied Peacefinder with a smile.

"Well, did we at least win?" asked Jadeclaw.

"We did," replied Peacefinder with a huge grin. "We won."

King Steadfast had mounted a horse and had rode into the battle along with his soldiers. He wasn't much of a fighter, but he wanted to show everyone that he wasn't afraid. He certainly achieved that, and when they beat back the human army and watched the dragon retreat, he was right there with his army to celebrate their victory. He then organized the medics who were running around, trying to help injured soldiers- both human and dragon alike. King Steadfast the 25th earned back his respect that day.

Back at the forest where Bubbletail and Firesneezer were now doing an extended victory dance, Daybringer contacted King Evergreat to inform him of their victory, and King Steadfast to let him know about Malon and Veralus, and the fate of both. Malon was sitting next to Daybringer, his head down. He had also seen the entire battle, but watched without any emotion. Now Daybringer turned to him.

"It seems you are the unkillable human after all," said Daybringer, translating his words through the orb. "Had we not nabbed you from your camp last night, you would be the one who fell from Doomswing today, and it would be your broken body on the ground now. But, as always, you managed to cheat death."

Malon looked up to Daybringer, as if he wanted to say something, but remained quiet.

314

"We'll hand you over to the Ravensthorn city guard as soon as we have the opportunity, then your fate will be decided by King Steadfast," said Daybringer.

Malon felt neither happiness for surviving the doomed battle, nor sadness for losing the jewel and being captured. He just felt regret. He felt like his entire life amounted to nothing. But, somewhere in the back of his mind, came the thought that he might yet be able to change that.

The next few months brought historic changes to the world. With the help of the Orb of Understanding, dragons could once again communicate with humans. The kings of both kingdoms met, and agreed to mutual friendship and assistance. Dragons helped humans re-build their ruined cities. Humans helped dragons learn new things about farming, cooking, and building. Trade between the kingdoms opened up again, and soon humans were visiting dragon cities on a regular basis, and dragons were doing the same in the human kingdom. The study of human language became a priority in Sagestone, and humans did their best to try to learn the very different language of the dragons. A time of peace and prosperity returned to the world.

# EPILOGUE

The ceremony was held in the royal courtyard, and attended by the entire Kingsguard as well as the king himself. They sat in the center row, while Peacefinder, Daybringer, Lavender and Honeywing were all sitting together to the left , while a rowdy group of family and friends were sitting to the right. Jadeclaw stepped onto the stage, her bright red sash looking splendid across her glistening armor. She had fully recovered from her injuries, and to honor her bravery, the king promoted her to be the leader of the Kingsguard after Crimsonshield retired. Jadeclaw had never been happier. But now she stood in front of the gathered crowd with a stern look on her face.

"The Kingsguard are the most elite soldiers in the king's army," she said in a booming voice so that all could hear. "There is no battle we will run from, no enemy we will not face, no challenge we will not conquer," she continued. "Becoming a Kingsguard is a great honor; one that most dragons have to work years to achieve." She stopped, and looked up at the gathered crowd. "But once in a while, a dragon is found that shows unusual bravery, intelligence, and spirit. Today, we honor not one, but two such dragons."

At this moment, the doors behind the stage opened, and two small dragons came out. They were wearing gleaming armor, fitted to their smaller size, and armed with the famous spears and shields of the Kingsguard. But even though the helmets were made especially for them, they were still a little too big and they flopped over to one side of their head, leaning awkwardly.

Lavender couldn't help but giggle. They stepped onto the stage to join Jadeclaw.

"Bubbletail and Firesneezer have fought more monsters and have been in more life and death situations in a few weeks than most Kingsguards experience in their entire lives. In every case, they showed the qualities we all admire." Jadeclaw stopped, looked at them, and smiled. Then she continued. "When I asked them if they were serious about joining the Kingsguard, they said they were. When I asked them if they were willing to train and learn and push themselves harder than ever before, they nodded in agreement. And now, it is my honor to present to you all, the newest members of the Kingsguard. This just proves that sometimes, the smallest dragons can make the biggest difference." The courtyard erupted in cheers and applause.

Bubbletail and Firesneezer took off their helmets and waved to the crowd, grinning. The cheering went on and on. The king stood and saluted. They all took their turn congratulating the two dragons, who were beaming with pride.

After the ceremony, they all met up in the garden next to the courtyard. It was a lovely spring day, and the trees were blooming with purple and pink flowers.

"I love this garden," said Lavender, as she gently stroked a blooming flower bud. "We should think about adding one like this to the orphanage," she said to Honeywing.

She fondly lifted a butterfly to a willow tree and it fluttered around the lush leafs with joy. After the battle, Lavender and Honeywing were both welcomed to join the king's council. But instead, Lavender asked the king if he would support the founding of a new orphanage; one that took in both dragon and human orphans. King Everwise agreed happily, as did King Steadfast, and so Lavender and Honeywing opened the world's first House of Hope Orphanage. They helped kids and dragons learn, grow, and find new homes. It was considered a huge success, as many of the kids were able to learn both dragon and human languages, which made them very special and important to the world.

"What about you, Daybringer?" Lavender asked. "Would you like to add a tree flower garden to your mountainside retreat?"

Daybringer smiled, looking at each of them. "If I do, will you come help me tend the garden?" he asked.

"Of course!" replied Lavender, grinning from ear to ear.

He had finally retired, and now lived in a lovely cottage high up in the mountains, where he had begun to write a book about his life, his experiences as a Seer, and their adventures together.

Peacefinder was sitting nearby, listening in and smiling. She had remained on the king's council, but she was now the ambassador to the human kingdom, making her one of the most important dragons in the kingdom.

"Peacefinder, did you have a chance to collect the manuscript from Ravensthorn?" asked Lavender.

Peacefinder stood up and walked over to her. "Yes I did," she said. She then reached into her satchel and took out a stack of hand-written pages. They were written in human language. "You'll have to get them translated," she said.

"That's ok, I'll ask one of the kids at the orphanage to do it. It would be a great way to improve their language skills. And how is Malon?"

"King Steadfast was kind to him," said Peacefinder. "He believes that even the worst person could still make something of his life. Of course he's still in jail, but he's doing fine. And now that you've asked him to help you write his experiences with orphanages and how they could be improved, he's really motivated to help," she continued. "Thank you Lavender. Your heart is so kind that you gave the guy who was once our greatest enemy a chance to redeem himself."

"Yes," said Jadeclaw. "That's what she's known for. The kind-hearted dragon that smashed a jewel with a sword so hard that all that was left of it was dust."

They all burst into laughter. Doomswing had been chased all the way to the northern mountains, where he disappeared in a snowstorm. Nobody has seen or heard from him since, but with the Jewel of Dragonsmight shattered, Doomswing was no longer powerful enough to threaten anyone.

Then Bubbletail and Firesneezer showed up, and they all laughed and cheered some more. Lavender looked back on her life's journey and all the unexpected twists and turns. She was an orphan once, just like Malon. But her positive attitude and kind nature allowed her to overcome the things that made Malon dark and angry and bitter. She felt some new-found sympathy for him, but she also felt lucky. And now, surrounded by her friends and her mom, she felt like the luckiest dragon alive.

Lilia Barć has enjoyed writing and making up stories since she was just 5 years old. She came up with the story for Dragons of the Past, Visions of the Future at the age of 10, and wrote it with the help of her dad, Jarek Barć. This is her chapter book debut.

In addition to writing, Lilia loves reading, gymnastics, playing with her friends, and drinking bubble tea.

Made in the USA
Columbia, SC
31 August 2024